A KISSING RIDGE NOVEL

Copyright @2025

Bull Riders Don't Swoon by R.M Neill

www.rmneillauthor.com

This is a work of fiction. Names, characters, places, and incidents either are the products of the author's imagination or are used fictitiously. Any resemblance to actual person, living or dead, businesses, companies, events or locales is entirely coincidental.

AI was not used to create the cover art or any part of the story within. This story was created entirely by the author and their sometimes too vivid imagination.

Cover by: DuffetteReads

Photography: CJC Photography

Model: Draven Barcia

Edited by: Jenn Reads Books

Contents

Note from the author   VII

1. Griff   1

2. Jamieson   13

3. Griff   25

4. Jamieson   29

5. Griff   39

6. Jamieson   49

7. Griff   61

8. Jamieson   73

9. Griff   83

10. Jamieson   93

11. Griff   105

12. Jamieson   115

13. Griff   125

14. Jamieson   135

15. Griff   143

16. Jamieson 153

17. Griff 165

18. Jamieson 177

19. Griff 187

20. Jamieson 197

21. Griff 207

22. Jamieson 217

23. Griff 227

24. Jamieson 237

25. Griff 249

26. Jamieson 259

27. Griff 267

28. Jamieson 275

29. Epilogue 285

Acknowledgements 293

About the author 295

Also By 297

Note from the author

Please be aware that this book contains mentions of alcohol abuse, an alcoholic parent, and caretaking of an alcoholic parent. There are also mentions of physical abuse off page by a former lover of one of the MC's.

Should any of these topics be sensitive to you, please do not continue reading.

One
Griff

Eight Years Ago

January—second year of University

"That one with the white splotch. Have you been on him? Cauliflower is his name."

The bull rider standing next to me, Jordan, shakes his head. "No, I don't think so. I'd remember a name like that."

Well, that's the truth, isn't it? Who was mean enough to name a fierce bull after a vegetable? If I was a bull rider, I'd remember it.

"I think he'll be a re-ride for whoever draws him."

Jordan scoffs. "How can you possibly know that?"

His lips quirk, not with a telltale, *I'm better than you smirk*, but more like the kind that says he'll humour me and go along with the joke. Both annoy me, but just once I'd like one of these guys to take me seriously.

"I just know. I can tell."

Okay, maybe that sounds lame, but there's nothing I can describe in words how I just seem to know what a bull might do. I just...know.

My dad used to call it a sixth sense, like the dog whisperer. I've learned I have the skill of rapidly analyzing behavioural clues and making predictions. Sadly, it seems not to work with humans. I still don't understand those cues.

"Ya gotta give me more than that if you think I'm gonna listen to a rookie bull fighter." He struts off to join his group of *cool guys.* The rodeo cowboys who have been here for a few years and established their names. I know there's a pecking order, and that's fine. But if he draws Cauliflower, I will gloat so hard when that bull lies down on the job.

"Do you really have a way to know that?"

The tallest of all the bull riders here and the one who is definitely the best cocks his head as he waits for my answer. I've paid attention, and he's an anomaly for the bull rider group. He's all legs and twig thin, but I bet he's the strongest guy here. He shouldn't be as good as he is, but he carries himself with a confidence I both envy and admire. It's almost like he knows he has a hidden talent and doesn't understand it either. With some extra muscle and more practice, he'll be at the top of the sport. Not that I'm an expert or anything. It's just the vibe he gives off. Like he knows he's destined for something great, but doesn't know how to get there.

"It's a gut feeling. I can't explain it, but after watching a bull a few times, sometimes for just a few minutes, I can pick up on little things and make a good guess."

It's only my second year at Red Deer College, and I'm here on a scholarship, but not for rodeo. Rodeo, I just sort of fell into. While I'm not about to climb onto the back of a two-thousand-pound bull for fun, I learned that my sixth sense with bulls had value in other ways. Not one to miss an opportunity to earn extra money, I jumped at the chance to be a bullfighter at the rodeo team practices.

"So, what about this one?" The guy asks me as he points down the chutes to the bull staring right at us.

"Black Knight. He's gonna throw his rider off in less than two seconds."

The guy's eyes widen, and he leans in closer. "How?"

"Well...he's going to burst from the chute, one spin, buck..." I swirl my finger in the air, "and then on the second spin, which he'll take to the left, the poor rider is gonna eat dirt."

Silently, we watch the next rider take his time to settle on the back of the bull. At the bull rider's signal, the bull bursts from the chutes and does exactly what I predicted. Almost. He made the second spin to the right, but close enough.

"Holy shit." The guy next to me breathes, awe lacing his voice. "Are you like telepathic or something?"

Laughing, I shake my head. "Nah, dude. I told you, I just notice things fast and have a crazy memory. Then I get a feeling."

"I have to ride the black one with the bent horn, Pothole. Any tips?"

"I don't remember that one. Show me?"

I know it's supposed to be my turn to sub in for one bullfighter shortly, but this guy is the first bull rider who hasn't just brushed off my statements. I want to hang around him a little longer. Plus, he's kinda cute.

He points to the bull in question in the chutes, and I remember it from an earlier rodeo. "I haven't paid too much attention to that one today, but last week he was right ornery, so I'd just hold on for the ride."

He holds out his hand with a booming laugh. "I'm Jamieson, by the way, and while I'll let that answer slide as a no-brainer, I'd like to talk to you more about your bull watching."

"Griff," I say as I take his hand with a smile. "Nice to meet you, and yeah, I'd be happy to."

"I need to get in position, though, so I guess I'll see you out there?"

My name is called, and I wave back in acknowledgement. "Yep. It's my turn to get out there, too. Good luck."

We head in our opposite directions, and I enter the practice ring, switching out one of the other bullfighters. Something about limiting our time in the ring for injury and insurance purposes since we're students and not part of the rodeo team, but whatever. It's easy money, and sometimes it's kind of fun.

Jamieson can ride a bull so well, he makes it look effortless. Some of the older riders give him lip or talk down to him, but they're just afraid of losing their top-dog status. He has a unique form of bull riding, and while it seems awkward, it sure works for him.

When it's his turn, I pay more attention to how the bull behaves in the chute, but it's not a bull I'm overly familiar with, and I have no gut feelings about it either. I smile, though, when I recall how Jamieson's face fell when I told him to hang on before a friendly smile graced his handsome face again and he laughed.

If I'm honest with myself, I probably noticed him more than the other bull riders because he was attractive in a way that I liked. A smile on his face all the time and an air of confidence, but not cocky. He just gave off vibes of an all-around good guy, and I liked that.

The gate opens, and the bull exits the chute, bucking and spinning with Jamieson on top in his unique form. The entire time, I'm watching every muscle twitch and head shake of the bull and filing it away for later.

When the buzzer sounds, I ready myself to distract the bull if he needs it. Jamieson usually dismounts in a controlled manner. I remember that about him, too, because it's hard to pull off when unpredictable animals are beneath you and again, he makes it look like my grandmother could do it.

But something is off today, and he's still on the bull, his calm exterior crumbling as panic grips him while he fights to free his hand from the rope. The other bullfighter in the ring stands slack-jawed and I'll allow myself to feel anger for his inaction later.

"Hey! Hey bully! Over here!"

In the fraction of time it takes the bull to swing its head towards me, Jamieson has the tension release from his bull rope and dismounts. With the bull too close for comfort, he heads straight towards me.

Jamieson stumbles through the sand past me and I step behind him to push the bull's head away. Pothole notices the open gate at the end of the arena at the same time he registers the rider is off his back. With one snotty bull snort, he turns and jogs down the chute out of the ring.

That was a little too close.

"Hey, you okay?" I call to Jamieson, who climbed up the railing to safety behind me.

"Um, yeah. I got my hand stuck and..." he drops to the ground and stares at me. "You distracted that bull just long enough for me to get free."

I shrug. It's my job after all, but I also know some luck was involved and we're both lucky to escape unharmed.

"It's what I'm here for."

Jamieson shakes his head as he walks backward to the exit. "True, but you saved my ass and I'm buying you a beer after this." He points a finger at me. "I'll find you, Griff, but you're not leaving here without me!"

"Okay!"

He disappears behind the gate and I shake my head with a smile before refocusing on the next bull rider.

Maybe being involved with rodeo isn't so bad after all.

"So, where are you from?"

Jamieson tops up my glass of draft beer from the pitcher before grabbing another chicken wing from the platter. He waited for me like he said he would and now we're in a pub a few blocks from campus.

"A shitty town you've probably never heard of. Fox Grove, Alberta."

The town is so small, the guy who operates the garbage truck also notarizes your government documents. He can also marry you if you're not picky about the time of day for your ceremony. It's a spit of a town, consisting entirely of mobile homes not fit for Canadian winters. The only decent place to shop is a mom-and-pop store that's like a Dr. Frankenstein version of Walmart and Canadian Tire with a burger joint on the side. The burgers only get served if the staff show up to work and most days it's a crap shoot.

Oh, and a Pizza Hut that definitely has no business being there, but it's still operating, despite the odds.

Let's just say I'm in no rush to go back.

Jamieson's jaw drops. "You're kidding. I know it well. I'm from Kissing Ridge. We always had to drive through when we went up north to rodeos."

"Kissing Ridge is a heck of a lot better than Fox Grove. At least you have your own high school. I had to take a bus for forty-five minutes on the highway every day, and staying after school for anything was never an option."

Jamieson nods as he swallows, his mouth full, and it's not just a nod to acknowledge your sentence. That nod is of understanding because he's been there. It's a powerful thing when someone can just *know* what you mean without saying much more.

"Okay, you got me there. But Kissing Ridge is so small the town knows what I'm doing before I do."

We both laugh and I hold up my glass for a toast. "Here's to small-town boys making it big one day."

"Cheers to that! It's always been my dream to be a bull rider. I'm on a rodeo scholarship and I don't intend to fuck it up and let my grades slip. Some of the rodeo team don't really care. They're all about the parties and rodeo and don't care if they flunk. What about you?"

After swallowing some of my burger, I nod in agreement.

"I'm on an academic scholarship. Taking my bachelor's in psychology. I want to be a social worker when I grow up." We both laugh, and Jamieson frowns into his glass of beer.

"I'm in education. Teaching kids has always been something I like. My dad wanted me to take over the family business, but he's a pharmacist. No way do I want to take that on. Not to diss my dad or anything, but I'd rather wipe kids' noses than recommend hemorrhoid creams to seniors and count pills all day."

I laugh when Jamieson makes a gagging noise as he reaches for another chicken wing.

"Pharmacy is cool, though. A family business would be something. How come you're not interested? Other than the counting and creams."

We both chuckle, and he shrugs as he licks off a finger.

"I guess I like bull riding too much."

"I mean...why can't you do both?"

"Probably because I don't want to spend all my time counting pills for people when bull riding is over. It's fucking boring." He laughs and takes a swallow of beer. "Seriously, though? I'm not that smart. It's only my second year here, and I barely got through my first year of education. Like...it was almost-kicked-off-the-rodeo-team bad. If I tried a pharmacist program, I'd flunk for sure."

"I can help you. We probably have some classes in common, or if it's something I understand, I can help. I'm the academic scholarship, remember?"

His lips turn up in a giant smile. "Really? I'd fucking love that! I had a tutor last year, but they weren't very patient with me. You seem like a guy with infinite patience. I'll pay you in beer and chicken wings."

"I won't turn down free food, but I'd do it for free. I mean, teaching someone is a great way to reinforce your own knowledge. And since you actually want to teach someday..."

I let my words hang as he nods in thought, and I hope I don't come across too nerdy.

"You sound like a professor."

My cheeks burn, and I raise my beer to my lips. "Sorry."

"Don't be. I like you, Griff. I think we're going to be great friends."

Jamieson and I trade stories of our first year here, what it's like back home, and what our goals for the future are. I love how we just flow together, and being friends with him is easy. He was right when he said we had a vibe, and I like it.

I kept to myself in high school. Most of the kids in my town had the sole ambition of getting high as often as possible. I steered clear of that because I wanted a better life than what I had.

Not to mention, there weren't a lot of gay guys around. If I ever wanted to discover that side of myself, leaving town was the only option. After spending what I like to call my formative years alone in our double-wide trailer with my dad passed out drunk on the couch most nights, I wanted better and I wasn't about to hide who I was.

Before I get far more attached to Jamieson, I need to know where he stands with having a gay friend. No sense waiting. That would just suck more, and I'd hate to have him brush me off because he doesn't want to hang out with a gay dude or protect some kind of macho bull rider image.

"Have you ever gone to the themed nights the LGBTQ+ club hosts here?"

My voice doesn't waver, and I hold his gaze while I wait for his answer.

Jamieson smiles, and my shoulders relax. "Once. It was rodeo themed, and they brought in a mechanical bull. How could I say no?"

"Ha, I suppose that would be hard to turn down. I was at that one." Swallowing, I lay it on the table. "I wasn't about to miss sexy cowboy wannabes in cut-off shorts. Even went home with one."

Sort of. We kissed outside before he told me his mom was picking him up soon, and that sort of killed the entire mood for me.

Jamieson nods and studies me for a beat. "So, is this you telling me you're not straight?"

Swallowing at the directness of the question, I nod. "Will that be a problem? I like your company, so if you end up being an asshole about it, I'd be largely disappointed."

Jamieson, to my surprise, laughs a full-on laugh and holds a fist out for a bump. "Dude. Not a problem at all. I like a taste of the same sex once in a while myself. Trust me. If you're gay, it's not an issue."

Thank god. We may only have just met, but I feel like Jamieson is someone who will be my best friend until one of us dies. Maybe even after that.

"I think we just became best friends." I joke.

He raises his glass in a toast. "Here's to a new rodeo partnership and new best friends. Oh, and hometown heroes!"

"I'll drink to that!"

We finish our food and beer before finally leaving the pub together, chatting away like we've known each other forever.

"Hey, before I forget, let me give you my number. I have a stats assignment due soon and if you could explain some shit to me, I'd be eternally grateful."

"Oh, are you planning to be a math teacher?"

Jamieson shrugs with a smile. "Maybe? It's the subject I'm better at, so I picked that."

After passing him my phone, he enters his info and sends himself a text before returning it to me.

"I have an exam soon too, so that works out. We can study together. I'll be in touch." I pocket my phone as we fall into step next to each other.

We both live on campus, but in different dorms, and after the short walk, we stop outside of mine. Jamieson waves goodbye as I enter my building, and I watch him for a beat as he trudges along the path towards his.

Once in my room, I collapse on my bed and laugh the best laugh I've had in several years. It's pure joy, and it feels good.

Something tells me Jamieson will change my life.

And I like that.

Two
Jamieson

First semester, third year university

"Holy shit! Griff!"

The hand holding my phone shakes as I pass it to my best friend with my exam results open.

"You passed! I knew you could do it!"

Griff pulls me to him in a bear hug, and I curl my large body around him. "I couldn't have done this without you. Your tutoring made the difference, Griff."

My throat grows tight, and I squeeze him closer. "Because of you, I'll graduate."

Sure, graduation is still another year away, but this was the hardest year. If I didn't get through it, I wouldn't be back for the final year, which is mostly in-school placements and actual teaching. The hardest part for me is now done.

And I wouldn't have gotten here without the infinite patience of my very intelligent best friend.

"You still had to write the exams and retain the information, Jamie. Don't sell yourself short."

Griff's mouth moves against my T-shirt because I still have him crushed against me, but I hear him. He's the only one who calls me

Jamie, and I kinda like it. It's something that's just us. Easing back, I'm delighted to see the shine in his eyes.

"You're crying for me. Such a softie." I choke out a laugh as a lone tear runs down my cheek, and I swipe it away. Fuck, I'm never this emotional. Passing midterms shouldn't make me tear up. Although I suspect it's the relief that I'm still on the rodeo team that sprung the waterworks.

"I'm crying because you still get to do what you want. You want to be a bull rider, and now, with school going well, you can." Griff squeezes me once more before I let him step away.

"I still have to finish this semester and next year."

Lord knows I still have lots of time yet to fuck up school, but this is the first deal to keep dad off my back. Passing allowed me to stay in the program, but a 70% meant I could stay on the rodeo team.

That was my dad's rule, and while I understand where he's coming from since he's paying for my degree and doesn't want me to put all my hopes into bull riding, I also wish he'd just let me do what I want.

"You can't give up on me, in class or on a bull. You need to be there."

Griff smiles a soft smile. It's one I've only seen aimed my way, and I'm so grateful I took the chance to make a new friend that day. He's been there for me at every corner, and that just doesn't happen much anymore.

He swings an arm around my shoulders and leads me away from campus. "We should go celebrate. It's wing night at the pub. You love wings."

"I do!"

Griff and I walk to the pub on campus, and his arm shifts from my shoulders to circle my waist as he speaks about me and how far I've come. He says how proud he is of me, and I don't doubt a single word. He's the best, most sincere, and supportive friend I've ever had.

"You've done a lot, too. Don't think I didn't see that email about the dean's list." My arm around him squeezes as I flash a smile down to Griff. "You're the smartest guy I know, and you helped me while doing your own work. Plus, holding a spot as a bullfighter. Never sell yourself short, Griff. You'll do amazing things someday."

Griff dips his head as we walk, and it's nice that he doesn't boast like some of my teammates, but then again, I brag about him whenever someone will listen, so maybe it evens out.

"Thanks, Jamie. That means a lot."

"You're welcome. I mean it."

Griff's eyes lock with mine, and for a moment, I consider pecking a quick kiss on his lips. Which is new. And weird. I playfully push him into the bushes as we walk by instead. He doesn't fall, but the scowl he aims my way is vintage Griff.

"What the hell, Jamieson?" He brushes a few stray twigs from his hair and throws them at me.

"I thought I saw a wasp on you. I saved you!" Slapping my hand to my chest, I pretend to be offended, and a small smile forms on Griff's lips.

"You're such a loser. Just for that, you're buying the beer."

I was going to anyway, but at least the weird moment is over.

Griff is just a friend.

"Okay, here's what I think."

Griff grabs my shoulders, and I puff out a breath. It's the final major rodeo on the college tour, and I wouldn't be here without his weird sixth sense about bulls. I'm convinced he's a mind-reading Dr. Doolittle. It's the only thing that makes sense.

"You drew Master Slaughter. He's tough, but I think he's tired today. Something tells me he's going to buck with half a heart and all you need to do is keep your form to score higher."

I stare at Griff and shake my head. "No, that's impossible. He's a major bull, Griff. He won't just have an off day like that."

"I'm telling you...he is. Trust me. He's not been quite right the whole time I've watched him in the chutes. That bull is going to straight buck, no spins. Hang on and make it look easy, like you always do." Griff smiles and claps my shoulder. "You good?"

"Yeah. Yeah, I'm good. Thanks Griff. I'll see you in the ring."

"You will. I've got your back, Jamie. Don't forget that."

Griff jogs down the small aisle behind the loading chutes and I step away from all the bulls and rodeo action. Before I enter the line up behind the scenes with the other riders, I always take a moment by myself. Maybe I'm a little superstitious that way, but once I made it part of my pre-ride routine, I couldn't stop.

Today's an indoor event, so I find a quiet hallway in the facility and lean against a cool brick wall. Griff's words still sound in my ears, and he's never been wrong yet. Not only has he tutored me through some challenging classes, he's been a huge part of my success in the ring, too.

He's not just a bullfighter. He's an intuitive guy. Smart, funny and the best person I've ever met. Closing my eyes, I envision myself on the back of Master Slaughter, riding flawlessly as the bull behaves exactly like Griff says it will. My attention then turns to Griff in the ring, keeping not just me, but all the riders safe.

For something he said he fell into by accident, he's a natural. I don't know how I'll be able to compete without him after we graduate. His gift is my advantage and not only do I not want to give that up, but I don't want to be separated from him after graduation, either. It's been hard to focus, knowing we have different paths ahead of us soon.

But there's no time for those thoughts now. This is the time to ride as well as I can, score mega points, and give us a reason to celebrate tonight.

Pushing off the wall, I count to twelve backwards—not to ten. I don't like zeros—then return to the chutes.

"Hey! There you are!" My coach grabs me by the elbow and pulls me aside. "You had to draw a new bull. Master Slaughter didn't pass the vet check. You can't ride him."

"Who do I have now?"

This is fine. It's all fine.

"No Mercy."

"Oh, well, that sounds no better than Master Slaughter, but it is what it is, right?"

Coach slaps my back, oblivious to my internal Zen unravelling. "You got it, Jamieson. You'll be fine."

I sure fucking hope so. Griff is in the ring, and I know nothing about this bull. I hate going in blind, but there's nothing I can do about it.

"Calm blue ocean, Jamieson. You can do this. It's fine. You did it before Griff, and you can do it again." I mutter as I take my place in the line with the others.

One by one, the riders mount their bulls, and I watch in a detached way as they all ride well enough. I cheer when I should, groan when it's required, and assist in the chutes.

Then it's my turn, and while I internally berate myself for depending on my friend's intuitive bull reports so much, he was right...again.

"You good, Jamieson?"

"Y-yeah."

No.

But the chute swings open, and my bull charges out, bucking and spinning. I maintain my form as best as I can, but I'm sliding to one side, and my grip on my bull rope has loosened.

With one final buck, I go flying and somehow still land on my feet. Blindly stumbling forward, about to face plant into the sand, familiar arms wrap around me and haul me into a hard chest. We both fall to the ground, and I land on Griff with my full weight.

"Look out!"

Griff rolls us to the side and covers as much of my body with his as the ground shakes around us, and Griff grunts in pain.

Then it's all over as fast as it began, and everyone in the ring rushes our way.

"Get a stretcher!" Someone yells, and it's then I register Griff's low groan.

"Griff? Are you hurt?"

"Something hurts, but I think it's minor. Don't worry about it, Jamie. I got you."

Griff is lifted off me as more people and more commotion surround us. Blood flows down his leg, soaking his sneaker and discolouring the tape around his ankle as he's placed on a stretcher.

"Where are you taking him?!"

Is that me sounding so hysterical?

"The hospital. He needs stitches for sure." The paramedic turns to me. "Did you get hurt?"

"N-no, but I don't want him to go alone."

"Follow us then."

Griff reaches for my hand as I walk beside him on the stretcher. "Stay, Jamie. I'm fine."

"Never. I'm not letting you go to the hospital alone."

He doesn't try to fight back.

Griff simply nods and squeezes my hand before we both enter the ambulance.

"I can drop by later with a pizza if you're up for visitors."

The line is quiet, but Griff finally answers. "Yeah. I'd like that."

"Do you need me to pick anything up for you? Library books, new porn?"

The quiet chuckle is my reward, and my shoulders sag. "I think I'm okay for both. A pizza and human company sound good, though."

"I'll be there in an hour."

It's only been five days since Griff went to the hospital, but it feels like five years. He needed thirty stitches along his calf where the bull's hoof grazed him enough to cut deep. But he also knocked his head hard and, while not concussed, it was still a head injury that came with a massive headache.

He's been ordered to rest and keep off his leg as much as possible. Since then, he's been in his dorm room and keeping to himself.

And it's been the longest stretch I've gone since I met Griff that we haven't seen each other. Pizza doesn't seem like enough to say thank you for saving my life, but what else can I do for him?

If he hadn't caught me and rolled us out of the way, that two-thousand-pound bull was coming straight down on my back. If I weren't dead, I would have wished I were, and my career would be over.

After stopping to get his favourite pizza, I quickly duck into the campus store and find a 'Get Well Soon' card with a giraffe wearing a scarf and a thermometer in its mouth. It's something that Griff would absolutely laugh at. Borrowing a pen, I scribble a quick note and shove the card in my pocket before winding my way through the dorms to Griff's.

"Knock, knock," I call and slowly turn the handle before poking half my face through the door. "Are you decent?"

"Does it matter? You've already got your head inside. Get in here."

After closing the door behind me, Griff sits up from his pillow mountain and slides to the edge of his bed. He eases his bandaged leg up onto a chair and attempts a smile. After placing the pizza on the bed next to him, I plop onto the floor and flip the pizza box open.

"I got your favourite."

Griff's mouth twitches in a small smile. "You don't like sausage on your pizza, though."

"I can pick it off. More for you."

"Thanks, Jamie." He gives me a tired smile, and after grabbing a slice and taking a few bites, he finally looks like the friend I miss.

"Um, so are you still hurting a lot?"

Griff tilts his hand back and forth and swallows. "Some. It's an improvement, though. Doc said I could take the bandage off today and start with slow movements until the stitches come out."

"And the head?"

"It's okay. I had a bitchin' headache for the first few days, but that's good now, too. How have your practices been?"

"We just had the one, and it was in the weight room." Griff nods, and silence settles between us. "Will you ever be back, Griff?" I whisper, and he jerks his gaze to mine.

"Why would you ask that? I don't want to quit."

"I guess I wasn't sure. It was scary, and we haven't talked much since it happened. How are you...you know...mentally?"

Many rodeo men have walked away from the sport when traumatic things happen. I read about it after the paramedic told me to monitor Griff for any behavioural changes.

He picks at the sausage on his pizza before he replies.

"I acted on instinct to protect you, Jamie. I really didn't think about what I was doing except that I was keeping you safe. That's my job, and I'll never let you down. I'm fine. Yes, it scared me, and I thought about the what-ifs for a few days, but as long as you ride bulls, I'm going to be in the ring to protect you."

A lump wells in my throat that's definitely not from the pizza.

"Thanks. I've, um…thought about the what-ifs, too. If…if you hadn't been there, I might not be sitting here with you now. I know that." Griff opens his mouth to protest, but I hold up a hand. "No, Griff, let me finish. Please." He motions for me to continue, and I suck in a breath. "You saved my life. Whether or not you want to acknowledge that, I do. You're my best friend, and I want to thank you for being there."

Griff remains quiet, and I eat my pizza while I give him a moment. We've been close like no other friendship I've ever had since we met, and this has brought us even closer. It's opened my eyes to who is really there for you. Few people would be in the position to take a bull's hoof for me, but if they were, I'm not sure how many would do what Griff did.

Finally, his giant smile returns. "If I say you're welcome, can we put this mushy stuff behind us and get on with things?"

Holding a piece of pizza up in toast, I take a bite. "A hundred percent. Let's eat this before it gets cold, and I'll help you clean up. When's the last time you did the laundry? It smells like an old sock in here."

Griff tosses a pillow at my head, and I bat it away, laughing.

"I was sentenced to bed rest, asshole. Don't rag on my lack of cleaning."

"I know for a fact you said you'd do laundry before this even happened." I point to the mountain of clothes in a heap in the corner. "That's not five days' worth of laundry."

"Remind me why you're my friend again." Griff moves the remaining pizza out of my reach with a grin.

Yeah, we'll be okay.

Three
Griff

The Last Week Before Graduation

I'm certain karaoke with Jamieson making up words for sea shanties is not what I want to do tonight. As entertaining as it is, I'm barely holding it all together. A significant chapter of our lives is about to end, and all I want is Jamieson to myself.

I should tell him how I feel. We've chatted about me staying in Kissing Ridge permanently. I secured a regular bullfighting rotation on the rodeo circuit, and Jamieson gets his dream to compete as a Canadian bull rider. It makes sense on paper for us to stay in the same town.

I didn't apply for the master's program in psychology like I'd planned, much to my professor's disappointment. He assured me I'd be accepted easily, and I might even qualify for partial funding, but I just couldn't do it. Jamieson is my focus.

He needs me while he's on the circuit, and I can't just walk away from that.

Is it stupid to put my future on hold because I'm in love with my best friend? Absolutely. But my heart wants to stay close to Jamieson.

If people can take time off after high school before they start their education, I can take time off before extending it. The reason doesn't matter.

"Griff!" Jamie jumps off the stage and throws his arms around me. I breathe in his essence and try not to bury my face in his neck. "Let's dance with..." He spins swiftly to the attractive blonde next to him. "Simon!"

Simon gives me an appreciative once-over and a little wave. "Hi. I'd love to dance with you both."

Jamieson whispers in my ear. "He's cute right?"

We follow Simon to the dance floor, and despite my inner turmoil, I agree. "He is."

Simon, with his short blonde hair, warm brown eyes, and a smile you can't help but return, is attractive in that magazine model way. Flawless skin, a perfectly tight body, and just the right amount of mystery. Jealousy strikes when he bats his eyelashes at Jamieson and playfully throws his arms around his neck.

Jamieson smiles at Simon with a promise on his lips, and I'm not sure why I'm even here. I don't get those looks from Jamieson, no matter how hard I wish I did.

The three of us dance and pass Jamie's beer around. He never could hold much alcohol, and while we're all pleasantly buzzed, we're also sober enough to understand the proposition put forth by the incredibly cute Simon.

"I want to take both of you home. My roommates are already gone, and I want to end this year with a bang." Simon runs a hand up each of our chests and tilts his face up to Jamieson. "Or a blow. I'm not picky about how it goes down, but you two are fucking hot."

Jamieson turns to me, and we share a silent conversation through eyebrow quirks and head tilts before I cup Simon's cheek and kiss him softly. "Lead the way."

I don't know why I've agreed to this. Yes, I find Simon attractive, but he's not the one I want. Threesomes aren't even on my fantasy list. Yeah, I'm an anomaly in literally everything in life, but Jamieson wants to do this, so I agreed.

Because I'll never say no to him.

Simon lives in a townhouse only ten minutes away, but the walk there takes us closer to twenty. Jamieson and I exchange kisses with Simon the entire time, along with the odd grope. Watching my best friend kiss another man is hot, but a low-key jealousy still burns. He never once reaches for me to kiss, and I try not to dwell on it.

Once inside Simon's townhouse, every moan and harsh breath are amplified by the emptiness of the space. A single chair remains in the living room with a small TV on the floor, and that's it. Clothes come off, and Jamieson is naked with Simon, while I'm still in shock that I've got myself into this situation. But the pull to be naked with Jamieson is greater than the need to back out.

Simon multi-tasks and undresses me while making out with Jamieson.

"I don't really want rug burn." He chuckles and takes our hands, pulling us down the hallway. "Let's move this to the bedroom."

I stand back in the bedroom doorway, watching the two of them kiss and grope, unable to bring myself closer and touch what I've always wanted. My dick aches being this close, but this isn't the type of sex I want. Jamieson, yes, but not like this.

Simon falls onto his bed and beckons me closer.

"Come on, Griff. I promise this is the best sex. Get your tight ass over here."

"You heard him, Griff. Come on. Join us."

I should be happy that this is how our university days will end. An exciting romp with a beautiful man shared between us. But it's not my style.

Simon is a filthy talker. He's painting pictures with his words that almost make me blush. A wave of insecurity slams into me, and I can't stop it. This isn't what I want. I don't want to share Jamieson, and I can't stand watching another person make him moan like that.

Fuck!

Even though my dick throbs watching the scene in front of me, I slip out the bedroom door and find my clothes on the floor in the empty living room. After pulling them on, I quietly slip out and hope like hell Jamieson doesn't come after me.

What was I thinking?

I hoped to end the evening with a deep conversation with my closest friend, sharing intimate details and secrets that I guard closely. Secrets I don't share with strange men like Simon.

So much for ending our year on a positive note.

Four
Jamieson

"I can't believe you're really doing this. It won't be the same without you."

My friend Jackson laughs as he pulls me into a rib-cracking hug.

"I'll be around for a few rodeos this year, yet. I'm just easing myself out of it and into a new career. I'm over forty, J. I may be fit, but I need to think ahead." One of his dogs races by us in the yard, chasing after a ball. "I want to be here for the dogs and Riley, too. This is what I've always wanted."

Watching the contentment ooze off Jackson takes the sting away. I'll miss him on our rodeo trips, but it's hard to not be happy about his new life plans.

"Hey, you!" Riley, Jackson's boyfriend, joins us and offers Jackson a glass of iced tea with a kiss. Jackson beams as bright as a Broadway marquee and grabs Riley's hand.

"Hey, yourself. Do you need me to start up the barbeque yet?"

"No, it looks like Gabe has that under control."

The three of us turn towards the grill and, sure enough, Riley's best friend, Gabe, has an assembly line set up and seems to enjoy the task.

"So, Jamieson, is this your year? Jackson thinks it could be your turn to make the finals." Riley leans into Jackson, giving him a side hug and they're too damn cute.

"Well...I don't know. I mean, it's always possible. I've been training hard over the winter. My fitness is prime, but you never know what bulls you might draw. That's the wild card in this business."

"True, but don't discount your talent, J." Jackson bends to scratch the beagle's ears before throwing the slobbery ball across the yard that the dog dropped at his feet. "Every athlete peaks and my gut says this is your time. You've even bulked up. Your strength and endurance, your technique...I've never seen you this good."

Jackson's words ease the uncertainty in my brain. I know what he says is true, but I've never been one to brag about my achievements. Heck, I don't even like to acknowledge when I'm mediocre. It always feels icky to me, but I have no issue talking up the attributes of my friends.

"I owe it to you and all your help in the gym this past winter. You inspire me."

"Me?" Jackson cocks his head.

"Yeah, you. You're like the brother I never had. Watching you finally make it to finals and fall in love last year...seeing you achieve everything was inspiring. I applied myself and was more disciplined because you proved it was possible."

Jackson's eyes are all shiny and I didn't mean to be so intimate, but he really did all those things for me, and I'll miss his steady presence at our campsites.

The beagle returns, Carrot is her name, some kind of inside joke with Jackson and Riley and he throws the ball for her again before sipping his iced tea.

"As an only child, I can say the same about you, Jamieson. It's been my pleasure to work alongside you and watch you grow."

Riley rubs Jackson's back with a warm smile. "And you still will. Just not as often. Rodeo is what you love. I know I'm the new guy to the group, but this isn't over. It's just a change, Jamieson. He's still here for you and rodeo will always be a part of Jackson."

Jackson nods and kisses Riley softly before turning to me.

"What he said." Jackson glances around the yard that's filled with our rodeo friends and family. "Where's Griff? Didn't he come with you?"

"He was supposed to, but he called me last minute and said he was running late, and he'd meet me here."

Griff never runs late. He's always punctual and never out of line. But this winter he's been different. He's cancelled our plans multiple times at the last minute and if I didn't know better, he's been avoiding me.

He's been my best friend since we met at university and my sister likes to say we're attached at the hip. I wish he'd let me in on what's bothering him so much. We've always been close and lately it feels like he's pulling away and I can't help but wonder if it's something I did.

"Is he okay?"

"As far as I know, he is."

Jackson nods in thought and Riley excuses himself to help Gabe when a large burst of flame rises from the BBQ.

"Should you go help them?"

Jackson smiles and shrugs. "I'll wait it out. But I should make some rounds and say hello to people." He smacks me on the shoulder. "I'll catch you later, J. And don't worry, you'll be fine this year without me."

After Jackson leaves to mingle with everyone, I duck behind his barn and pull out my phone. There are no texts from Griff, and the ball in my stomach clenches. He should be here by now. It's what we always do to start the rodeo season. One last get together with our friends and families before we spend most of the summer away at events.

Even my sister is here and she's so city I'm surprised she shows her face at something as low key as a backyard BBQ.

I hit dial and wait for Griff to pick up, but it rings and rings with no answer. Stuffing the phone in my pocket, I stride towards the front of Jackson's house. Maybe Griff is already here and didn't turn his phone on.

Not seeing his car, I call him again. Not because I think this call will end any differently, but because I need to feel like I'm doing something.

"Come on, Griff. This isn't like you." I mutter as the unease grips me tighter.

Finally, the telltale wheeze of his old car's engine sounds in the distance and I walk to the end of the driveway to watch Griff's white Ford Neon come into view. When he finally parks along the shoulder of the road, he walks towards the house with his hands in his pockets and his head down.

"Hey, I was worried something happened to you. You're never this late."

Griff's head snaps up, and I immediately inhale a sharp breath.

"Jesus Christ, Griff, what happened?" I growl before pulling him into a tight hug. I welcome the relief that swamps me when he hugs me back. "Are you okay?" I whisper, and his head nods against my chest before he steps out of the hug.

My hand instinctively cups his cheek, the one that's turning shades of purple right in front of me. Griff pulls away as soon as I touch it.

"I'm sorry. That was dumb."

Griff squeezes my wrist, assuring me it's okay. "I almost didn't come, but I know it's tradition. I didn't want to let you down."

Something tightens in my chest over those words. This is what he's been keeping from me, and I don't like that it caused physical pain. That someone did this to him.

"I would have come to you, Griff. You're my best friend. Why didn't you say anything?"

His eyes flash in anger. A sharp turn from the softness a moment ago. "Because I don't want you to look at me with pity like you are now, okay?"

"It's not pity. I just want to help you."

Griff hangs his head again. "I'm sorry. I know you do. It's just...I'm almost thirty years old and I shouldn't put myself in these positions, but..."

Griff shrugs and trails off, but I know. He never talks about his relationships much, but this one set off alarms I should have paid more attention to.

"Just tell me he's out of the picture now, please?"

"Oh yeah. You don't need to fight for me, Jamie. The trash took itself out."

Griff wants me to let it drop, but I can't.

"I will kick this fucker's ass into the next province if he even gets close enough to breathe on you again." Reaching out, I gently brush my fingers across the bruise on his face. It takes a lot to make me angry, but this mark on my best friend's face has turned my normally sunny demeanor dark. "You should report this, Griff. He assaulted you."

Griff closes his eyes and shakes his head slightly. "I can't, Jamie. I don't...I'm not bringing this up with the police and..." He sighs. "I just don't want to, okay? Please let it drop." He whispers.

Saying no to Griff is hard, but if that's what he wants, then I'll give that to him.

"Come on. Let's get into this shindig." Hooking my arm through his, I pull him along to the house and choose to let the heaviness of whatever happened slide. He knows if he needed me, all he'd have to do is call and I'd be there faster than The Flash. I have to believe he'd call if he truly needed me.

"I'll warn you now, Riley's friend Gabe is manning the grill, and I already saw a wall of flames, so we might be stuck with salads tonight."

Griff groans and laughs, and I know he's okay. He squeezes my arm through his, and when his gaze catches mine, I read the silent message. We've always connected non-verbally, and that hasn't changed.

Thank you.

"My mom and dad are here. Even Kara came."

"Maybe I should ask her if she has that good makeup with her."

"It's my sister. What do you think? She never leaves the house without a bag as big as a carry-on suitcase, and I bet she has makeup."

Jackson notices us walking up the driveway and, bless him, he doesn't even flinch when he notices Griff's bruised-up face.

"Hey, buddy! Glad you could make it, but I'll warn you now. The burgers look like hockey pucks, and the lawyer boy needs to stay away from the grill." Jackson makes a disgusted face, and Griff's laugh rings out, further easing my anxiety.

Jackson's dog, Tramp, trots over to Griff and waits. Tail wagging and ears perked.

"I can't believe you keep coming back for this." He reaches into his pocket and unwraps a peanut-butter-filled pretzel from a small piece of plastic wrap. "You know, I have to remember to keep buying these things just for you now. I hope you're happy."

Tramp barks and sits as Griff offers him the treat with a fond smile.

"If I need to pay you for all the peanut-butter pretzels you're buying, let me know." Jackson chuckles as the dog gulps his treat and runs back to the yard to keep playing.

"I'll consider it even since you feed me occasionally."

"Deal." Jackson motions to the backyard. "Join us when you're ready."

Griff takes a deep breath and stares after Jackson before turning to smile at me.

"Let's kick off your season then, Jamie."

The smile almost reaches his eyes, but I let it go and nod before hugging him once again.

"Let's do it."

"Griff! Do you have, like, a cup of noodles or anything I can eat before we go?"

He still hasn't packed for our first rodeo trip of the year. Since there's still time before we absolutely have to leave, I might as well eat while I wait. Opening the cupboards, I find a box of Ritz Crackers instead and tear into them.

Griff exits his bedroom and drops an oversized duffle bag on the floor with a sigh.

"Are you ever not hungry?"

That's a valid question. "I'm gonna say no."

He grins with a shake of his head. The bruising on his face is now yellowish and doesn't look quite so painful. It's amazing the difference a week makes.

"I think I'm almost ready. Just let me change and have a look in the bathroom again."

"Griff, I swear, you're just as bad as Kara sometimes. If you forget something, we'll buy it. And it's only for four days."

His voice carries down the hall in his small apartment. "I know. But you know how I am."

I sure do. I know he's going through every single drawer and cabinet in his bathroom right now, *just in case.* I've mentioned before that we can just buy what we forget, but he always brushes it off.

He finally returns and shoves a hairbrush into his already over-stuffed duffle.

"A brush?"

He shrugs and passes a hand over his short hair. "I might need it."

Setting the crackers beside me, I stand and open my arms. "C'mere."

Griff wraps his arms around my waist and squeezes me back. I wasn't always such a touchy person. But after Griff put himself in front of a bull for me at university, I couldn't help it. It's like an urge to always let him know I appreciate him, because what if next time we aren't so lucky? Thankfully, Griff doesn't mind me always hugging and touching him.

He rests his head against my chest, and I breathe in his lemon-soap scent. I wonder if we could find lemon meringue pie on the drive?

"Sorry. I'm just all over the place, and I need to get it together."

"You will, Griff. You're human."

He pushes away from me and clears his throat. He opens his mouth but then closes it before huffing a breath and turning down the hall. "Right. Let me get changed, and we can finally get going."

My best friend disappears into his room again and closes the door while I collapse on the sofa with the box of crackers.

The cushions crinkle, and I stand up to move the pile of papers I fell on. A familiar university logo sits on top, and before I can stop myself, I'm reading.

"We are pleased to offer you a position in the masters program beginning August 15th. Please return your answer by May 23rd with a deposit."

What the hell? He's doing his masters and didn't tell me?

Pushing aside the questions I want to ask, I flip the paper over and shove it back before sitting back down with my crackers.

Today is May 23rd, but we're heading out to begin our rodeo circuit together.

"I think I'm ready, Jamie," Griff calls as he walks back into his living room. "Let's get this started, eh?"

He's my Griff. Happy and surly all rolled into one, and he's never kept secrets from me. At least I think he hasn't. He told me about the date, who was a bit too physical, and that he was going to break up with him. Which was a relief because he sounded like a Class-A asshole. I still think he should have pressed charges.

But this? He might leave, and he's staying quiet?

"Everything, okay?"

Griff's hand touches my shoulder, and I jump up.

"Sorry, I zoned out." He smiles again and motions to the cracker box. "Bring those along and we'll stop for a burger at the truck stop you like."

At the mention of burgers, I'm grabbing his bag and pushing him out the door, allowing myself to forget what I just read.

Because Griff won't leave me.

Five
Griff

"This is gonna be so weird without Jackson and Hunter. I mean, you know you're my buddy, but it's like we're kids on our first road trip without Mom and Dad, you know?"

Jamieson, who can't stay quiet if his life depended on it—or stop eating—grins at me from the passenger seat of his truck. I'm only driving because he drives a vehicle like he rides a bull: *hang on tight and let's see where this takes us.* That's not exactly joyful for a passenger.

"It will be different for sure. I'll miss having them around."

Not that we won't see them. Jackson is just dialing back the number of rodeos he does this year. He's not quitting. Since Hunter is his partner in the ring, he's also hanging back. I'm happy for my friend who finally found love and is easing into a new career with a hydroponic gardening business and all the other projects he and Riley have on the go, but I'll miss Jackson's steady presence on the road.

Especially since I'll no longer have a buffer between me and Jamieson. Jackson is the only one who knows I intended to quit the life of being a rodeo bullfighter. When Jackson announced his reduced schedule, I knew what it meant.

Jamieson would lean on me even more.

There was no way I could go through with my original plan and do my masters in psychology now. As much as it hurts to always be so close to him but never have him, I'd never be able to leave Jamieson like that. Not with everything we've been through.

So here I am again, dreading what lies ahead for the next few months. Still in love with my best friend like I have been since we met in college all those years ago.

"Oh! I was thinking—"

"That's never a good idea, Jamie." I love saying that just to see him scrunch his eyebrows at me.

"Rude." He tosses a cracker at me, and I laugh when it sails in front of me and hits the window. He keeps eating crackers from the box, forgetting my teasing, and continues. "I was thinking if you're up to it, maybe we could do some longer trips this summer? We always had to rush back because of Hunter's ranch or something Jackson has going on, but since we're both younger than them and this is our job...maybe we could slow it down?"

Jamieson has never been one to slow anything down. He's always a rush here and rush there kind of guy. Hurry and wait, so this takes me by surprise.

"What did you have in mind?"

He shakes the empty cracker box and frowns.

"When we go to the rodeo in Manitoba, it's close to the Ontario border. I looked at the schedule and I might like to explore Ontario for a few days before coming back home and stopping at different rodeos on the way back. Only if you want to, though."

The truck tires hum along the pavement as I roll around the scenarios in my head. Extra days with Jamieson doing something that might feel like we're a couple is probably not the best idea.

But I've never been to Ontario as a tourist either. From the corner of my eye, I can see Jamieson doing that thing he does when he's anxious. He alternates chewing his top and bottom lip while nodding his head like a bobble head on the bumpiest side road.

"I'm not opposed. I'd need to plan for it, of course. Financially."

Not that it will cost buckets. Knowing Jamieson, he'll want to take the camper and go to some kind of pretty park to hike. Which actually sounds nice. We're used to sleeping in a camper together and I've never taken a real vacation either. Ever. Maybe I can handle this one last time before I tell him I'm quitting rodeo and getting serious about pursuing my education again.

"Oh, for sure." His smile damn near blinds me and I have to remind my brain it's not a lover's smile. It's a happy best friend and nothing more. "Actually, part of the reason I'm asking is that there's a bull riding event near the town where I got my tattoo. Remember when we did that extra leg to go to the Big Money Bulls event last year? I saw the shop, and he had an opening, so I did it then."

"I remember. You whined about how much it hurt after."

"It did!" Jamieson mock-pouts before smacking my arm. "Oh! We're already at the truck stop. I might grab an extra burger for the road. Do you want one?"

"How do you not weigh as much as a bull? I swear to god, I don't know where you put all the food you eat."

Jamieson ignores me as I pull into the busy truck stop with our camper and find a spot near the back next to all the transports.

"Anyway, the tattoo guy's name is Marko, said he knew a place we could stay if we ever came back close and wanted to. His boyfriend lives on a ranch or something."

"Well, that's nice of him. No hotel bills would be nice."

"Nope. He said we'd just need to worry about food, and the place is ours for as long as we want."

Even though my brain shouts no, my heart can't get on the same train. It's hard to say no to Jamieson. Especially when he seems so excited about it.

"It sounds great, Jamie. Let's do it!"

When my best friend whoops with excitement and beams that smile back at me, the one with full dimples that makes my skin tingle, I know I'm not getting out of this summer with my heart intact.

"Hey, Griff! Good to see ya!"

Mitchell, one of the longest-serving bullfighters on the circuit, smacks my shoulder in greeting.

"Hey Mitch! They let you back here again, did they? I thought you were gonna quit."

He snorts. "If I do that, they might be forced to offer your grouchy ass more rodeos. I can't let that happen."

"Always a comedian, aren't you?"

Mitch laughs as he sits beside me and tapes his ankles. "Gotta keep it light in here, sunshine. So, how're things? I heard Jackson is partially retired. Without him and Hunter, is it just you and Jamieson from Kissing Ridge now?"

"Yep. There's a new crop of youngsters coming up soon, though. That's something Jackson and Hunter are working on, too. Kind of like a rodeo skills camp or something."

"That's so, Jackson." Mitch shakes his head with a fond smile. "So, you're the only one left to keep Jamieson in line? You've got your work cut out for you."

"Heh, yeah, but I've been doing it for years. Ever since we were naïve university kids. I'm used to it."

Which is true. Ever since we met at rodeo practice and he took me for a beer after, I've been following Jamieson like a shadow. From keeping him safe at the bar to being his fake emergency call when he had to get out of a bad date, I've been there.

Without Hunter to follow him to the bar, someone needs to monitor him and tell him when to stop singing sea shanties. The guy seriously can't read the room while singing. Which means it's up to me. Or at least that's what I'm telling myself, anyway.

Mitch tosses his tape into a duffle bag and stands with a slap to his thighs. "Well, see you out there, sunshine."

Mitch has always been a role model to me. We both put ourselves into the paths of dangerous bulls to keep the riders safe as a job with zero hesitation. While most of us, I admit, are a little unhinged most days, Mitch has always been steady. He's a guy I could picture at a desk job. Mitch is likeable and always put together, right down to his pressed button-up shirts. He says he loves this life, though, and I see it every time we work at an event together.

It took me a few years to be truthful to myself and admit that I wasn't always happy being a bullfighter. Yes, it takes a skill that I seem to have, but knowing the way Jamieson is and not trusting anyone else to keep him safe, I accepted the offer to be a regular on the rodeo circuit with him. It's easy enough to make sure I work the same rodeos as he competes in. For the few that I'm not working, I still go with him and give him my pre-ride report.

It keeps him calm and performing his best while he rides, and I sleep better, knowing he's safe. I'd call that a win-win.

The music pounds through the ground as the announcers hype up the crowd for the bull riders. Jamieson already went through his pre-ride routine, and now I do mine.

It's nothing as intricate as his. I simply take a moment to ask the universe to keep us all safe tonight, and I pat the scar on my calf to remind me how close I came to losing Jamieson.

Nothing intricate. No big chants or anything.

Just gratitude.

And an extra wish for Jamieson.

I'm exhausted and pissed off.

Every bull rider but one so far has been an asshole. Who stays in the ring and plays to the crowd just steps away from an angry bull who would stomp you into the ground without a second thought? Have some damn thought of your safety, for fuck's sakc.

My throat burns from yelling at the assholes while almost taking a hoof to the head. Thankfully, there are only two more riders to go tonight, and Jamieson is up next.

My heart always lodges in my throat when I watch him in the bucking chute. His six-foot-two frame should never ride a bull with such grace, but that's Jamieson for you. He always seems to do the unexpected.

He drew a solid bull. A strong bucker and if Jamieson keeps his form, they should score high and end in the money. His head nods, and the chute doors open. His bull doesn't stray from its usual pattern, and he looks comfortable out there. I think he might even be smiling.

The buzzer sounds for his eight seconds, and I spring into action, waiting for his dismount or to lure the bull away. He hits the ground and stumble-runs towards me as Mitch draws the bull's attention to the exit chute.

"All clear, Jamie."

Jamieson immediately stops running and bends to brace his hands on his thighs.

"Thanks, Griff. Great ride, huh?"

Jamison sags, and I grip his arm tighter as I lead him over to the exit.

"Yeah. Should be a good score. You okay?"

He nods. "I shouldn't have skipped my pre-ride snack. Just a little woozy."

"Jamie," I practically growl his name. "The one time you *need* to eat, and you don't. You can't be crashing while on a bull!"

Jamieson eats constantly, but he needs to eat before he rides. His metabolism is one I'll never understand because the adrenaline of an eight-second ride is enough to make him lightheaded. He learned that early, and we always make sure he eats something light before he warms up.

Soft brown eyes stare at me through the cage of his helmet. "I know, Griff. But you're in the ring, and I know you'll keep me safe when I fuck up. I'll go have a snack now."

Then the fucker slips through the gates and into the back. His score of 88 booms from the speakers in the announcer's voice, and he's in the lead. After the last rider has a great ride and bumps Jamieson into the second spot, he's the first to congratulate the winner after the event.

I listen from the bench where I unwrap all the tape from my ankles.

"You're always so smooth out there, Jamieson. I don't know what it is about you, but you've just got it." The other bull rider, Cody, playfully punches Jamieson in the shoulder. "What are you doing after? Do you want to get a beer?"

My hands shake as I keep my head down and focus on my task. Here it comes.

"We're always at the bar after. I'll see you there." Jamieson can't help being friendly. It's just the way he is, but Cody isn't looking for a group drink.

Cody hesitates. "Oh, yeah, of course. Maybe I'll buy you a drink later."

"It should be me buying. You won, after all."

Clearing my throat, I draw their attention as I toss my used tape into the garbage. "He's right, Cody. Winners don't buy their own drinks."

He flashes me a tight smile. "I'll see you guys later, then."

It's so small I almost miss it. Cody thinks he snuck in the perusal, but I notice. Jamieson never does, though. Male or female, if you're not throwing yourself at him, he doesn't pick up on flirting.

Which is a whole other kind of heartache for me when I need to spell it out and watch him hook up with people who aren't me.

"Let's hit the showers before the drinks."

We fall into a comfortable walk, his six-foot-two and my five-foot-eleven amble together easily, and he throws an arm over my shoulder. We find the truck in the back parking lot and, after tossing our gear in, Jamieson turns to me.

"Sorry for scaring you in the ring. I was really hyped up for tonight, and I knew I should've eaten something, but I...I just didn't. I'm sorry, and I'll try not to let it happen again."

"It's fine, Jamie. You're just being you."

He huffs. An annoyed sound I don't hear often from him. "No, it's not fine, Griff. You have a hard job, and I was selfish for not thinking about how that would affect you. I worry too, you know."

"What? Why would you worry?" He does that thing again where he bites both of his lips, and my heart rate kicks up. "Jamie? What are you worrying about?"

With a sigh, he levels me with a gaze that almost kills me.

"Sometimes I worry you'll get sick of my bullshit and leave. I know I'm a lot, but...I need you and...yeah, I just don't want to stress you out with my stupidity."

God dammit. Why would he say something like that now, after all these years?

Clearing my throat, I pop my hip into his. "I'm not going anywhere, Jamie."

He huffs a breath. "I notice you didn't disagree with the stupidity part."

Laughing, I shake my head. "Let's call it poorly calculated risks instead."

And just like that, we slip back into our usual roles, and everything is as it should be. Me pining for Jamieson and him remaining clueless.

Six
Jamieson

A new town, a new rodeo, and a sort-of new bar.

The honky tonk tunes have my fingers tapping against my jeans and the line dancers are on fire. Me, though? I'm drunk.

"So, where do you stay when you travel for a rodeo?"

Blinking to get my focus back on the cute blonde girl next to me, I bend closer. She's super tiny. Or maybe I'm a giant. Either way, it's a long way for words to travel, and I'm not sure how I even heard her question from way down there.

"My buddy and I usually have a camper and stay nearby. Sometimes we do hotels. Depends on our moods. He's moody, but in a good way." Some people don't think that but I do. "Did you know he saved my life?"

Where is Griff, anyway?

"Wow, that's incredible. I'm glad he saved you. How sad would it be if I didn't meet you tonight?"

She bats her pretty eyelashes and rests her hand on my stomach. She does that a lot. I imagine it's because she's short. What else would she do with her hand?

"Right? I like to meet people, and I can't do that if I'm dead."

Unless I'm a ghost. But that might scare people to see a ghost. No, I definitely can't meet people if I'm dead. I should ask Griff.

"Everything okay over here?"

"Griff!" Throwing my arm over his shoulder, I smile into his scowly face. He always looks constipated when we go out. I wonder if he eats enough fruit? "I was just telling," motioning to the pretty girl whose name I don't know, "this beautiful lady, that if I were a ghost, I couldn't meet people."

Griff's gaze darts to the woman, and she smiles at him.

"Is that right?"

She nods, and her hand slips into my back pocket.

"Yeah. He's full of all kinds of stories." She sips her beer and stares up at me. "So, are you two at a hotel or your camper this time?"

What an odd thing to ask. We're at a bar for fun. Our sleeping arrangements aren't important. "Do you like sea shanties?"

"Uh, sure. Why?" The woman says, but I can tell she doesn't know what I'm talking about. I need Griff.

"Griff!" I shout, but I already have my arm around him. "We need to sing, buddy!"

Griff's scowl softens, and he shakes his head as he plucks the drink from my hand. He leans in close to my ear. "This girl clearly wants to hook up with you, Jamie. Do you want to?"

Griff's breath is warm and tickly on my ear, and his hand rests on my forearm. He has nice hands. They're thick and strong.

"Is it hot in here?" Where did all this sudden sweat come from? It's like I'm wearing a wool sweater in the middle of July. Not that I've ever done that. If I did, I bet it feels like this.

"Are you feeling okay?" Griff's hand tightens on my arm.

The pretty girl—*what the hell is her name again?*—squeezes my ass through my jeans pocket and blinks up at me. Right. Griff thinks she wants to hook up.

"Do you want to come home with me?" I blurt.

She licks her lips and presses against me closer. "I thought I was obvious about that. But yeah, I do." Her gaze cuts to Griff, and she gives him a once-over. "Your friend can join us."

Griff waits for me to respond, but my brain just went back to the one time in university that Griff and I almost shared the same guy. He was hot, and I know Griff was into him, but once the clothes came off and we were pawing on each other, Griff left. He never told me why.

"My friend doesn't like to share, and since he's my ride tonight, I have to decline."

Wow. That sounds superb for being drunk. Oooh...I just used superb in a sentence.

"Oh." She steps away from me and eyes up Griff a second time. "I didn't think...I didn't know you were with someone. Sorry."

Without another word, she pats my stomach and leaves me with Griff.

"I would've dropped you off and given you a few hours alone, Jamie. You didn't need to do that for me."

Throwing my arm over his shoulder, I squeeze him tight.

"I don't think she likes to sing. Let's sing *Old Black Rum* and then get out of here."

He shakes his head but smiles, and I pump a hand in victory as Griff starts the song.

I join in and sway with him, and a few people around us do too. We all hang our arms over each other's shoulders and sway like we're indeed drunken sailors, and I love it. I could do this all night. But when we finally end the song, we added extra choruses to the end because creative embellishment is fun, Griff squeezes my arm again.

"C'mon, Jamie." He plucks the beer from my hand again and grips my elbow. "If you're not going home with anyone, let's go. We have a long drive ahead tomorrow."

Griff leads me out of the bar, and I see the pretty girl again and wave. Griff stops walking and leans in again. "You sure you don't want to take her offer without me?"

"Yep! I think I just want a snack and to go to sleep. Sex seems like too much effort right now."

Griff laughs and shakes his head. "Stop at Subway first, then?"

My stomach growls, and I pat my belly as we step outside the bar. It's quiet outside, but my ears still ring from the music.

"God, yes. A foot long with all the sauce, Griff. I want that so bad."

"Jesus, Jamie." He shakes his head with a huff as we walk to the parking lot around the corner. "I'll get you your food and no more pop. Drink some water before you go to bed."

He opens the truck door for me, and I flop into the seat, boneless and happy that my best friend is so good to me.

"I love you, Griff." My cheeks hurt from smiling at him, and he shakes his head again.

He bats my hands away from the seatbelt and buckles it in correctly. Huh, I guess I had it backward.

"There. Good thing you're a happy drunk or I'd never do this for you."

He starts my truck and checks all the mirrors before pulling out of our spot. He's so safety-minded. I like that, though. Most times, I don't think about that stuff. Seatbelts, yes. But other stuff, not so much.

"Remember when we went skating, and you almost punched me when I said I wasn't gonna wear a helmet?"

In the dim light of the truck cab, Griff's lips tick up in a smile.

"You were so close to me making good on that threat."

A loud snort laugh bubbles past my lips, and Griff laughs. This, of course, makes me laugh harder, and before I know it, we're both wiping tears from our eyes as Griff parks in front of a Subway restaurant and kills the engine.

"Nobody cracks me up like you, Jamie. Do you want to eat in or take it to go?"

Unbuckling my seatbelt—it's easier than the buckling part—I reach for the door handle. "In. I'm too hungry to wait." As we pause outside the fast-food place, I grab his arm. "For the record, where would you have punched me if I didn't put the helmet on?"

"What kind of question is that?"

"I just wanna know."

Griff doesn't answer for a beat, and I'm just about to ask again when he breaks the silence.

"Honestly? I wouldn't have been able to. I was going to tie your laces together so you wouldn't make it to the ice instead." Griff opens the door to the restaurant and motions for me to step in. "Get in. I don't need you waking me up with a grumbling belly in three hours."

My stomach growls on cue, and I step inside.

The aroma of fresh-baked bread makes my mouth water, and I order my usual. A cold cut combo with everything on it. Like...whatever is under the glass, I want some of it on my sandwich. Except mayo, that would be gross.

Griff carries the tray to a table and stacks two bottles of water in front of me with my sandwich before returning with his own cup of lemon tea and a very tiny sandwich.

"Griff, I need to ask you something. I thought of it earlier, and I forgot."

He sips his tea before nodding for me to continue. "Sure. What is it?"

He bites into his sandwich, waiting for me to speak, and I have to dig around again to remember what I just remembered I need to ask him. Brains are weird.

"Oh, right. Remember when we took that guy home just before we graduated? You never told me why you left. I thought you liked him."

Griff pauses mid-bite before ripping off another mouthful.

"I did like him." He sets his sandwich down and leans back, picking at the lettuce on the wrapper. "Why are you asking now?"

"I dunno. That girl tonight, I guess. I've never had a threesome, and it made me think of that night, and I wondered why you backed out."

Griff drinks his tea and pushes the rest of his sandwich towards me.

"Here, finish mine too, and we can get out of here."

"Bonus sandwich! You're the best!"

After wolfing everything down, I grab the second bottle of water as Griff stands up. I'm really sleepy, and my eyes close as Griff drives us back to the campsite.

I think we were talking about something. Oh well, if it's important, he'll bring it up again.

"Jackson! Where are you?"

It's been one busy week at home, and it seems like I've been at Hunter's ranch every day but have yet to spend any time with him or Jackson.

Finally, Jackson calls from the back of the barn. "I'll be right there!"

Nobody works as hard as Jackson. He says he doesn't do rodeo anymore, but he's been renovating Hunter's barn to offer rodeo clinics to younger kids who want to learn steer wrestling or team roping, since Hunter used to do that. On top of helping his boyfriend with his event planning business and restarting his hydroponic gardening, the man doesn't stop.

"Hey, Jamieson. What's up?"

"Nothing really. Just wanted to take a minute and visit with you. Feels like forever since we've talked."

Jackson tucks his work gloves into his back pocket and motions towards the ranch house. "You're probably hungry. Let's go have a bite and catch up. I know it feels like forever, but it's barely been a month since the kick-off BBQ."

Jackson bumps me with his shoulder as we walk. "You can admit that you miss me."

"Of course I can. I do miss you."

"I miss it some." Jackson's beagle cross, Carrot, races across the farmyard towards us, barking the entire way. "Better hold up. She needs to know what we're doing, or she won't stop barking."

The dog stops at our feet, tail wagging so fast she should take flight, and Jackson bends down to scratch her ears.

"It's just Jamieson and we're going inside. You know him." Jackson coos and my heart gets a little squishy watching my friend's face light up over his dog. "You're all muddy, though. If you need to keep a watch, it's from the porch. Hunter will kill me if I let you in like that."

Carrot barks once in protest and after snuffling all over me and getting more ear scratches, thumps herself down on the porch with a groan.

"The security system is satisfied now. Come on."

Following Jackson inside Hunter's place, my jaw drops. "Jackson, what's going on in here?"

Boxes line the hallway and there's some stacked in the living room. The familiar pictures on the walls are gone, leaving the holes and faded paint where they once were.

"Ah…it's not my place to say, but he's making some changes."

Jackson moves to the fridge and pulls out a giant bowl. After gathering us smaller bowls, he fills them with soup and pops them in the microwave.

"Tell me about your season so far. You're doing well?"

Nodding, I watch as Jackson moves around Hunter's kitchen, fixing us a late afternoon snack.

"Yeah, I am. I could do better, I think. The last rodeo I drew a bull that was kind of shitty, and they didn't let me re-ride. Griff was so pissed."

"How're things with the two of you?"

Jackson places a box of crackers on the table and a glass of iced tea for us both before returning to the microwave.

"We're good. It's weird for both of us not having you and Hunter around, but we're doing okay. We're talking about a sort of vacation after the next rodeo. You remember the place we got tattoos?"

Jackson nods as he sets a bowl of homemade chicken noodle soup in front of me. "Yeah, I do. Little town close to the Manitoba border. Bloomburg, was it? Hunter's ex lives there."

"Yeah, that's the place. I've never been a tourist in Ontario, and Griff hasn't either, so we're doing a buddies' trip thing." Taking a spoonful of soup, Jackson smiles.

"That sounds like fun. I think Riley and I should go away for a while. I just don't know where yet. My mom and dad said they'd come and watch the dogs for us. I just need to plan it."

"Downtime is important. You both have so much going on. I'd hate to see either of you burn out."

"Nah. We're good that way. We make sure we have down days. Which are currently Mondays. No work for either of us, and we take the dogs somewhere. Last week, we went further up the mountains to a path I'd not been to since I was a kid. You should have seen it, Jamieson. It was a breathtaking view and Riley didn't even know it existed."

Jackson keeps gushing over the hike, Riley, and his dogs. Happiness seeps from his pores as he talks. He was happy enough when we were touring together, but this kind of happy? It's different.

"I'm really glad it's all going well for you, man. It's like you found your place or something."

Jackson's spoon scrapes the bottom of his bowl, and he swallows his last mouthful.

"I've found peace, I think. Like...rodeo helped me be me. I met Riley because of that and now..." Jackson bites his lip while he pushes a crumb around the table. "I've just found a new reason to live. With the dogs. All of it. I'm just super happy, Jamieson."

I know he is, and I'll admit I'm jealous. He has everything he ever wanted, and it couldn't have happened to a better person, but a part of me wants that feeling, too.

"I'm happy for you."

"Thanks. Now tell me about this trip you're planning with Griff."

Jackson moves around the kitchen cleaning up our mess, and I help as best I can. Hunter can be particular about things, so I let Jackson make sure it's all set. He stuffs a piece of cheese in his shirt pocket as we're ready to go back outside and pats it.

"Carrot's reward for being a good girl."

"You spoil those dogs, don't you?" I say with a laugh, and Jackson laughs back.

"I don't even try to hide it."

Outside, Carrot pops up when she sees us, and Jackson dutifully offers her the cheese, and my chest tightens. I thought maybe he'd wax poetic about missing rodeo or maybe even be prying me for details about guys on the tour. Instead, he's just...content with his decision.

As we head back to the barn and I help him move more of the equipment around, I wonder if I'll ever have the contentment Jackson has.

I love riding bulls, but it never makes me feel like he does.

Maybe it's the being-in-love thing? I've never been in love either, so I don't know. But whatever makes Jackson so carefree and fun is what I want too.

I just don't know how to get it.

Seven
Griff

"Have you been eating, Dad?"

With the extended break between rodeos, I made the trip to see my dad in Fox Grove. It's been a few months since my last visit. Winter is unpredictable in these parts, and after Christmas, I stayed away.

Knowing he never takes care of himself made it all that much harder, but my tiny Ford Neon is no match for the cruel snowstorms of an Alberta winter. My biggest fear is that one day I'll show up to find him dead.

High-functioning alcoholism is shit.

"I eat," Dad grunts and barely looks my way. Instead focusing on the CFL game between the Roughriders and the Blue Bombers. He loves the gopher mascot for Saskatchewan. I've never seen a grown man so excited for a life-size gopher, but he is.

After rummaging through the cupboards and fridge, the only thing I found that wasn't prepackaged was a single apple not fit to eat. I knew ahead of time he'd likely not have much in the house, and I came prepared after a grocery run in Kissing Ridge.

"Frozen pizzas and cookies are all you have here, Dad. Do you eat fruit and vegetables?"

He huffs from his chair as he pops the tab on another beer. The third one in the last hour, but I won't comment on it. There's no point.

"It's expensive to eat that shit." He swigs from his beer and throws his recliner back. "Come sit with me. How's rodeo going? Have you met a nice girl yet to settle down with? You're a smart kid. Why don't you use that fancy degree you got?"

Gritting my teeth, I remind myself he's not doing it on purpose.

"Dad...we've been over this, and you know it. I'm gay. There will never be a nice girl to settle down with."

Dad wasn't always like this. Before mom left, he was fun and a... dad. But his heart never let her go and he turned to booze instead. When I was little, he tried to hide it. He'd bring home a Christmas tree from the side of the road, claiming it was a surprise, and drop a bag of dollar store gifts under the tree when I was asleep, telling me Santa ran out of wrapping paper.

Sometimes I took money from his wallet to buy fresh fruit and just plain food before he could spend it at the bar. He kept food in the house, but not enough for a growing boy who often visited the office to grab from the snack bowl when it was supposed to be recess.

He's not a bad man. He's just a man who's made some bad choices. I can't really fault him for that when I've made plenty of my own.

"Right, right. You told me that. Not a phase, you said. It's just my default, I guess, to ask if you've got a family of your own." He burps before taking another drink. "So, when are you coming home for good? I could use help around here."

Scrunching my nose, I tie up the overflowing garbage bag in the kitchen and wonder when the last time he washed the floors in here was. I'm certainly not moving back to be his maid.

"You could hire a cleaning service."

"I don't want a strange person here." He pats the worn sofa next to him. "Come on, Griffy. Sit with your pop for a while. I miss you."

It's hard to keep the emotions at bay when he slips into that voice and calls me by my childhood nickname.

"Give me a sec, Dad."

After dropping the bag of garbage outside in the can, I duck into the bathroom and cringe at the state of the cleanliness. Pressing a square of toilet paper to the dampness in my eyes, I suck in a steadying breath. This is why I hate coming here. It makes me far too emotional. I miss the dad I lost to alcohol and the family I never had.

Even walking by my childhood bedroom twists at my heart in ways I can't always understand, but I'll keep coming here for Dad and hopefully one day, he'll leave this pit. After making sure I'm not crying, I grab a seat next to my dad, and he smiles a genuine smile my way.

That's why I keep coming. He's my dad, and I love him. I love that smile and the memories of conversations on this very couch. He's all I have.

"Griffy. Want to order a pizza?"

"Sure, Dad. Cesar salad, too?"

His wrinkled face frowns. "If you're paying."

After calling the order in to the only pizza place here, my dad asks me about rodeo, and I explain again that I'm a bullfighter and not a rider. He never seems to remember that either.

While we wait for the food, I ask what I always ask when I visit.

"Dad...when was the last time you went to a doctor?"

"I don't need a doctor."

He presses his lips together in a tight line, and I know he won't say anything else on the subject. Sometimes I can get him to open up, but today isn't the day.

With a sigh, I change the subject. "I'm going to Ontario for a few days. A small vacation after my next rodeo."

"Oh, that's fun. Are all the boys going with you?"

"Just Jamieson. Jackson and Hunter are semi-retired now."

"A real boys' getaway, then. Good for you. I wish you'd come by more often."

Another reason it's hard to keep coming here. Guilt trips for not being here enough. Not that he's doing it intentionally, but every time he states he wants to see me more, I feel like I've failed as a son.

"There's nothing here for me, Dad. My life is in Kissing Ridge now."

The words are out before I can stop them, and Dad frowns at his almost-empty beer can.

"I'm here. Isn't that enough?"

His voice cracks, and an overwhelming sadness sits on my chest.

"You are, Dad, but...it's not a place for me. You know that."

The knock comes on the door for our pizza, and after paying the guy, I pull the coffee table closer and set the pizza down with some napkins for Dad. I don't bother finding dishes and use the plastic fork to eat the salad straight from the container.

Dad has an appetite for the pizza, at least, and his mood picks up.

"They're talking about building a Walmart here. Wouldn't that be something?"

He's also been saying this for at least five years now. I'm not sure whether it's the same story from five years ago he refers to, or if there's been new talk in the town. Either way, I let him chatter on about how it would be great to get milk and new socks at the same store to save on gas.

"Yeah, sounds great. I hope it happens for the town."

"Would you mind getting me another beer, Griffy?"

"Sure."

Folding up the pizza box lid, I take the leftovers to the fridge and get the beer for him as he asked. When I return, he's already half asleep in the La-Z-Boy.

His face, once handsome and so much like mine, has aged so much since I was here last. He's only sixty-two and should be enjoying his retirement. Instead, he looks like he's eighty with one foot in the grave.

"Hey, Dad, I'm going to go now. It was nice seeing you again." Setting the beer on the table next to him, I place a kiss on his forehead.

"You too, son. Don't be a stranger, kay?" He mumbles as his head turns to the side.

"I won't. I love you."

My dad doesn't reply. He's already passed out.

With a painful heart, I lock the door behind me and drive the two hours back home. Just like every time I leave, I wonder if it's the last time I'll ever see him.

"Griff!"

Jamieson's panicked voice sounds across the field as he strides towards me.

"What's wrong?"

"My bull got pulled out of the lineup. He wasn't supposed to be at today's event. Somebody fucked up."

Jamieson's hands clench at his side, and he chews at his lip.

"Okay. Calm down. Who do you have now?"

"Polaris."

Nodding, I grip his elbow and pull him towards the chutes. "I know that one. Good bull. Let's have a look."

Walking towards the bulls, Jamieson removes his hat and runs a hand through his short hair and puffs out a worried breath. Dropping his elbow, I move my hand to the small of his back.

"Breathe, Jamie. It'll be fine. You're good at this."

His jaw clenches tight, and even walking the tightrope of anxiety, he's so handsome and capable. I don't know why he can't see that in himself. Sometimes it's hard to remember that Jamieson was once a tall, skinny boy with hidden strength and a kind smile. It seems like so long ago we were both young kids at university searching for our places.

Now he's all man. Bulkier with chiseled features that would rival any marble statue. But there's nothing hard about Jamieson. That kind smile belongs to a soft heart.

A heart I'd be best to forget about if I'm to set him at ease over this turn of events and do my job properly. My visit to my dad's last week, along with Jamie mentioning our almost threesome in college, has had my emotions spinning off in all directions that I'm still trying to contain.

"Yeah, you're right. As always." He laughs softly and turns his warm gaze on me. "I don't know what I'd do without you, Griff."

It's a passing phrase, thrown out with surface meaning is all. He'd get along just fine without me, but at times like this, I like to believe it means something more.

"You'd ride the bull and score points. The same thing you did before you met me."

We stop in front of the enclosures, and Jamieson points out Polaris, a black bull with white spots all over one side. I remember it from last year. A fast-moving bull that was unpredictable. In the chutes now, though, he's calm. Like he's waiting to burst out and start a fight. The tiny hairs on my arms stand when the bull looks right at me, and I stare back.

"So, any feelings about him?"

None that I want to say out loud to him. Right now, he needs to be reassured.

"I feel like he's giving you your best score of the season tonight, Jamie. All you need to do is do what you do best. Hang on and make it look easy."

He snort-laughs and smiles my way so big my breath catches in my throat. "Didn't you tell me that the first time I met you?"

Smiling, I cock my head for us to walk away from the chutes. "I tell you that all the time, so it's possible."

The announcement sounds that the bull riding is about to start, and I pat Jamieson on his flak-jacket-covered chest.

"You're the best. My feeling is you prove it tonight. I've got your back."

He nods and squeezes my hand before I pull it away.

"Stay safe, Griff."

"You too, Jamie."

He walks back to his place where he gets in his groove before he rides, and I step out into the ring, ready to protect all the riders tonight, not just Jamieson.

But that bull has me uneasy, and it's odd for me to feel so off.

With a whispered prayer to whoever listens, I ready myself for the first rider.

It's been a great night for the bull riders so far.

Impressive rides and scores have gone up, much to the delight of the fans. It's a big money event, with top-notch bulls and riders. I wasn't kidding earlier when I told Jamieson something big was going to happen for him tonight. He's due for a massive score, and when Polaris stared me down, I knew it would be tonight.

It would be a perfect start to our short road-trip vacation if we could celebrate a massive win for him.

"Hey, Griff!"

Another bullfighter I know, Carson, jogs over. "Three more to go tonight. You doing okay? It's been a rough one."

The rodeo clown performs his skit while we get a break with some water on this *very* hot, early August evening. Carson hands me a bottle of water, and I chug it down before passing it back through the fence to the staff.

"Yeah, I'm okay. But...Polaris...be on your toes."

Carson quirks an eyebrow. He knows about my predictions and, like Jamieson, he listens. "He rank tonight?"

"I don't know. He's unpredictable, so be careful. It's just a feeling."

He nods and pats me on the shoulder, a silent understanding that he trusts me, and jogs back to his side of the ring.

The clown exits, and the music for the riders begins again. The first rider is on a bull I've seen many times. A real spinner and Carson signals with a twirling finger that he remembers, too.

Once it's out of the chute, the rider does well, and Carson and I work together to shove the cowboy out of the ring while the third bullfighter leads the bull to the exit.

There's a commotion in the chutes, and all heads swivel to find out what's happening. A familiar form leaps up off the bull as it thrashes in the chute.

"Stay calm, Jamie," I mutter as I watch from the side. Jamieson is always cool. Nerves never get to him when a bull acts up before it even leaves the chute. Thankfully, that seems to still be the case as he remounts and goes through his motions.

I wasn't lying when I told Jamieson earlier that this bull will give him his biggest ride. Something big is about to happen. I can feel it as sure as the clothes on my back.

Finally, Jamieson's head nods, and the chute opens in a furious flash of bull and rider. One buck slams the bull's feet into the fence before it lurches forward, angrier than it was when it started.

With every move the bull uses to throw him off, Jamieson remains relaxed. He's perfect up there, and when the buzzer sounds, my heart swells with pride. There's nobody better than him.

Jamieson tries to dismount with the help of a pickup man but can't, so he opts to dismount with them close by instead. Normally, a safe thing to do, and he's done it dozens of times. Except the bull doesn't keep bucking and head off to the exit like it does 9 times out of 10.

Polaris stops and turns, zeroing in on Jamieson's back as he stumbles through the sand towards me and the safety of the gates. My gut clenches with a flash of what happened to us, to me, specifically the last time a bull went off plan.

Time stands still.

Jamieson's face registers fear when he sees me launch towards him.

"Get to the fence, Jamie!"

He won't make it. It's a roar of white noise as Carson runs on the other side of the bull to distract him, and the pickup men try to lasso it. Polaris barely notices.

The lasso lands around the bull's neck just as I dive between it and Jamieson. The thud of the bull's head on my arm sends me flying backwards, and it's Jamieson who scoops me up and drags me out of danger.

With the bull roped and the two pickup men barely keeping the bull under control, the rodeo announcer distracts the crowd with Jamieson's score–97 points. Almost perfect.

"I told you this would be your best ride!"

"Griff, you need to get to the hospital."

"What? I'm fine."

Jamieson's mouth opens and closes with no words, and it's not until Carson walks up that I finally notice what everyone is staring at.

"Shit. I don't think arms are supposed to go like that." I puff a harsh laugh, but the sight of my left arm no longer straight and pointing at a weird angle sends a roll of nausea through me. "Well, fuck."

Jamieson's arm around my waist and his gentle voice in my ear is the last thing I remember before I pass out.

Eight
Jamieson

"Are you sure you're okay to do this road trip still? I won't be mad if you'd rather be home."

"It's a broken arm, Jamie. I'll be fine."

Nothing about Griff's voice leads me to believe he's lying. It *is* just a broken bone, and it could have been so much worse. I try not to think about that, but it creeps in when I imagine my best friend being hurt worse than a broken bone.

He offers me half the sandwich we picked up from the hospital vending machine on our way out this morning. I slept off and on in the waiting room chairs while they set his arm and cast it. There was no way I'd leave him there and ask him to call when done.

I stretch my neck, trying to work the kink out while I drive and eat.

"I told you those chairs weren't made for sleeping. You should have gone to the hotel and let me call you."

"I wasn't letting you call me. It's my fault you're...broken."

Just like the last time when he needed all those stitches. He did it for me then too, and I'll never forget it. I probably think about it too much sometimes.

"It's my job, Jamie. You know that."

Griff stares out the window as I drive us closer to the Ontario border. Our sort of vacation now changed from a fun time with my best friend to...something else I don't have a word for.

We crossed into Saskatchewan easily enough, but with only me driving while Griff slept off the anesthetic, I had a lot of time to think. That's not always a good thing.

"I know it's your job, but I feel responsible."

Griff shoves the empty sandwich container in a bag and leans back in his seat.

"I'm an adult and make my own choices, Jamie. I'd do the same in any situation out there, not just for you."

"Ouch. Way to make me feel special."

I'm joking, but Griff doesn't laugh.

"We planned to stop in Winnipeg tonight. Are you still okay with doing that?"

"Yeah. You need to rest some too, or you won't be able to enjoy this dude-bonding trip you planned."

Griff's playful grin returns, and I internally leap with joy.

"You'll be driving on the way back. You can take Saskatchewan blindfolded, with both arms broken, and still be fine."

Our old banter returns, and it eases the ache in my chest some.

When we arrive at our motel, it's not the greatest, but I'm just happy to take a hot shower and sleep in a bed, no matter how uncomfortable.

"Do you need my help with anything? If you want to shower, I can ask the front desk for a garbage bag and duct tape."

Griff laughs as he lies on his bed and closes his eyes. "That shouldn't sound so dirty, but yeah...I'd appreciate it if you could."

"Let me grab our bags, and I'll do that real quick."

Griff gives me a thumbs up, and for some reason, that gesture makes me smile. After dumping our bags and grabbing a room key, I walk back to the main office and ring the bell.

The older man who helped us before appears again with a smile.

"I didn't think I'd see you so soon."

"I'm hoping you can help. My buddy broke his arm yesterday, and we're not prepared for tonight. Would you have some duct tape and some plastic we could borrow?" The man's bushy eyebrows pop up, and my cheeks burn as I replay how that sounds. "To cover his cast so he can shower."

The man snorts and holds a finger up. "I think I can help. Give me a minute or two."

When the man leaves, I thumb through my messages on my phone.

Jackson asked if Griff was okay and congratulated me on my high score. Funny, I haven't given myself much time to think about the score until now. My biggest concern was making sure Griff was okay.

After answering Jackson, I reply to Carson, the other bullfighter, and ask him to spread the word that Griff broke his arm but is otherwise okay. When Carson asks if Griff will work the coming events, I pause. That's probably not a question I should answer, but if I know my best friend, he's working if he can function.

"Here you go. This should help."

Shoving my phone in my pocket, the man from the motel hands me a baggie with rolls of clear tape and several small garbage bags.

"Oh, thank you so much. I probably don't need this many."

"You'll need it for a while. The tape is surgical and waterproof. I had some leftover from when I had my foot cast last year. Just keep it and take it on your way. Your friend will appreciate that better than duct tape."

When he says the word friend, he makes it sound like something else. Something intimate.

"Um, yeah, he probably will. He has fine hair on his arms. You can't always see it, but it's there. It's super blond."

I don't know where waxing on about Griff's arm hair came from, but the man smiles.

"There is a lot we don't always see at first. Little things often sneak up, and then you wonder how there was a time that you never noticed before."

This feels like a bizarre conversation to have in a motel lobby with a stranger while my arms clutch medical tape and plastic bags to my chest.

Clearing my throat, I nod and hold up the bag of supplies.

"His arm hair thanks you."

Jesus Christ, Jamieson.

The man wishes me a good night, and I exit the lobby back down to our room. When I open the door, Griff sits, head hanging, with his cast forearm against his stomach.

"Griff?" After the door clicks closed, I flip the inside deadbolt and security chain. "Good news. Waterproof medical tape so it won't rip the hair off your arms."

"What magic did you work for that?" he jokes, but when he lifts his head, there's more than just the tiredness from the last twenty-four hours. A sadness I've only seen a handful of times when he spoke of his parents creeps at the edge of his normally smiling eyes.

"My normal charming self, I suppose."

"Probably." He rolls his eyes, and we both laugh.

"Here. I'll help you."

He yanks his arm further into himself. "I can do it myself."

"I know you can, but I want to help you." Griff's chest heaves as my hand takes his cast arm away gently. "You don't always have to do everything yourself, Griff. Let me help you this time."

Griff relaxes and allows me to place the bag over his arm. He watches as I wrap the tape and press it all together around his arm.

"I'll turn the water on for you. You go first. If you need me to help, just yell for me."

"Kay."

When I emerge from the bathroom, Griff is struggling with removing his pants with only one hand, so without asking, I grab the other side of his pants and help him out of them.

"Sit."

He does as I ask, and I take off his socks. The scar from the first time he put himself between me and a bull has faded on his calf, but it's there. A reminder of what Griff has done for me all these years.

"The water should be good now."

"Yeah. Thanks."

In just his briefs, he walks to the bathroom, and the door clicks behind him. For several minutes, I don't hear him in the shower or even a toilet flush.

"Do you need me —"

"For god's sake Jamie, I don't need you to wipe my ass! I'm fine!"

"Sorry!"

Finally, I hear him moving and the sounds of him in the shower after a toilet flushes, and I lie on my bed staring at the ceiling with the voice of the motel clerk in my head.

There is a lot we don't always see at first.

I think I just noticed something about my best friend for the first time in almost ten years of friendship.

And I don't know what to do with that.

"I thought you said we still had a way to go? Why are we stopping already?"

Griff raises an eyebrow, and I smile back.

"It's like you don't even know me. You think I'd take a road trip like this and not research all the food places I need to visit?"

"You just ate a pound of pierogies before we left Manitoba!"

I probably could have eaten more, to be honest. I've never tasted pierogies that fucking amazing.

"True. But that was hours ago, and there's a place that's supposed to have the most amazing blueberry ice cream in Dryden. We need a rest stop, anyway."

"You use any excuse to get snacks." Griff shakes his head, but he's already reaching for the small pack he has his wallet and phone in with sunscreen and whatever else I didn't see. When he showed me how much he loved this fanny-pack thing, because that's what it is, I couldn't tell him it's what retired men wear or that he was a blast from the 80s. He was so damn thrilled it would make hiking easier. It was like he discovered the moon.

"Well...yeah. Snacks are life."

I turn the vehicle into the parking lot of a truck stop and restaurant off the highway and stop at the gas pumps. While I fill the truck, Griff empties the garbage inside before joining me with a stretch.

"It's a perfect day. Too bad we're spending it driving."

"You're doing okay then? Arm isn't too sore?"

Griff shakes his head. "A little off and on, but nothing I need a painkiller for or anything. It's just getting used to moving with my arm."

After replacing the gas nozzle, we walk into the truck stop together. It smells like home-baked goodness and...blueberries.

"Oh god, do you smell that, Griff?" But he's already pointing to a giant shelf of fresh-baked goodies and baskets of blueberries.

"Look at this, Jamie. It's everything you love. Maybe we should get some to eat for breakfast while we're at the ranch."

Blueberry muffins, pies, tarts and jams line the shelves in various sizes and my mouth waters.

"I don't trust myself not to spend every dime I have here right now." I push Griff closer and cover my eyes. "Pick some stuff for us while I take a piss."

Griff's laughter rings out. "Go on then. I'll save your bank account."

Trusting Griff to feed me, I follow the signs to the washroom and take care of business. On my way out, I pause at a community bulletin board when a rainbow-coloured flyer catches my eye.

"No way."

Snapping a photo, I hustle out to find Griff holding two bags of goods waiting by the door.

"I didn't buy you ice cream, but the guy says the best place is a little shack as we drive out of town on the left. It's called The Cream Queen."

"It is not." I laugh.

Griff snorts as we leave the gas station. "It sure is. It's only five minutes away, so you can get your ice cream. I think I have you covered for snacks for a few hours, too."

"So, look at this." I pull up the screen on my phone and show it to Griff. "The town we're going to is having their Pride Festival right now! It'll be like old times. We can take in all the events and relive our youth."

Griff reads the poster I saved in my photos, and it's impossible to ignore the happiness that spreads across his face.

"Oh my god. They have so much stuff! I haven't been to a Pride event in years." He passes back my phone with a giant smile. "And we're still young, you asshole. So stop with the *relive our youth* shit."

"Well, you're the one wearing a fanny pack, old man."

Griff gasps and clutches at his pack. "You take that back! This thing is amazing!"

"If you pull white socks up to your knees while wearing shorts, I'll call for an intervention."

I try to keep my face straight, but can't, and we both burst out laughing as we pile back into the truck. Griff is the most relaxed I've seen him. Even with the broken arm and scare we had a few days ago, he's not looked this carefree since we first met.

"I'm really happy you agreed to do this vacation with me, Griff. It means a lot. I'm so excited to just be a tourist in this little town and not worry about bulls or training for a few days."

Griff rips open a package of Twizzlers and offers me two. "Or your diet? Because we've done nothing but eat since we left the hospital."

"Fuck the diet. I'm sure we'll be working off all my extra calories. Besides, my metabolism still hasn't slowed down yet. My body thinks I'm still a fourteen-year-old boy."

"That tracks. Most days, you still act like one."

Griff chuckles and tries to squish up against the door as I stretch across and push his face into the window.

"Ow, ow! My arm!"

Immediately, I sit back and pull away with both hands on the wheel and look for a place to pull over.

"Shit. I'm so sorry, Griff. Are you okay? I didn't mean to...I was just..."

Then the little shit laughs and I shoot him a glare.

"You faker. Don't do that. I nearly shit because I thought I hurt you."

Spotting the sign for the ice cream place, I put my signal light on and glare at Griff.

"Sorry, Jamie. I was just playing."

After pulling into the parking lot, I shove the truck into park and release a breath.

"Sorry. I snapped because...because I just don't want you to hurt. You've already done enough of that. Please don't joke about it."

Griff stares at me for a few beats before holding out his good hand. "Restart. I won't do that again, and you won't tease me about my fanny pack."

"And you're buying me ice cream."

My hand grips his, and we shake on it. The balance of the world restored that easily.

Griff pays for my ice cream, blueberry cheesecake explosion, and while we sit in the warm sun and eat our frozen treat before lunch, talking about what we plan to do in the next four days, it occurs to me that this is the first time since university I've felt this free. Free to be the person I was when I met Griff and not the young man hell-bent on becoming the best bull rider.

And I like it.

Nine
Griff

Travelling with my best friend has never been hard. We've always had an easy banter and understanding.

This trip is different. While our banter and teasing are still there, I know I'm hiding something big from Jamieson, and if I don't tell him, it will cause hurt I didn't intend to bring.

He parks the truck in an angled parking space along the main street. This town is so cute, it should be on a postcard. Rainbow flags hang from all the lamp posts down the street, and giant hanging baskets of flowers in a riot of colours hang literally everywhere there's still space.

"Griff, look."

Jamieson grabs my attention as we meet in front of the truck and he points to a crosswalk painted in rainbow with the words, *YOU MATTER*, through it. If my town did this when I was growing up, I would have made an enormous impact on my life. Simple gestures can go a long way.

"Wow. I know Kissing Ridge is progressive, but I don't think you'll ever see them painting a crosswalk like that."

"This is going to be amazing, Griff. Come on. Let's pick up the key and find dinner."

Jamieson leads me down the sidewalk towards the place we're supposed to pick up the key to our accommodations.

"This is it."

He pushes open the door to Dark Horse Tattoo, and I don't know what to expect, but it wasn't this. It's lush and welcoming, with a plant hanging in the corner and comfortable furniture. The walls are adorned with gorgeous paintings, some that border on erotic, but the one that holds prime wall space is a painting of a peacock.

"I'll be right there!" A younger man exits a side room after a beat. "Oh! You must be Jamieson?"

"Yeah, is Marko in?"

"He isn't. Kind of a last-minute thing, but he left you a key and some info. I'd be happy to answer questions you have on how to get to the ranch, though."

Jamieson chats up the younger man, Curtis, and I sort of listen while my gaze keeps returning to the paintings along the one wall. The peacock is so vibrant and stunning, it's hard to look away, but it's the smaller piece next to it that keeps drawing my attention.

"Griff? Did you hear me?"

Jamieson is suddenly next to me, and I point to the pencil-drawn art. "Look at this. I've never been one to appreciate art, but I can't stop looking at it."

It looked like a simple drawing from across the room, but the more I stared, the more it drew me in. It's not overly complex, but it calls to me in a way I can't put my finger on.

"All the art is by Marko, the guy who did Jamieson's tattoo. He's the owner of this place. He's also a supremely talented artist."

Curtis walks over to stand on my other side. "He drew this on his honeymoon. It's one of his favourites. Mine too."

The sketch is a man's hand holding a heart. The heart isn't perfect or anatomically correct. It's literally a cartoonish heart, but it's drawn with purposeful imperfections. It's scratched and missing a tiny piece on the edge, but it's smiling with a single tear on its cheek. The heart walks from one hand into the other, and the wedding bands are visible on the ring finger of each hand now that Curtis mentioned a honeymoon.

One hand is calloused, and the other is smoother but paint stained, and it's the way the damn heart has a hand reaching out to the empty hand that has me blink back something raw. Something I just can't put into words.

"Would he mind if I took a photo of it?"

"I don't think so. He knows Jamieson, so I think he'd be okay with it."

My hand shakes as I pull my phone out and snap the picture. If Jamie notices, he doesn't comment on it.

"Right, so you said there's a diner here we should eat at?"

On cue, Jamieson's stomach growls and we all laugh. Curtis explains how to find the diner and I take a last glance at the art on the walls.

"Thanks for your help, Curtis. Just in case I don't see Marko while we're here, please thank him for me."

As we leave Curtis in the shop, we walk along the sidewalk towards the diner. With it only a few blocks away, we leave the truck and enjoy the chance to stretch and experience this cute little town.

"I wasn't totally listening, but did Curtis say something about the place we're staying at not having a coffeemaker?"

Jamieson laughs and bumps his shoulder into mine. "Figures that's the only part you remember. But yes, he said that. But we can go to the main house after 5 A.M. and get coffee or we can just go to the coffee shop across the street from the tattoo place. They're open 7 days a week and are amazing. I stopped in when I was here last."

"You know I need time to wake up in the morning, so whatever works best."

"Griff..." From the corner of my eye, Jamieson chews at his lips and my shoulders tense at what he wants to say. "That drawing you liked...it uh..."

Jamieson stops walking and forces me to meet his gaze. "That night we fought before my ride, and I didn't want to listen to you about Homewrecker, you remember?"

"It's hard to forget, Jamie."

We fought for real for the first time—ever. It wasn't because he didn't want to listen to me, but more because I was still hurting over what had happened the night before. I said things in the heat of the moment that I wasn't proud of, but they carried a lot of truth I wasn't sure Jamieson picked up on. Maybe I was wrong.

"I'm sorry. You're the most important person in my life, Griff. I never meant to hurt you, and when I saw you looking at that drawing so closely...I think I get it."

My mouth runs dry, and I look into my best friend's eyes. The same hurt when I threw those mean words at him sits there, but also, there's something new. Maybe he understands after all.

"It's not my business what you do with your private life, Jamie. I was out of line that night, and I still regret what I said."

Jamieson was sucking face with a pretty girl in the corner while the boyfriend watched. He claimed to be cool with it, but I recognized the look on his face. The jealousy. The wish that she'd give him the same attention. Perhaps the girl was clueless and really loved the man like she claimed, and was only looking for something exciting. A roll with a cowboy is on every girl's bucket list, it seems.

But the way Jamieson had so flippantly ignored my request to let this one go and told me to get over it ignited the latent anger I wasn't aware was close to erupting. He dismissed me and the other man's feelings in such an uncharacteristic way I lashed out.

"You need to watch yourself, Jamie! People's hearts are real and breathe. Just because it seems like a good idea to you doesn't mean others aren't getting hurt. You're such a self-centred prick!"

"Oh, fuck off, Griff, with all your righteous bullshit. You're just pissed that you aren't getting laid. Why don't you find someone for yourself for once and just leave me alone?" he sneered through the haze of alcohol. "Oh, that's right. Nobody is ever good enough for you. I forgot."

He was right and didn't even know it was him I measured everyone against. Even in that moment, when he was the ugliest I'd ever seen him, I knew I could never not love him.

Jamieson sighs and rubs a hand across his belly, drawing me out of my sad memory.

"Not to be an asshole and change the subject, but I really need to eat." His lips tilt in that cute half smile.

"It's fine. We never did clear the air properly that night. This is good." I cock my head towards the diner. "But let's get you fed before you reach that cranky stage."

Jamieson's laughter lightens my heart, and he slings his arm around my shoulders like he always does when we go anywhere.

"You know me the best, Griff."

He chatters on about the diner and stuff Curtis told him, but I nod and half listen. I'm still stuck on that damn drawing and wondering if Jamie really gets it at all.

By the time we make it to the ranch, our bellies full of home-cooked food and bags of far too many snacks from the grocery store, the sun has dipped behind the trees. A bright moon illuminates the ranch's yard, and we park in front of the equipment barn as directed.

A sign above the small door on the barn says, *Loft Entrance*, and after grabbing a few bags each, we take the single flight of wooden stairs to the top. Jamieson doesn't use the key, it's always open. The key is for us to lock up when we go out. Part of what Curtis was telling Jamieson was that the ranch was safe and we don't need to lock up unless we want to.

He steps in and sets his bags on the kitchen island right in front of us and I flick on the light switch. It's a gorgeous open space above a barn. Renovated to be modern but rustic at the same time. Obviously, a bathroom needed to be installed and instead of a wood burning heat source, an electric fireplace sits in the seating area.

"Where's the...oh."

After setting my bags on the counter and walking towards the couches, there's an alcove that serves as the bedroom. With one bed.

Jamieson brushes past me and flicks on the lamp on one side of the bed.

"Looks like we're snuggling, Griff. It's a king, though. If I roll around too much, you should be fine on your side."

Jamieson states it all matter of fact, like we've had sleepovers and shared beds our whole lives.

"Don't steal the covers and I'll be fine." I joke.

It's a lie though. Sharing a room is one thing, but a bed? Where I can feel his heat and smell all things Jamie, and not be able to do anything? Jesus fuck, this is a disaster.

He laughs as he squeezes my shoulder. "I can't make any promises. You put the food in the fridge, and I'll go grab the rest of our stuff."

Jamieson disappears out the door, and I do as he suggested. Poking around the kitchen, it doesn't seem like there's much to cook with in here. A kettle and a small pot, along with a few plates and cutlery. Maybe the people who usually stay here eat in the main house too?

"Okay, this is the last of the stuff. Curtis said the Wi-Fi is good here and we should be able to use Netflix on the TV at a minimum." He peels off his T-shirt and tosses it towards the bed.

"I'm going to shower and probably just get some sleep, though. It's been a long day."

"Yeah, good idea. I'll find that tape and plastic bags for my arm and do the same."

Jamieson pops into the shower, and I cast a worried glance at the bed.

Jamieson was out like a light, lightly snoring, but in a way that always makes me smile. It's not a window rattling snore but this little grumble, like a cat's contented purr.

I laid awake on the edge of that damn bed so close I'd probably fall off if I ever fell asleep. The last few days have been...exhausting. My mind just won't turn off.

The ache in my arm has settled, but the one in my heart has doubled in size over the last two days. Jamie taking care of me, even while I was at the hospital, jostled the feelings loose. The ones I thought I had covered well and locked away.

Everything was fine. Until it wasn't.

The acceptance into the master's psychology program that I ultimately declined. My dad drinking himself into an early grave while I watch, helpless to do anything but hope for a miracle. The torch I have for Jamie still burning bright against all my attempts to extinguish it.

Everything has washed to the surface like debris on the shore after a potent storm.

My life feels out of control, all because my heart wants someone who doesn't feel the same.

Jamieson twitches in his sleep, and I turn my head on my pillow towards him. He's still handsome when he sleeps with his mouth hanging open and that purring snore. His long body finally at rest and splayed over three-quarters of the king-sized bed.

It would be so easy to shuffle closer and have a part of him touch me while he sleeps. I could pretend he's mine.

Or I could make a fucking decision like I originally planned and get on with my life. Accept the admission and forget about my dad, and just do one thing for myself that doesn't make me hurt.

With a sigh, I adjust my arm across my chest and attempt to get some sleep.

Ten
Jamieson

"This has to be one of the cutest towns I've ever visited. Don't you think, Griff?"

He's still eating candy from the cool retro candy store we found earlier. I think that's all he needs to make this trip a success. Unlimited penny candy in a brown paper bag. It definitely made him smile more today.

The dark circles under his eyes concern me. I don't want to pry and be all up in his face like a mother hen, but I'm positive his arm hurts more than he's letting on.

"It's definitely cute. I really want to try that burger place we saw earlier for supper, but I don't know if I have room for food. I ate a lot of candy today."

Griff frowns into the tiny brown paper bag, and I peek over his shoulder. "You ate the whole thing?"

He clutches the mostly empty bag to his chest with a half-laugh.

"Don't be so judgy! You ate that giant cookie from the bakery *and* candy."

"This is true." I laugh. "But I'm still a bottomless pit, remember?"

We amble along the sidewalk again. The crowds from the Pride celebrations show no signs of slowing down, and I tug at Griff to stop at a face painting booth.

"There's nobody in line now. Let's do it."

Griff rolls his eyes, but I know he wants to. That little half smile of his is a dead giveaway.

"Hey fellas." A young woman with the brightest purple hair I've ever seen gestures to the single chair across from her. "Who's first, and what do you want? Rainbows, glitter, unicorn? A slogan or flag?"

I sit first since it was my idea, and I look at all her offerings on the table.

"Can I get a bi flag and something cowboy-ish?"

She taps her lips with a red-polished fingertip before reaching for her face paint. "How about a rainbow horseshoe next to the bisexual flag?"

"Perfect!"

As the woman gets to work with her art on my cheek, Griff watches from behind her, and I swallow the lump that's lodged in my throat since I sat at the hospital with him. I thought it was a fear of losing my best friend, but even after the doctor assured me he wasn't near death's door from a broken bone, it didn't go away.

It didn't go away when I buckled him in my truck to take us on this vacation, and it didn't go away after we sort of cleared the air over the only fight we've ever had that happened over a year ago.

And now it's still there when I watch Griff shove the last cherry twist from his candy bag into his mouth as he watches the girl paint my face.

"You look awesome, Jamie. That horseshoe is cool."

"Do you know what you want, sugar? He's almost done."

Griff nods with a giant grin.

"Yep. I want the gayest flag with glitter."

I burst out laughing as the woman hands me a mirror to see her work. "Glitter? For real?"

"Yep." Griff bumps me with a hip to get me out of the chair and sits in front of the woman, who opens her glitter pot with glee. "I've always wanted to get glittered up for Pride. In university, they didn't have big festivals, and then we're often busy with rodeo and miss all the parades and festivals. This is the first time I get to glitter."

"Well, I'm so happy for you! And I'm so honoured I get to be your first."

Griff's ears get a little pink, and I watch as she paints the flag on his cheek and smooths glitter over the top of it. She does the same design on both his cheeks and then paints a stripe of red glitter paint up his cheek and under each flag when she's done.

"Take a look." She hands him the mirror, and Griff's smile is the brightest I've ever seen.

"This is..." His eyes catch mine in a flash, and that lump comes back. "This is amazing. Thank you."

Griff drops a donation into the jar the woman has out for the local LGBTQ+ youth shelter, and I do the same before we spill back out into the masses of people out celebrating.

Stuffing my hands in my pockets so I don't scratch at the face paint, we keep walking until we reach the intersection. While we wait for the light to cross the street, a poster in a shop window catches my eye.

"Oh my god! Griff! Look at this. We have to go."

A bright neon poster exclaims the Cowboy Olympics are on at the Burgatory from 6 to 10 P.M. as part of the Pride celebrations. They even have Jell-O shots on the menu.

Griff laughs before pulling out his phone and punching in the address to Google Maps. "Jell-O shots make my stomach turn. That's one memory I'd like to leave at university." He looks up at the street signs and back at his phone. "It's the next street over, and I said earlier I should get a burger. Do you really want to go when we're supposed to be away from rodeo?"

"Of course! It's a blast from the past. Jell-O shots, cowboy games, and rainbows. And food! Can't forget the food." Griff laughs as we walk towards the next street. "Food first. I'm starving, and you should get something other than sugar in you."

"Okay, okay. I'm convinced."

Throwing my arm around Griff's shoulder, I hug him close. "I know we go to bars a lot when we're touring, but...this is different. I'd love a good techno dance night, you know? Where we can just dance and not be fawned over for belt buckles."

Well.

I haven't even started drinking, and that truth sort of slithered out. Griff doesn't say anything, just quirks an eyebrow.

"Does that bother you? Your groupies? Because you have them. You know that, right?"

"I mean, yeah, I know. I recognize faces in the bars, even though it's a different town. They're out there, but it would be nice to just switch off for once and just be me and not a bull rider."

We walk in silence because it's the first time I've said that out loud and acknowledged it myself. My alcohol tolerance is shit and I like to party with my friends, but there's always an expectation.

Bull riders are the draw of any rodeo. It's a sexy and dangerous sport. The bar scene is how I burn off the excitement from a ride. It's like I have a huge adrenaline dump that takes hours to go away.

Inevitably, the buckle bunnies find you while you're there. Men and women. I prefer women, but there's been the odd man I didn't turn down. All of them were just part of scratching the itch and living up to the wild cowboy image.

A group of shirtless young men with their arms linked together sing as they march down the sidewalk, confident and carefree. I envy that.

"Hey, Jamie. You okay?"

Forcing a smile, I nod.

"Never better, Griff. Well, not true. I'll be better once we eat."

The sign for the Burgatory comes into view, and my stomach growls like it knows there's food nearby. Griff's face lights up as he laughs and smacks me across the stomach.

"I swear your stomach is its own person. Let's eat and see what the Cowboy Olympics are about."

"I like your plan." Opening the door to the restaurant for Griff, we step inside, and I know he feels the same thing I do. When I look over, Griff has this faraway look as his gaze bounces all over the place.

"Oh my god, Jamie. It's just like the pub on campus. This is wild."

The only thing missing is the stage for bands and the colours of our university, but the whole aesthetic is so damn accurate it's like walking into a time machine.

"Hey, guys. Table for two?"

An older man in a tight plaid shirt, form-fitting Wranglers, and a smile that could melt the polar ice caps greets us. He's...very attractive.

"Please." Griff returns the smile and lingers on the man's face. That lump in my throat comes back, and I throw my arm over his shoulders.

"Near the action, please. We plan to be here for a while."

"Cowboy Olympics is...not at all what I expected."

Griff bends over, wheezing, after we went outside to run a hay bale relay. We didn't win, and I'm a little embarrassed about that.

"Who the fuck runs with hay bales?!"

Thankfully, it's the last event of the Olympics. An Olympics made to make us thirsty and order more beer and Jell-O shots...and possibly kill us.

We threw hay bales over high jump bars, ran an obstacle course with a wheelbarrow and then ran a race with a god damn hay bale. My shoulders scream louder than after a bull ride, and Griff is still wheeze-laughing.

"We can't tell Hunter about this. Or Jackson! They'd never let us hear the end of it. Promise me, Griff."

Those two would probably challenge us to the same events just to prove they're more fit than two guys a decade younger than them.

"My arms are still on fire, Jamie. We should be in better shape than this." Griff laughs and I move in to massage his arms. A few times in university, we'd overdo it in the weight room and Griff would get these crazy muscle spasms. He'd sometimes drink pickle juice to help, which is completely disgusting, but my fingers are magic and smell better than pickle juice.

"Here," I motion for him to step closer, and he steps up, resting his head on my shoulder as I massage his biceps through his shirt. "Is it getting better?"

"*Mhmm*," Griff sighs into my shoulder. "Much better."

"How's your arm? You probably shouldn't have been doing all that with a cast on."

Griff steps back, but my hand still massages the biceps of the broken arm. "It hurts. I won't lie and say it's fine. It's probably not the smartest thing I've ever done, but it was worth it."

Despite my concern that he overdid it, I grin back. "Totally."

The atmosphere in the bar has switched to a dance party. Strobe lights and flashing drink cups light up the dance floor as dance beats vibrate under our feet. Most of the current dancers are younger, in their early 20s, or perhaps even some with fake IDs and are teenagers. I don't judge them on that. We all do things to be a part of the crowd we want to run with, and it's not always the right thing, but it sure is fun.

Griff sways his hips to the dance music, and it reminds me of the time we went to a rainbow night at the campus pub. Griff was always the most relaxed on those nights. He always walked with a shield, and his smiles didn't come as easily...unless he was with me, I noticed.

Those nights with the dance music and sweaty bodies with no eyes passing judgement were when Griff was the most Griff-like. My best friend wasn't always a force in the bull riding ring with a stern face and an almost super-vigilant stance. He had a laugh that was infectious and dance moves that should remain private. Griff could have even the quietest mouse in the corner talking because he was that personable.

It's a side of him I've not seen in years, and I wonder if he knows it's been that long.

He points to the backdrop in the corner where two guys attempt a choreographed dance against the logo for a popular social media platform.

"Do you think it's a new dance challenge? I'm never up on the stuff that's going around."

Snorting, I wave down the waitress walking by with beer in buckets of ice and grab two before pushing bills and a large tip into her hand.

"You want to try it, don't you?"

Griff tilts his hand back and forth as he sways to the music and attempts one of the dance moves the other two are doing. He almost falls over and drops his beer.

Cackling, I take his bottle and set it aside as he scowls. "Knock yourself out and practice. I'll wing it if you want to try."

Griff just smiles and wiggles to the music. And then backs into the girl behind him.

"Oh, I'm so sorry." He places a hand on her arm. "Are you okay?"

She just smiles and pulls him closer to me. "I'm fine. I've been watching you two, and I need your help."

Griff and I exchange a glance, and he shrugs.

"So, what do you need help with?" I ask. I'm positive it's about the dance thing, and I can practically see the yes coming off Griff's lips before she even asks.

The girl blushes and turns to Griff. "Um, I'm scared to tell my best friend I like her more than a friend. But there's this video challenge where you sort of surprise them with a kiss and see their reaction. I think it's the easiest way for me to tell her because I'm not fantastic at words."

Griff's eyes widen, and he stares at the girl. "Do you think she likes you? Aren't you afraid of fucking up the friendship if you know...if you just kiss her like that?"

The girl shrugs a shoulder with a small smile. "I think she might feel the same. But if she doesn't, we're solid. I'll get over it, and it will be awkward, but I'll have taken the chance. I don't want to wait, and this is the perfect time, but I'm not good with words and...I just...fuck, I'm nervous, you know. Like I want to kiss her so bad but..."

I jump in since Griff seems to be at a loss for words.

"Show us the video and we can do a practice run."

"Oh my god, that would be amazing!" She pulls up a video on her phone, chattering the whole time like she's known us forever. How can she be shy with her crush and so chatty with us? She shows us a few different attempts, and we agree that the one where she sings a line of a song and then leans in to kiss her is the best.

"Here. We can practice it." I pull Griff over and notice the paleness of his cheeks. "Hey, you okay?"

"Yeah, I'm fine." He smiles at the girl. "What song is it?"

"Doesn't matter." I wave her off. "We're just lip syncing, anyway. We don't even have to kiss." I whisper so the girl can't hear. "Just pretend so she gains confidence, Griff."

"Right. Okay."

Griff and I mimic the dance move, and when we face each other for the confession and kiss part, Griff steps up and takes my face in his hands. He leans in and doesn't pause. His lips press against mine softly with a breathy sigh. And again. On the third time, I don't let him pull away and circle my arms around his waist, pulling him closer and kissing him back. God, he tastes like the cherry twists he ate earlier and lemon Jell-O. That's so perfect for him. Sweet with a bit of bite when needed.

And now I'm kissing Griff.

Griff presses against me with a strangled cry. His fingers slide into my hair, curling tightly as he keeps kissing me. His tongue pushes past my lips and slides against mine with a reverent hunger that short-circuits my brain. My mouth doesn't want to leave his because this kiss is by far one of the best I've ever had, and I really like cherry twists. When we finally break apart with swollen lips and heaving chests, I don't know what to say.

"Um, guys? Thanks for your help, but I think I'll just leave you. Thank you!"

"Hey, sorry...good luck." But the girl has already disappeared into the crowd.

My thoughts scatter like dandelion fluff and Griff looks like he wants to throw up. It wasn't that bad of a kiss, was it?

"So...on a scale of one to ten, how do I kiss?" My voice isn't as calm as I hoped, and I swallow the lump that'd returned.

Griff cracks a small smile. "Eleven."

"Nice." My mouth can't work because I'm staring at Griff in a whole new way. And I want to kiss him again. "Um...Do you —"

"Can we just get out of here? Please?"

"Whatever you need, Griff."

Without another word, he weaves his way through the bar while I follow him.

My best friend just kissed me...and I liked it. I liked it a whole damn lot.

Kissing Griff was not on my list of things to do on this trip.

Eleven
Griff

Outside the bar, the night is still clear and warm, but I suck in a breath like I just dove in the deep end and I'm only now resurfacing for air.

I don't know if I'm walking in the right direction, but Jamieson walks by my side, so it must be right. I'm not sure what I'm more rattled about. The fact I kissed him or that he kissed me back. What the fuck do we do now?

"Do you want to talk about what just happened?" Jamieson rumbles beside me and I guess that answers my question. Although I could say no, I don't want to talk, this conversation has been a long time coming. "I'm sorry."

"For what exactly?" Jamie's hand on my arm has me finally stopping my feet from moving forward, and I puff out a breath while keeping my gaze on the sidewalk. "Are you sorry you kissed me or sorry that I kissed you back?"

"I'm sorry I made things complicated."

Risking a glance, I lift my gaze to his handsome face. The face paint is still there, his bisexual flag still bright and un-smudged, and for a moment I wonder how make-up can do that. How do we wash it off?

Jamieson's face still smiles as he waits for me to answer. Like he's not at all freaked out about it while I'm a horrible mess, wondering if I just fucked up the best friendship I've ever had. Hell, the only one I've really had.

Oh, god.

"Hey, hey...Griff. Take a breath." Jamieson is at my side and somehow my ass is on the sidewalk with him next to me. "I think you're having a panic attack, Griff. Or hyperventilating or something. You looked like you were about to faint."

"God, I'm so sorry."

Jamie's hand on the back of my neck forces my head down to my knees while his voice soothes me like a scared animal. "Don't be sorry. I've got you. Just don't pass out because I don't think I can lift you into the Uber tonight. You're a big dude, and my arms still hurt from slinging hay bales."

That makes me smile, and the fog and tightness in my chest retreat some. He doesn't sound like he's even affected by what happened, which again...helps me breathe, but we need to talk about it. This is too big for me to stuff away like all the other feelings I've not dealt with my whole life, and likely might be the one thing that finally cracks me open.

"Our ride is almost here. Why don't we go back to the ranch and talk about it over blueberry muffins?"

Jamieson's stomach growls as a car pulls up to the curb, and he stands and offers me his hand.

"I don't know where you put everything you eat."

He opens the car door for me, and I slide into the back seat while Jamieson settles in next to me. He tells the driver where we're going, and I lean back, listening to their easy conversation.

Jamieson has always been like this. He can talk to strangers so easily and always has something to say. He's always polite and likeable. Even now, the Uber driver chats away and comments on the Pride activities and gives us tips on how to get the face paint off.

After Jamie pays and we're walking up the stairs to our loft, the panic grips me again, and the shakes set in. What if I just fucked everything up?

"Griff...sit down, please."

He grips my elbow and leads me to the couch, where I all but collapse against it. Bags rustle in the kitchen, and water runs before the couch dips next to me, and Jamieson settles by my side.

"I'm sorry, but I'm starving. I'm not making light of anything, Griff. But I brought you a muffin and flavoured water. That watermelon stuff you like."

Turning my head on the couch to look at Jamie, he already has crumbs stuck to his lips, as he's likely on his second muffin. Reaching out, I take the glass of water he mixed for me and swallow it all down before picking at the muffin.

"You don't have to eat it," he says as his hands reach for my plate, and I shove it closer to him.

"Go on. I bought them for you, anyway."

Jamieson loves blueberries in anything. I knew he'd love these muffins, and it's why I bought so many.

"You do that a lot. I never paid much attention until recently."

"Do what?"

Jamieson finishes his muffin and takes a drink from his glass. "Put everyone else ahead of yourself."

He chews at his lips, both the top and bottom, and I brace myself for what's about to come. A long overdue conversation that I both dread and need.

"Griff..." He scrubs a hand down his face and leans forward, resting his elbows on his knees. "How come you never said anything before? That kiss was...it meant something. This wasn't you kissing me because of some trend on social media."

His voice is hoarse, almost pained, and I'm not sure what to do with that.

"It's not exactly something that's easy to talk about, Jamie."

He turns his head towards me, and there's a flash of hurt in his gaze that I feel to my soul.

"I'm your best friend. You can come to me with anything."

I laugh a dry laugh and stare up at the ceiling beams.

"And say what? I've been in love with you practically since we met. For ten fucking years I've pined over you and hoped that maybe one day you'd just look at me and see me as more." Jamieson sucks in a sharp breath.

"It's true, Jamie. Do you know how much it hurt me to see you leave with a different man or woman every time we went out?" I don't let him answer, because he can't possibly know. "I've been dying a little inside with every day that passes without you looking at me like that."

It feels good to get that off my chest, even if it is to Jamieson. The one person in this world I can't stand to lose.

"I didn't know you felt that way."

Remorse in his words sets a spark of hope in my chest, even when I feel a little like an asshole for just dumping it out like that.

"I still do. I'm sorry if kissing you made things awkward, but it was the moment and—"

"I kissed you back, Griff." Jamie's voice is thick, and his swallow is audible in the small room. "I kissed you back because I wanted to." He turns his head towards me, eyes always soft for me. "I don't regret it."

Puffing out a shaky sigh, I look away. "Where do we go from here? I can't just pretend it didn't happen."

"No, me neither." Jamie hangs his head again and bites his lips. Funny how the urge for me to pull the flesh away from his teeth is now ten times stronger than before. "I...I need to know something."

"Okay. What?"

"The guy you were dating earlier this year, the one who hit you, why? Why did you give yourself to someone like that when you could have been with me? I'd never, ever do that to you. Or anyone, really."

I allow my lips to curl into a small smile and make a joke. "Are you saying I have a shot?"

Jamieson doesn't laugh. Instead, he sits back and turns to face me. "Maybe."

Jamie usually has a very expressive face. I can read him well, but not right now. "Don't joke about this, Jamie."

"I'm not. Tell me why he hit you. Tell me why the only men you've dated have treated you like shit and not once have you let me meet them. Why, Griff?" Jamieson pushes off the couch and paces the small area.

He runs a hand through his hair that's getting a little long, but I like it that way. I hate that he's worked up over something I did, though.

"They didn't deserve to meet you."

He pins me with a hard stare. "Don't. Don't feed me bullshit, Griff. You tell me it killed you to see me with other people, but did you ever think how I felt about you being treated like garbage? Hearing you tell me how these men were assholes and used you for sex? I watched and listened and hoped every new guy would be different for you."

Jamieson stops pacing and stands in front of me. "When you showed up with that black eye at Jackson's place, I..." He swallows and closes his eyes. "I wanted to kill the asshole." Jamie kneels on the floor in front of me and places his hands on my knees. "I've seen you stand up for yourself and others before. I know you're a strong person, so help me understand this."

My heart races so fast it might explode in my chest.

"It's not a simple explanation, Jamie. There's a lot of shit with me. If I'm being honest, I should probably seek therapy and not try to become a therapist."

Jamieson's eyes flash to mine. "While we're dumping secrets...I saw the letter from the university on your couch. We'll come back to that."

Swallowing hard, I stare into the eyes of my best friend and see nothing but care and concern. Maybe I've fucked things up this whole time by keeping things to myself. I should have trusted him more with all my secrets. Even if I never admitted I was in love with him, I should have leaned on him. Instead of protecting him, I've hurt him.

"There was no sex, Jamie." Squeezing my eyes closed, I continue. "Well, I considered what we did sex, but I was garbage because they didn't get what they wanted."

"What? I don't follow." His thumbs rub circles on my thigh, calming me. Offering me the comfort I always refuse to take. This time I need to go all in. It's Jamie, for fuck's sake. I kissed him, and he's still here, talking things out like a rational person, while I fight the urge to just stuff it all away and pretend everything is fine.

"I don't like penetrative sex," I blurt and run all the words together because if I say it too slowly, I might change my mind.

Jamie doesn't blink. He just waits for me to continue. "He hit me because he said I led him on. It's not a dating app. It's a fucking app, right?" I laugh dryly and turn my head away. "There's a stigma in the gay community towards men who don't like anal. I try to hide it until I can't, then I make an excuse to cut ties so they don't find out. That guy was...overly aggressive, and he caught me off guard."

Jamieson remains eerily still. Even his thumbs have stopped moving on my thigh.

"He hit you because he wanted to fuck and you weren't into it?" His voice is a scary growl, and his hands grip my thighs. "Griff? Is that what you're saying to me?"

"Yeah, that's it in a nutshell." As hard as it was for me to tell him that, the tension in my shoulders loosens.

Jamieson stares at his hands for a few moments before he runs his fingertips over my cast. "The night I waited for you when you broke your arm. Two things went through my mind. I hated that you were hurt because of me, and all I wanted to do was take care of you. It was like a repeat broadcast of the same commercial. You know, like those Sarah McLachlan ones where they show you all the animals and ask for money?"

Despite the image those commercials create, I nod. "The ones that make you cry and get your credit card out."

"Yeah. I wanted to cry, and there was this thing...this, I don't know, a feeling, I guess. It was this lump in my throat. This overwhelming feeling that you needed me. I know that sounds stupid, but while I sat there knowing you only had a broken arm, all I could think about was what if it was worse? What if I lost you one day? What if I never met you? All the fucking what-ifs I could think of and that damn lump never went away."

Jamieson's chest heaves like it took great effort to say all that. Perhaps it did.

"I can't stay away from you, Jamie. You're a part of me. The only way I'm leaving is if you tell me to."

He shakes his head with conviction. "No, Griff. I need you to stay. Please. We're on the same page with that, right?" He pushes himself up and hovers close to my face. "Can I kiss you again?"

All the air leaves my lungs, and I swallow hard. Is this actually happening? "Yes," my voice is barely a whisper as Jamieson brushes his lips over mine. It's a slower kiss. Much different from the passion-fueled one in the bar. This one is so tender, my heart aches for not saying something sooner. Maybe I could have had this years ago if I'd been brave enough to reach for it.

He rests his forehead against mine and my hands grip his arms on either side of me. "We'll figure this out, Griff. If you want to try, I mean."

His warm breath fans my face, and I swear I can feel the pulse on his forehead against mine.

"You want us to be...dating?"

"Yeah. We have too much between us to ignore this. If you want to, I'm here." Jamie releases a shaky breath. "I like kissing you."

"Can we do this slowly?" I breathe as I slide a hand to cup Jamieson's face. "I have a lot of stuff to work through, and I'm probably messier than a pulled pork sandwich at a Rodeo Days' food truck."

Jamieson's stomach growls, and neither of us can hold the laugh inside.

"It has a mind of its own, I swear." He chuckles as he helps me off the couch. "But yeah, Griff. I don't want us to keep hurting each other. I can slow down for you."

"What about the whole sex thing? That's, I mean, most guys—"

"I'm not *most guys*, Griff. There are far too many other ways to have an orgasm. It's not a deal breaker." My body leans into his, and I circle my arms around him as he hugs me back. "And I like messy."

"I've seen you eat. I know."

Jamieson pinches my ass. "Asshole."

But we laugh as we strip down to our boxers, and he holds the covers up for me. He doesn't hesitate and pulls me against his chest, being careful to make sure my arm has support.

For the first time in years, I fall asleep quickly.

Twelve
Jamieson

During the night, Griff and I changed positions, and he had his cast arm over my chest and a leg thrown over mine.

I've never felt so at ease sleeping before. Even with the scratch of the plaster against my chest, and a warm body pressed against mine. He just felt right being there, and I don't want to speculate too much, but I think Griff has needed someone for a very long time.

Maybe I have, too. If I'm being honest, there's been a lot about my life I've shoved aside just to pursue bull riding. I created a rift with my father when I refused to interview for teaching jobs after I got my degree. My sister and mom get it. But Dad...not so much. He wanted me to follow in his footsteps, and instead of trying to understand his point of view, I made it all about what I wanted.

I should have paid more attention to Griff and noticed more than what was on the surface. Maybe he wouldn't be hurting so much if I had.

My bladder screams at me to get up, and I shuffle Griff gently off me.

"Jamie?" he mutters, and I set his arm on a pillow.

"Go back to sleep. I'll find us coffee and be back."

Griff mumbles something and squeezes the pillow next to him as I pad softly to the washroom. After washing up, I grope in the dark for a pair of shorts and a T-shirt and quietly let myself out.

The sun is barely awake yet, just enough glow to tell you it's early. My phone says it's not too early to get coffee at the farmhouse, though, and that's what I plan to do. But I detour towards the field beside the barn first.

Intent on watching the rest of the sunrise, I'm surprised to find a man leaning on the fence with a mug in his hand, staring at the horizon. He turns when he hears me, and even in the low morning light, the intensity of his blue eyes catches me off guard.

"Morning. You must be Marko's friend staying in the loft."

"Hey." I offer a hand to shake. "I am. Jamieson. Nice to meet you."

"Alec," he offers and turns back to the field. "What brings you out here so early?"

Settling next to him, I watch a little bird swoop after a fly before vanishing as quickly as it appeared. "Honestly? I was going to search for coffee at the main house, but I came here to think instead."

Alec sips from his mug. "It's a great place to think."

We stand together quietly. Just two strangers watching the sunrise, and I think of Griff. All the memories, how we kissed, how I felt when he showed up with that black eye, and finally, his eyes last night...so sad and lost. Completely at odds with the sometimes grumpy but one hundred percent confident best friend I know and love.

"Can I ask you something?"

Alec turns to me, mug still in hand and his hair still mussed from sleep.

"Go for it."

"Have you ever known someone your whole life and thought you knew them, but then one day something changed and everything shifted? What you felt all this time was maybe not what you thought it was?"

Alec's answering smile is as breathtaking as the sunrise.

"I think I can confidently say yes to that. Most of it, anyway." He drains his coffee mug and frowns. "You sound like you need to get something off your chest. You're welcome to join me on the porch if you'd like. I'll get you a coffee." He gestures to the smaller house to the side of us. "My husband is sleeping late, or I'd invite you in. He owns a restaurant in town, and last night was a long one. I don't want to wake him up."

Something warms inside my chest about that, and I follow him without a second thought. When we reach the porch, he turns.

"What do you take in your coffee? Have a seat, and I'll bring it out."

"Oh...milk or creamer is fine. No sugar."

With a nod, he disappears inside, and I ease into a wooden rocker on the porch. It's so *Little House on the Prairie* that I can't help but smile. A few chickens scratch around off to the other side of the house and the bray of a donkey sounds from the barn.

Alec returns and passes me a mug before settling on the other rocker next to me.

"You have a great place here."

"Thanks. I love it."

Sipping my coffee, I gather my thoughts and wonder what it is I should say to this stranger. His presence and offer to listen are comforting. Unbiased opinions are hard to find, and I think it's what I need right now.

"I came here with my best friend for a brief vacation. We've never visited much of Ontario, and we were at the bull-riding event in Manitoba. I figured we were close enough to take some time off and visit at least Northwestern Ontario."

"You're a bull rider? Cool. I used to rope. I loved rodeo...until one day I just didn't anymore."

"Wait. *Alec*, right? You're the one that used to team rope with Hunter?"

He smiles and nods. "That's me. That was a long time ago. You're from Kissing Ridge then. How is he?"

"Semi-retired. He and Jackson are both cutting back. Jackson has a new boyfriend and Hunter is...I guess just going with the flow."

Alec sits back, rocking in his chair and sipping coffee like there's nothing better in the world to do and I kind of envy his calm.

"My best friend kissed me last night." My cheeks burn at my sudden blurt of sensitive information.

Alec pauses his rocking for a moment. "Oh?"

"I know you don't know me, and it's a lot to spill on you, but I knew I cared about him before he kissed me. Like, it was more than an I-love-you-as-a-friend type thing, but not quite an I'm-in-love-with-you type thing, if that makes sense?" I don't even know if it makes sense to me right now, but it's the best I can do to describe this odd feeling that hasn't left since the hospital. "And he's got some heavy shit he's carrying and has been for a long time.

I feel like the worst friend for not calling him out on it sooner. Now we've kissed and I'm sleeping with him in my arms, and it feels like it's all so right, but..."

I take a sip of the incredible coffee before heaving a breath.

"You're afraid you'll fuck it up because you don't know what you're doing and losing his friendship would devastate you?"

Blinking, I turn to stare at Alec. "Um, yeah. Mostly."

"I don't have advice except to be patient and let him work through his issues. Stand beside him while he does. Support him like it sounds like you always have, and if you're truly in love with him...it will work out. It's not all smooth rides. He'll probably push you away, and that hurts, but recognize it's only him protecting himself. He's just as afraid as you."

"For someone who doesn't have any advice, that's a lot of advice."

Alec tips his head to acknowledge that and continues. "Life experience comes in many forms. I've stood beside people and still lost, but I've also remained patient and won. I wish I could tell you it all comes up roses, Jamieson, but it might not. Just hold on like it's the ride of your life at rodeo finals and hope you land on your feet."

My lips tilt in a smile at the words that sound so similar to Griff's.

"Is this one of those *it-builds-character* situations?"

Alec lifts a shoulder. "Something like that." He stands and reaches for my mug. "I'll fill two for you. Go back and talk with him over coffee."

After setting the coffee mugs down so I could open the door without spilling or scaring Griff awake, I set them on the kitchen counter before peaking over to see if he's moved.

His good arm is over his eyes, and his cast arm sits to the side. The covers have slid down, displaying his naked chest and the V-line of his pelvis. I've never paid attention to that part of him, but now that I have a moment to appreciate it, I do. Griff is as fit as he has to be, but not overly muscled. His shoulders are bulkier than his pecs, and he has a sandy blond dusting of hair on his chest leading to his groin.

I'm not sure I've been with enough men to say I have a type, but I like what I see now.

"Are you staring at me?" he rasps, breaking me out of my creeper mode and I lick my suddenly parched lips.

"Just appreciating the view, baby."

Griff pulls his arm away from his face and raises an eyebrow. "We're on to pet names already?"

My cheeks burn as I realize it just sort of slipped out, just like the affection I have for him. Both catch me off guard, but not in an uncomfortable way.

"Well, I brought you coffee, so if you don't like the name, I get a pass on that."

Carrying the cups over to the bed, Griff pushes himself up and leans back to accept the mug. I place mine on the bedside table before making myself comfortable next to him.

He takes a sip and hums. "It's good coffee. I'll allow it."

"Would it be crossing lines if I kissed you good morning?"

Griff holds my gaze, and I watch all the emotions flash through his eyes. Hope, tenderness, lust and finally fear. It feels like an eternity before he finally answers.

"Not at all. I'd actually like it. A lot."

Taking his mug, I set it next to mine on the nightstand before turning to him and cupping the back of his head before leaning in.

"You know I'm competitive and I won't turn down a challenge," I whisper across his lips before kissing him again. But it's no quick peck. Licking past his lips, Griff opens for me and kisses me back. I love the way his lips feel and how his hand rests on my chest.

He's both soft and hard, open and guarded, but most of all, he's giving it back to me with a vulnerability I can practically taste. While my skin tingles with all the possibilities of what we could do together, I know neither of us is ready to go there yet. But this? Making out with Griff fills a crack in my being that I've ignored.

Finally pulling away, we stare at each other. With swollen lips and wide eyes, Griff looks like nothing I've ever seen before.

"Was that better than nice?" I rasp.

His finger runs along my bottom lip. "You know you have a habit of chewing your lip. I've always wished I could reach out and save it from your teeth when you do that." He leans forward quickly and kisses my cheek. "Much better than nice. It was perfect."

Griff, my best friend who protects people from bulls in the ring and has had his fair share of bangs and bruises from bulls, blushes. The pink spreads to his neck, and I'm awestruck that after all these years of knowing him, I've only just begun learning about him.

"What do you want to do today?" I ask as I pass him his cooling coffee mug.

Griff grins. "I saw a sign at the waterfront yesterday that said we could take a boat tour to a beach. I'd love to do that."

"I'm game."

"Really?"

"Yeah. Why not? We don't get to do much beach stuff, so that could be fun. There's like a million lakes here, so we should enjoy one."

Griff reaches for his phone and pulls up the photo of the sign he took with all the details, then calls to book us a spot. When he ends the call, he's beaming.

"I got us a spot on the early afternoon tour. They take us to the beach, and we even get one of those sun shelter things."

"A cabana?"

"Yeah, something like that. She said the towels are provided and there's a roaming bar, like on a golf cart, but we're free to bring any food or drink. It sounds like it's an island resort, but just for day trips."

Griff is giddy about it until his gaze falls on his cast.

"Oh. I forgot about this." He raises his arm with a sad smile. "Should we still go?"

"We'll pack bags and tape, and we can wade up to our waists to cool off. It's still a day in the sun and relaxing. You want to go, so we'll go."

"It won't be as fun to not swim."

Griff stares at his cast, and I suspect he thinks the situation will somehow dull my enjoyment of it.

"I'll have a great time without swimming, and so will you. Why don't we pack what we need, get some breakfast, and then stroll around that boardwalk we saw in town?"

He nods and drains his coffee. "I need sunscreen, too. If I'm lying on the sand all day, I'll need it or I'll be as red as a lobster."

Griff has always been fair. With his sandy blonde hair and lighter complexion, he's often used sunscreen even just in the rodeo ring. The one time he didn't, he burnt his nose and was actually kind of cute when it was peeling.

He slides out of bed on the way to the washroom, and I notice him. I mean, really notice him. The way his toned ass fills his boxers and how solid his torso is. Griff is strong. Even his legs are muscular and not thick, but sturdy. I don't understand how a man with so much strength could allow someone to hurt him physically. His guard had to be so low to get caught like that.

Griff pauses and looks over his shoulder.

"I see you looking, Jamie."

A laugh bursts from my mouth, and if he had said that months ago, I'd likely have joked about it and not noticed his secret smile. Or maybe the smile would be hidden, too. This total change in how we speak and act with one another is almost like a new dimension, but I like it. No... I think I love it.

This is *my* Griff, because he's always been mine. It's just different now. Nobody has made my chest ache like Griff has the past few days. I'm not always the brightest guy, but if I'm honest with myself, I think he's always been in my heart. But just like him, I was afraid to examine it too closely.

"Yeah, I'm looking. I like what I see, too."

Griff laughs and blows me a kiss, then steps into the bathroom. He doesn't wait to see if I catch the kiss.

But I catch it anyway.

Thirteen
Griff

"**T**his place is gorgeous, Jamie! Oh my god! Look at all the sand!"

If I didn't have a cast on my arm, I would dive off the boat to swim to shore. Sure, the people on the dock would give me some serious side eye, but I'm vibrating like a toddler on Christmas morning.

I'm at a mother-fucking beach!

I grab Jamieson's hand, pulling him off the boat at a jogging pace and towards the beach shelters.

"We have four hours out here, babe. Don't use all your energy in the first fifteen minutes."

It's the second time Jamieson has called me babe. Each time he does, my whole body tingles like it's not sure if it's itchy or cold. It's weird to hear him call me that, but holy hell, do I love it! Nobody has ever called me anything so simple and made it sound like a royal title.

I've been called a lot of things, none of them with genuine affection like Jamieson does. A simple endearment so common and yet unique to us flips the switch from soft butterfly wings in my gut to flapping Canadian Geese running across the water before flight.

"I know. It's just…I've never been on a vacation like this. Well, ever actually."

Jamie tugs on my arm hard enough for me to stop power walking, and I turn to face him.

"You've never been on a vacation? Ever?"

Jamieson's brows knit as he thinks through our history, and he has every right to be confused.

"Um…no. My dad never…" Puffing out a breath, I squeeze his hand. "Can we get settled, and I'll explain after?"

Jamieson nods in agreement, and I continue along the path to our little slice of beach. Shelter #7 sits on the corner before the beach curves around and gets a little rockier on the other side. It's no beaches of white sand from the vacation channel, but it's groomed and, well, sand.

We drop our bags inside the small tent, which is more like a giant umbrella pinned to the sand with flaps at the back to provide some privacy than a fancy cabana. I think it's perfect. More so since I'm here with Jamieson.

The water is mostly calm, only lapping at the shore when tired waves from a boat's wake finally reach us. A couple at the shelter next to us run into the water, hand in hand. The man pulls the woman to him and dunks them underwater as they laugh and sputter, and I feel the weight of Jamieson's gaze on me.

When I turn, he's still standing next to the shelter, watching me with a question on his handsome face. There's so much I've kept to myself the past few years, not wanting to burden him with any of it. He's always so carefree. The sunshine I need when life feels too dark. I didn't want to dull any of his shine with worry about me.

But now he knows the biggest thing I kept hidden, and rather than push me away and make it weird, he's all in. That still doesn't seem real.

Turning back to the water, I watch the couple laugh and float before they kiss, and I look away again to find Jamieson beside me.

"Is that what you think you're missing with the cast? You wanted me to drown you in the lake for fun?"

His voice is low as his hand slides across the small of my back, and I shiver.

"Sort of. It's an experience, isn't it? To play around in the water with someone you're with? Then you dry off in the sun after and feed each other grapes."

Jamieson kisses my cheek with a small laugh. "What TV shows are you watching, Griff? And who brings grapes to the beach?"

"Who doesn't? They're healthy and portable. Sweet. They're good snacks."

"Griff...talk to me. Not about grapes. Tell me what's been going on." His hand lightly squeezes the back of my neck. "Please?"

Nodding, I take his hand. Once our towels are down, we settle in our little spot of shade, and I close my eyes.

"I don't know where to start."

Jamieson's hand finds mine, and he laces our fingers together. "Tell me about not going back to school. Why did you turn it down? If you applied, you were serious about it."

"I still am serious about it, but I applied because...it was my ticket away from you. My excuse to put distance between us. If I could go to school, then I wouldn't have to pine for you, and it wouldn't hurt anymore. Maybe I could find someone to have a healthy relationship with."

Fuck, each word felt like a knife slicing my throat to say out loud, and Jamieson probably felt each cut as the words hit him.

Jamie remains silent, so I open my eyes and turn to look at him.

"You were going to run away from me and not say anything?"

"No. Yes." Frustrated, I bring his knuckles to my lips and dust a kiss to draw his gaze to me. "I was going to tell you. Every time I wanted to, I couldn't because I was afraid of us drifting apart if I left rodeo. I was afraid you'd forget me, and in the end, I just couldn't do it."

"I'd never forget my best friend, Griff. I'd have been sad you were no longer with me, but I would've understood. You have to live your life and not mine."

"There's more, though." Swallowing hard, I look back out over the water. "I didn't want to spend the money on school because I think my dad will need care soon."

"What kind of care? Is he sick?"

God, I have fucked up *so* badly with Jamieson. First, assuming if I left he'd forget me and now not telling him the truth about my dad.

"I think he's close to liver failure. Maybe a heart attack. Honestly, every time I visit, I'm surprised he's still alive."

Jamieson puffs a humourless laugh. "You kept *this* from me? What the fuck, Griff? What's going on? You should know me better than to think I'd judge you or not support you with any of this."

The hurt in his voice doesn't go unnoticed and I'm grateful he hasn't told me to fuck off yet.

"Remember when we graduated, and I told you my dad couldn't make it because he was sick and didn't feel up to travelling, so I told him to stay home?"

Jamieson nods.

"Well, he definitely didn't feel up to travelling because he's an alcoholic. Not just a guy who drinks a lot, but an alcoholic, and he's slowly killing himself. He didn't come to graduation because that weekend was the first time he ended up in the hospital over it."

Tears I'd hoped I could contain flow freely as I finally share with Jamieson how bad my dad's condition really is.

"He's what you call a high-functioning alcoholic. He does his job and stays just sober enough to keep it. The minute he's home, he's drinking until he passes out. He doesn't eat properly, and last year he took early retirement, so now he doesn't even have a reason to get up in the morning." My vision blurs, but calloused thumbs wipe at my wet cheeks, and I continue. "The last time I saw him before the season started, he'd already taken on a yellow tint, but he won't go to the doctor. He's all I have, Jamie and I can't just...leave, or not try, you know?"

"Griff...hey, come here."

Jamieson pulls me into him and tucks me underneath his chin and lets me sob, which is embarrassing, but his arms around me are a comfort I desperately need. He kisses the top of my head and murmurs that he's got me and to just let it all out.

When I'm finally done having my mini breakdown, Jamieson lets me pull away.

"I wish you hadn't kept all that from me. I understand the part about not wanting to upset me, but fuck Griff, I've never not been here for you. You should have told me about your dad. You're killing yourself by not talking about it."

It's hard not to hear the disappointment in his voice and I know I screwed that up, but how was I supposed to tell him my dad was drinking himself into an early grave when the worst thing he ever had to deal with was fighting with his dad about not going into teaching? There's no comparison.

"I'm sorry, Jamie. We can get past it, though, right?"

His eyes roam over my face for several seconds. "We will, and I'll tell you why." He offers me his open palm, and I slide my hand into it. "You're the one with the degree that understands human behaviour, but I'm the one who understands *you*. You've saved my life, Griff—twice. You calm my squirrel brain and boost my confidence whenever I need it. Sometimes even when I don't. You give to everyone but yourself, and for too long, I selfishly let you."

He swallows hard and tugs me closer. "We'll get past it because there's always a place for you in my life. Because I love you. I always have. If you had never kissed me, I wouldn't have known how much." He dips his head and brushes his lips over mine. "I was perfectly happy coasting along and having fun riding bulls with my best friend at my side. But there's always been something missing."

A charge hovers between us, and I wonder if we were supposed to come together like this. Not when we first met, but later in life, when one of us was seeking comfort in new ways. When we're both more mature and aren't guzzling Red Bull to stay awake and study for exams.

Jamieson licks his lips and squeezes my thigh. "Now let me slather you with sunscreen so we can explore this beach you're so excited to be at."

I toss him the sunscreen from my fanny pack and peel off my shirt as I step out into the sun. I'm woefully white, and Jamieson chuckles when he spins me around and presses his very tanned hand against my pale chest.

"It should be illegal for someone to remain this pale all summer. Don't you ever take your shirt off at the ranch with Hunter?"

Jamieson squirts sunscreen into his hands and slides them down my chest. I can't control the ripple of goosebumps or the way my nipples pebble under a mostly innocent touch. The bastard notices, of course, and slows his movements.

"I n-never take my shirt off because...it's...fuck I can't think when you do that, Jamie."

His low chuckle has me snap my eyes to his. "Griff likes nipple play. Noted."

His hands go back to work massaging the sunscreen in, and I stare at the tattoo on his chest. He got it last year on a whim, and it's a hoofprint of a bull. He went back and added a bull rider on his biceps. Both of them suit Jamie, but I prefer the hoof print because bulls do stomp and mark us forever.

"If you want to return the favour and put some on me, I won't complain."

Jamie's voice sounds far away as I lean closer to his chest tattoo. I must be seeing things.

My fingers trace the initials in a lighter shade of black inside the hoofprint, and Jamieson goes still.

"Is this what I think it is?" My voice cracks, and Jamieson gently takes my fingertips away and kisses them.

"Yes."

"What does it mean to you?"

Jamie's gaze locks on mine, and he presses my hand over the tattoo.

"When I asked Marko to add your initials to it, it was to remember that you were a part of my success as a bull rider. That you made a mark just like the bruises from bulls and to honour my best and closest friend."

A hysterical laugh escapes my mouth as I stare at my best friend. "You tattooed my initials on you, Jamie."

"I did, and I don't regret it. Especially now that you're not just my friend."

I've seen this tattoo many times. We've changed in hotels and the camper, and I've seen him take his shirt off working at Hunter's. But I never looked this closely, because that would have been especially painful. I didn't know he added to it when he got the second tattoo, either.

"Are you upset?"

"What? No! I'm...fuck...I want to kiss you."

His arm wraps around my waist and pulls me closer. "I like that idea."

Our mouths meet in a clash of lips and tongue, and it's still so odd that I get to do this now. That Jamieson wants this. Just as much as I do, if the way he's kissing me back and holding the back of my head so I can barely take a breath is any indication.

My cock comes to life, and I press my body against his. A low hum of approval from Jamieson ignites a burn that's been smouldering for the last ten years.

"Fuck, I want you to make me come so bad, Jamie."

He laughs at me and holds me close.

"I thought you said you wanted this to go slow?"

"I made an error in judgment."

"We're literally standing on a public beach, Griff." With a huff, I drop my head to his shoulder, and he flexes his hips, poking me with his growing problem. "Don't think I don't want to, but I'd like to not get arrested out of province." He tilts my chin up and takes my lips in a tender kiss. "The first time we do that, I'd like it to be just us and not include the random strangers who might walk by."

"Why did I suggest coming here?" I groan.

"Actually, let's get ice cream and you can tell me all about that."

"There's ice cream here?"

He points his chin back towards the dock. "There was a little building near the dock, and I'm positive it said ice cream. Let's take a walk, then cool off."

Pressing on my dick, I raise an eyebrow. "I need to cool off first."

He snickers and tugs me over to our bags. "Sure. I'll wrap your arm, we'll wade out and get our dicks wet in the un-fun way, then we'll get ice cream."

Honestly, his calm shouldn't surprise me. Jamieson can maintain his composure on the back of a bucking bull. Common sense says he can do the same while sporting an obvious hard-on in his swim shorts.

And when you finish the deal off with the promise of ice cream, that's just the mark of a true professional in calm.

Fourteen

Jamieson

"The sunset out here is gorgeous. I wish we had more lakes near home to do this."

"Me too."

Griff presses back into my chest as I hold him close. The boat we took to the beach has an upper deck and we've come up here to enjoy the sunset, along with a few other couples. It's a stunning view.

I don't just mean the sunset either. Griff has always had a tender heart. I knew that when I met him, but he often kept it hidden. Today he showed me all of him and I can't stop seeing him in a different light. He's an attractive man. I've always thought that too, but now that I've peeled back a few more layers, his inherent goodness is more beautiful than any sunset.

After we found ice cream and walked along the beach, he shared with me how vacations held mixed emotions for him. His mother left when he was just a young boy, and he had no memories of family vacations. His father often broke his promises to him, and Griff held onto those broken promises so hard he caused himself physical pain.

When he was only ten years old, he wanted so badly to visit a beach and collect seashells from the ocean. His dad said they'd take a road trip once school was out and visit a place in British Columbia. They talked about it and planned for a month. When school ended, his dad kept brushing it off and making excuses until poor ten-year-old Griff realized it would never happen.

Griff forgave his dad because he figured out it was the grief and the alcohol, and his father often said things he didn't mean. But he never let the wound heal. Meanwhile, my parents took us to Cuba and Mexico during spring break almost every year. While I left Griff during reading week to go catch some sun in the middle of Canadian winter, he smiled and wished me so much fun, promising he'd enjoy his week off.

He didn't.

He made a quick trip home in his shitty car to check on his dad before coming back to the dorms to study or pick up an odd job for a few days, like waxing floors in the cafeteria. Griff never once complained or said anything about it to me, choosing instead to hear me rave about the resort and how amazing it was to sleep on the beach during the day and party at night.

I realize we come from different backgrounds, and it was a privilege my family had, but not once did he ever let on that perhaps my life was one he envied.

"Hey, where did you go?" Griff tilts his head back, and the freckles along his nose are a little more prominent after the sun today. He still smells like coconut sunscreen and his smile is so fucking happy it just gets me right in the feels. This is the spring break he never had. The elusive vacation he wanted as a ten-year-old, and he did it with me.

My chest aches with the emotion that swamps you when you come to realize someone made you their number one, their most important person, and guilt scratches alongside that realization. We could have shared these things for years, but I lived fast and free, chasing casual sex and allowing my family to spoil me with things Griff never had.

I press a kiss to the side of his neck and squeeze my eyes closed. Christ, I've never been emotional like this. I squeeze my arms tighter around Griff, pressing him so close. I wish I could crawl inside and mend all the bruises on his heart.

"Not complaining about the hug, but it's hard to breathe, Jamie."

With a watery laugh, I release my hold, and he turns in my arms to face me. The sun has almost disappeared, and the dock is in view. In a few short minutes, this magical day will be over.

"Are you okay?" Griff brushes a stray piece of hair off my forehead, and the creases on his forehead deepen.

"I'm fine. More than fine. I had an epiphany of sorts, and it kind of caught me off guard."

"Should I ask what it was?"

An announcement sounds for us to return inside the boat while it docks, and the other couples head to the stairs. Damn if I don't want this moment or night to end, but reality is a bitch sometimes.

"That I don't want this day to end, and I've probably been in love with you for a long time."

Griff's lips part in shock.

"Gentlemen, we need you to take your seats, please." A staff member calls out since we're still not down on the lower deck.

Clearing my throat, I apologize to the woman and lead a silent Griff down the stairs to our seats on the lower level. Our day in the sun may be over, but our night isn't.

"We already have to drive back tomorrow. Then a rodeo in Saskatchewan before we're home in our own beds again."

Griff tosses his towel over the back of a chair and eases next to me on the couch. We had dinner at the diner when we got back from the boat and then took turns in the shower. I gathered up a few things in the loft I'd left lying around and ate the final blueberry muffin while Griff showered. I wasn't hungry, but it occupied me for a few minutes at least.

"Are you okay to work this rodeo with a broken arm?"

Griff raises his eyebrow. "Of course I can. The pain is mostly gone, and I can still use my arm fine." He finishes pulling off the tape to remove the bag I placed while he showered. "It's like armour if another bull tries to get me. I can bonk him if I need to."

He shifts to look at me, and I meet his gaze. "Are *you* okay with it?"

"It's not my decision to make."

"That's not what I asked."

Letting my head drop back, I stare at the ceiling and remember waiting at the hospital. How I just had this pressure on my lungs that if Griff didn't walk out of there completely fine, I might just deflate forever. "I don't want you to get hurt again."

His knee bumps against mine, and I squeeze my eyes closed.

"Jamie…you risk injury yourself every night on those bulls."

"For eight seconds. You're out there for every single rider."

I'm totally irrational and I know it, but I'm pulled from my spiralling thoughts with the weight of Griff straddling my lap and his palms sliding up my neck.

"I don't want to fight about this. It's been the best day of my life, and I want to end our time here with something better than a fight."

He presses forward and nudges his groin against mine, and I suck in a breath. "You want to finish what you wanted on the beach?"

"Yeah." He pulses his hips and drops his lips to my neck before kissing my tattoo. The one with his initials in it…that I foolishly told myself meant nothing more than friendship. Even Marko assumed it was something else and I was so fucking obtuse. "Can we? Are you okay with it? It's not like… it's not the sex you're used to, I guess."

"You're right. It's not." My hands grip his firm globes and pull him tighter to me. Griff's lips part with a sigh at the contact, and I know without a doubt, this will change my life. "Because the sex I'm used to is just getting off with people, Griff. I already know this will be different and not because of the no penetration thing, if that's what you meant."

His neck flushes pink as he huffs a long, shaky breath. "You're sure you're okay with that? It's a big ask."

Fuck those fucking fuckers who ever made him think he wasn't good enough as he is. I hate seeing him so unsure of himself. My Griff is strong and confident and always will be, even if I have to build him back up one orgasm at a time. Sex can be beautiful in every way with the right person, and Griff is my person.

"Yeah, babe. I'm more than sure, because me and you?" Reaching up, I pull his mouth to mine. "We're gonna light up the night every single time."

Griff melts into me with a moan, and I'm consumed with the need to have him come undone because of me. For me to bring him to the ecstasy he's been missing with these lesser men. To just once, not think of myself first anymore and treat Griff right.

Tapping his ass, I whisper against his lips. "Take it off."

Griff pushes off and stands in front of me. His hands slide under the elastic of his briefs before he shoves them down, stepping out of them and standing before me, naked. Suddenly, my loose-fitting sweatpants feel far too tight and I'm struggling to push them down. I've been with men before, and while I've enjoyed my encounters, I've never felt the snap like I feel right now. The indescribable pull that has me reaching for Griff before he's even settled back against me.

"Jesus, Griff. You're sexy." Bumping my nose against his, I breathe in the lingering scent of sunscreen even after a shower and my lips curve into a smile.

His shaky breath hits my skin before his lips find mine in a frantic kiss. Like he's afraid this is the only time we'll do this.

"Jamie...I..." Griff rests his forehead on my shoulder while he moves his hips. A slow rock that brushes against my rock-hard cock every time he draws back. It's the intimacy of the entire action that holds me back from mauling him like a starving animal. Almost like he's afraid of what this means.

My hands roam and map every line and curve on his back until they rest on his ass, content with their final destination. He sits back, chest heaving as he reaches between us and runs his thumb over the tip of my cock, before touching it to his lips with a sexy grin.

"One day I'll know the taste of every inch of you, but right now I'm probably gonna shoot the moment you touch me."

"I want to see that."

Griff reaches back and guides my hand to his length. Never letting my gaze leave his, I stroke him slow and firm, watching as his body coils over me before releasing the sexiest, horniest moan I've ever heard. Griff's load lands hot on my dick after a few short pulls, just as he predicated, and I'm not mad about it. He let himself go, fully and completely, just for me. No more hiding.

I pull him down to my lips with my free hand and kiss him. Nibbling his lip and scraping along his stubbled jaw.

"You just came on my dick, and I've never been so turned on. Make me come, Griff."

Like him, it doesn't take much to send me over the edge because every inch of my body is on fire for him. A live grenade and any touch from Griff pulls the pin.

With a groan, I drop my head back and come hard. Spurts of cum hit my stomach and chest and I have to blink my eyes a few times to clear my vision.

"Holy shit, Jamie," he pants as he leans forward to feather kisses across my jaw. "Just...holy shit," he says again before pressing his lips to mine.

Sweaty, covered in cum, and with Griff's lips on mine, I couldn't be more content.

"You're right. That's better than arguing," I puff against his lips.

"We should clean up...again." He laughs softly. "Then get a decent sleep before we have to drive tomorrow."

"This wasn't how I thought this vacation would go. What do you think the guys will say when we get back?"

Not that it matters to me, but I want to know where his mind is on the issue.

"I think they'll be happy if we are. Any regrets?" Griff slides his nose along mine, and the tender gesture shifts my emotions again.

"One." Griff stiffens, but I meet his gaze. "That I didn't buy more blueberry muffins."

My stomach growls, and I grin.

Griff kisses me with a laugh, and I honestly can't think of another time I felt this complete.

Fifteen
Griff

This thing with Jamieson is both odd and exhilarating.

Do I want to shout at everyone to back off because this bull rider is mine? Fucking right, I do.

But I'm also worried about what people might think. Jamieson could do better than me, I'm sure, and there are a few cowboys on this circuit he's hooked up with over the years who are likely wondering what he sees in a bullfighter like me.

The old nagging thought of him being distracted while he rides because of me rages to the front of my concerns.

"Hey, buddy! I didn't think you'd be working. I heard about the arm."

Another bullfighter that I've become friends with, Dalton, smacks my shoulder as he sits next to me.

"It's just an arm. I can still work."

"Oh, true. I guess I thought you might take some downtime before getting back to it."

My memories are still fresh from the getaway I took with Jamieson, and my lips turn into a smile.

"I did. I went on my first vacation the day after it happened. I'm rested and ready to get back to work. This was the first stop on the way back home and Jamieson can't miss it."

Dalton pauses while lacing up his shoes and casts a sideways look.

"Did you and Jamieson go away together?"

Fuck. I didn't ask Jamie how he wanted to make this public or if he was even ready. There's no way Dalton can tell we did anything. Friends go away together all the time. I'm honestly the most prepared guy I know, and yet after eight hours together in a vehicle, we didn't discuss this once.

"Uh, we—"

"Hey, babe. You almost ready?"

Where the fuck did Jamieson come from? He stops in front of me and leans down to kiss my cheek before smiling over at Dalton.

"Hey, Dalton. It's been a while." He offers a fist that Dalton bumps before going back to his shoes. Jamieson bites his lip and sends an apologetic glance my way.

"It has been. You don't come this way much. Must be following the Bullarama tour?"

"Yeah. I really want to get to the National Finals this year, and the bulls at these events can score higher, so I'm going a little farther from home."

Dalton sits up and looks between us. "See you out there." He nods to me and smacks Jamieson on the shoulder as he walks past. "Good luck tonight."

After he's left, Jamieson plops beside me on the bench.

"I'm sorry I did that. We should've talked about how to handle this. I just came looking for you and saw you struggling to answer his question." He sighs and turns those soft eyes on me. "I'm sorry. I kind of want everyone to know."

"Oh." I breathe and look at my shoes. I should have known Jamie would charge out and just tell everyone. "It won't distract you, though, tonight, right? I think that's been on my mind too much."

"What do you mean?"

"I want you to focus on riding and scoring high. Part of what worried me about us together is that I'd distract you while you ride."

Maybe my ego is too big, worrying about thoughts of me in the ring distracting Jamieson, but all it takes is a split second of your mind wandering to bring disaster.

He bumps his knee into mine, and I turn my head to find his warm gaze on me. "It won't distract me while I'm on the back of a bull. You have my word."

"Protecting you out there is second nature to me, Jamie. It's all I ever wanted to be good at." As soon as the words leave my lips, I huff. "Well, that sounds incredibly obsessive of me."

Jamieson laughs low and squeezes my thigh.

"You're one of the best, Griff. I'm not just saying that." He scuffs his booted foot on the floor. "I think I just want everyone to know that you're mine. That's why I kissed you in front of Dalton. I don't know; maybe it's a primal thing, but I wanted him to know."

The way my belly swoops at his words makes me feel like a boy with my first celebrity crush.

"Okay. So we can just let people know then, and it won't interfere with our job."

Is it possible for it to be just that easy?

"I'm okay with that if you are."

Jamieson offers me his hand, and I take it, kissing his knuckles before releasing it again and standing. "Okay."

"Let's check out my bull for the night, then."

We fall into our pre-event routine, and the comfort I always feel with Jamieson at an event returns. There's something to be said about routines settling your nerves.

"I have Bust-A-Nut tonight. It's the brown one over there with a splash of white on his face." Jamieson points to the bull, and I bark a laugh.

"Bust-A-Nut? Really?" Shaking my head, I walk closer and observe the bull. Nothing odd except his name and no strange vibes. "Is he new? I'd remember a name like that."

Jamieson shrugs. "I guess so. I'd remember a name like that, too." His eyes darken as he steps closer. "Tell me, Griff, what do you think about me riding Bust-A-Nut to completion tonight?"

My skin flushes with heat as Jamieson's breathy words drift across my ear.

"You said this wouldn't interfere with work, Jamie." My voice is hoarse, and it takes all my willpower to not pull him into me and kiss him breathless.

"Sorry." He steps away and stuffs his hands in his pockets. "I'll just ask you again later." He winks and I try to stuff the image of a naked and desperate Jamieson aside. I fail and send him a scowl, which makes him chuckle more.

"Right now, I get no vibes from this bull. Just hold on and do what you do best."

Jamieson's lopsided smile always does things to me, but now that I know what those lips feel like against mine, it's hard to think of anything else.

"You know...you said that the first time I met you."

"It was true then, and it's true now."

There's a new vibe between us, thrumming through the air as bulls snort and rattle bars. Our new dynamic scares and thrills me in equal measure, but I won't let it distract us.

"You need to do your pre-ride ritual. I'll see you out there."

As I pass Jamieson, he reaches a hand out and grabs mine.

"Stay safe for me, Griff."

The words we both feel stay behind our lips. Instead, I squeeze his hand. "Back at you, Jamie."

The group of cowboys we normally hang around with wave their goodbyes as Jamie and I walk towards his truck.

"You're sure you don't want to go to the bar tonight, Jamie? You had an incredible ride and must be vibrating."

He really did. Tonight, he scored one of his highest scores and on a bull neither of us knew. He won points, getting closer to finals, and he won money. Jamie often takes a while to come down from rodeos like this, and singing at the bars with a few drinks has been his way to work the adrenaline high out.

We pause at the back of his truck and throw our gear in the back. When I turn to get in the driver's side, Jamieson grabs my arm.

"I *am* vibrating, but I'd rather work my adrenaline off with you." Jamie crowds me against the truck and flicks the brim of my ball cap. "You never did wear cowboy hats like the rest of us when you're finished work." He dips his head next to mine, and I shiver as his breath washes over my skin. "I like it."

"Y-yeah?"

A low rumble in his throat sounds as he twists the hat backwards on my head. His knee presses between my legs, and I bite my lip to stifle the moan threatening to spill out. Being the object of Jamie's desire is overwhelming. If this is how intense he'll be every time, I question how I'll survive long term.

"Is this too much? I can back off if you want me to, but ever since I kissed you in front of Dalton, I've been thinking about a new way to work off the high of a good ride."

I take a moment to form words because Jamie's lips are on my neck, and I swear every time he breathes on me, it makes me want to drop to my knees.

"N-no, not too much. Not really."

Jamie pulls back, and his gaze roams my face. "I can dial it back, Griff. Just say the word."

"I'll tell you. It's just...I'm still nervous with you. This is a lot." He immediately steps away from me, and it's not what I want. My hands grab his hips, and in the low light from the moon above, Jamie's face softens as I struggle to get the right words out. "I want you. Always have. I just don't know how to accept this...affection."

It's not just because it's Jamieson either. Not all my partners were violent when they learned about my sexual preferences, but most of them had unkind reactions. I became conditioned to brace for the worst with every admission about the type of sex I didn't like. For every time Jamieson acts positively, it's like a delayed processing reaction. I need extra time to register that he's real and genuine.

"Okay. I'll turn it down a notch, but I still want to be with you, baby." His voice lowers. "I know you like it when I call you that, and I bet you're blushing."

Laughing softly, I press a kiss to his lips that he returns with a hunger I don't know if I'll ever be able to satisfy. It only takes a moment for me to get caught up in the heat between us, and it's Jamie who breaks the kiss first.

"Get in the truck, Griff. For the first time in my life, I don't want food after a rodeo. I want you."

He doesn't even wait for my answer and walks to the driver's side, sliding behind the wheel and starting the truck. I walk to the other side on wobbly legs and climb in.

"You sure you don't want to stop for food?"

"I'll order room service if I have to."

Okay, then.

I have to admit, not going to a bar after a rodeo is a welcome change.

It's nice not to be around crowds and have a little quiet after the chaos of a bull-riding event.

Once in our hotel room, Jamie waited for my signal. He didn't push. In fact, he didn't say a word when I ducked into the bathroom alone and said I was going to take a shower.

That was fifteen minutes ago, and I'm still standing at the counter, clutching the surface like I might fall over if I let go. I can't even put my finger on why I'm overthinking this so badly. It's Jamieson. He's listened to every concern I've had so far, and not once has he shown my sexual preferences to be a turnoff for him.

A normal person would talk to their partner about why they're hiding out in the bathroom. Communicate like a mature adult and all that. I guess I'm so used to keeping it all to myself that this part is harder than I thought.

A soft knock sounds at the door. "Griff? Is everything okay?"

I open the door to find Jamie standing there with my tape and plastic bags for my cast dangling from a finger. "I figured you'd come back out when you noticed these weren't in there, but you've been in for a while...how can I help?"

"I'm...having a moment." I laugh, but Jamie doesn't.

"Don't do that. If something is bothering you, then you need to tell me."

He sets the tape and bags on the counter and strips off his shirt. My gaze drops to his tattoo, and I draw courage from that. That he already etched me on his heart, and I need to move beyond this fear of him rejecting me.

"I'm afraid of not being enough for you. That you'll want the kind of intimacy I can't give you."

Jamie hums and reaches for my shirt. It's over my head and on the floor before I register what he's doing. "I think I know myself well enough to know I'm not missing out on anything." He motions for me to stick out my cast and places the plastic over it. He folds it tight, and my free hand holds it while he gets the tape. "I understand that you've had some shitty people in your life who have some questionable thoughts on what makes a man a desirable partner. I also understand why you'd be sensitive to that."

He rips off the tape and squeezes it around the top of my arm, making sure it's a tight seal before tossing the tape on the counter. "But I don't understand why you think I'm like them."

"I don't think you are." My voice is hoarse, and I reach a hand to the top of his jeans and pop the button. "I know you're not, but I'm...touching you like this and kissing you can be overwhelming. Sometimes I'm all in and I want to stay naked with you all day." Pushing away my nerves, I trace the zipper on his jeans with a finger. "Sometimes I feel like a shy virgin who hasn't touched a dick before."

Jamie remains motionless as I surge ahead and unzip him. Then I tug at his pants until they fall and puddle at his ankles.

"What do you need from me right now?" Jamie's voice is hoarse as I run my hand over his bulge.

"I want you to get me out of my head. I don't want my past to be between us." Swallowing hard, I force all the insecurities out of my head and focus on the gorgeous man in front of me. "I trust you."

"You'll tell me to stop if you need me to?"

"Yes."

I expected him to steal my breath with a kiss, but he presses a kiss to my forehead instead and pushes me aside to turn on the shower.

He chuckles when he steps back in front of me. "Were you hoping for something else?"

I playfully push at his shoulder. "Yes. Don't be an ass."

His eyes darken as he reaches for my pants. After making quick work of the zipper and button, he drops to his knees and pulls them down my legs, and my mouth goes dry.

"Is this better?"

"Oh, yeah."

He peppers kisses on my thigh while his fingertips slide under the elastic of my briefs, and he drags them down. If he moves a little to the left, my dick will slap him in the face. But no, instead, he sits back on his heels and makes me step out of them before standing up with a giant grin on his face.

"Hate me yet?"

"Is this your idea of getting me out of my head? Making me so frustrated that I beg for you?"

"I don't know. Is it working?" Jamie smirks and loses his briefs before he spins me around to face the shower.

"You know damn well it is."

"Good. Then let's keep going."

Sixteen
Jamieson

If Griff wants me to help him forget about all the ways the assholes he's been with have made him doubt he's a desirable man, then I'm going to do it.

But not in some run-of-the-mill cheerleader way where I talk and reason with him. Oh, no. I'm a man of action, and Griff has heard too many empty words.

Once he's under the shower spray, I turn him to face me and reach behind him to squirt shampoo in my hand. If our dicks touch, it's only accidentally on purpose and I press a kiss to his nose when he sucks in a breath.

He closes his eyes and lets me wash him. His hair first, and then his body. Since I'm in a devious mood, after I soap him up, I rub up against him while he's slippery.

"Sharing a shower saves water, so why not take it further and share soap? That's a good idea, right?"

"I had no idea you were this cruel." Griff's lust-thickened voice in my ear draws a laugh from my lips.

"You're adorable when you're grumpy." I turn him around and hold his back against my chest with my very hard cock sliding through his ass cheeks. My Griff has a very fine ass. He does a lot of squats in the gym, and it shows.

He moans every time my dick bumps against his balls and he twists his head in search of a kiss. Griff kisses me with the passion you can't fake. He's in this and he wants it. Most importantly, he hasn't asked me to stop.

But I do because sex in the shower is great and all, but he still has his arm wrapped up and I want to have his dick in my mouth without fear of him slipping or smacking me in the head with his cast. Or a million other things that can wrong in a shower.

"Rinse, please."

"What?"

His dazed question makes me smile, and I pull him back under the spray with me. I rinse us both off before Griff catches on that he won't get to come in the shower. He's all dazed and loopy, and this might be my new favourite thing.

After drying his arms and removing the plastic from his cast, he snaps back to reality and launches himself at me. His mouth is everywhere, along with his hands, and I don't even mind the scratch of the cast on my skin.

"I've never in my life needed a dick in my mouth like I do now. Fucking A+, Jamie. Your torture worked, and now I need you."

I should care that I made him drop to the porcelain floor so hard his knees will bruise, but once his lips are around my cock, I'm pretty sure it's not bothering him, so why should it bother me?

"*Holy fuck!*"

Griff swallows me. My cock is literally past his tonsils and waving hello to his...whatever the part is that you swallow with. He hums in pleasure and pulls me closer to him, burying his nose at the base of my dick.

I'd like to say I lasted longer than three seconds, but that's probably a lie because I barely have time to grip his hair and yank him off before I cover his face and chest with my load. His face is a picture of bliss, and he licks what he can reach with his tongue while I gasp and try to return to planet earth because I definitely left this realm for a moment or two.

"I was supposed to suck you off first." I think I'm pouting because I definitely sound like a kid at a birthday party, disappointed he didn't get to blow out the candles for the birthday child.

"Then you shouldn't have teased me that much." Griff pushes off the floor and stands in front of me. His good hand is still jerking himself like he was while on his knees. His breath comes in short pants, and I know he's close.

Cupping his balls in my hand, I lower my head to flick my tongue over his nipple.

It's game over as Griff jerks his body closer and cums over his fist and onto me with a string of curses and words I can't decipher.

He rests his head on my shoulder, and his chest heaves against mine.

We stand together for a few minutes, and I smooth a hand up and down his back, pressing kisses to his temple.

"That was one of the hottest things I've ever done," Griff mumbles into my shoulder. There's just something about praise after sex that makes a man feel like he's every superhero rolled into one, and I puff my chest with pride.

"I'm happy it worked, then. Feel better?"

Griff lifts his head and kisses me. It's tender and lazy and so fucking perfect.

"I feel like I could sleep for a week. That orgasm came from…I don't know where, but I can barely stand right now."

"Then let me tuck you in after we clean up again."

He nods, sleepy and sated and fucking adorable.

"I want to be the big spoon."

"Whatever you want, Griff."

Griff still lay sleeping.

Despite his insistence on being the big spoon, he plastered himself to my front during the night. His head on my chest and our legs twined together are the most perfect things in the world. Even the drool that's leaking down my chest.

This past week together has done more than just bring us together as a couple. It bonded us closer than we've ever been. We have a lot to work out, and Griff should probably get some professional help. I'm no expert, but after witnessing his panic over me rejecting him purely because of the way he prefers sex, I know my words and actions can only go so far. But I'll do what I can.

Life throws all kinds of curveballs at us. My best friend in love with me for years wasn't a pitch I could even jump away from. It kind of smacked me right in the gut, and I'm still in a daze.

A good kind, though, because nobody knows me like Griff, and it feels like this is where we're both supposed to be. If I didn't think the world revolved around me for the last ten years, maybe I could have saved Griff some of his hurt, too. That's something I might need my own therapy to work through, but one step at a time, I guess.

We need to drive home today, and all I've done is lie here and alternate staring at the ceiling and Griff's sleeping form at my side while replaying all my life's choices. Caffeine is about to become my favourite food group.

My phone lights up, and when I glance over, it's a text from my dad.

Dad: I know it's early, but your sister said she saw on the rodeo site that you had one of your best rides ever. I'm proud of you and wanted you to know that.

Leave it to my sister to be the one watching so closely. But hearing from my dad and reading his works is the kick-start I need to make changes. Easing myself away from Griff, he mutters and clutches a pillow to his chest as soon as I stand. Grabbing my phone along with a pair of jeans and a T-shirt, I dress quickly before stepping quietly into the hotel hallway.

The sun isn't up, but it will be soon. The bustle outside on the highway has begun, and the hotel staff nod as I make my way to a quiet corner in the lobby and find a chair.

I hit call, and my dad picks up before the first ring is even over.

"Jamieson. I didn't think you'd be awake this early. You didn't need to call."

My dad's voice is more surprised than I'd like, but I know he hates to text, and I want to hear his voice.

"I was awake. Hard time sleeping, so I thought I'd call you."

"Is there a reason you're awake?"

My dad's voice carries amusement, and I smile at his innuendo.

My phone buzzes with an incoming text from my sister with a congratulations message, and for a moment, my heart aches that I have family texting me and congratulating me while Griff doesn't.

"Just Griff. He hogs the blankets." My dad remains quiet, and the lump in my throat that seems to be present whenever I think of Griff grows bigger. "Um...he's more than a friend, and I have a lot to tell you."

"Son...in case I never made it clear before, your sexuality was never an issue with me. I just want you to find someone who loves you and treats you well." My dad's voice is the gentlest I've heard it in a very long time. "If it helps, I've always liked Griff."

"I have so much I need to tell you, Dad. I..." I squeeze my eyes closed and puff a relieved breath. "Thank you for saying that. It helps."

"Anytime you're ready, you call, or even come over. Your mom always loves to make that macaroni salad you like."

I huff a small laugh. Dad may be comforting me, but he'll never actually come out and say what he wants. At least not for this. He wants his kids to choose to visit their parents and not do it out of guilt. "Thanks, Dad. Tell her I'll come over tomorrow."

"I love you, Jamieson. I always will, okay?"

"I love you, too, Dad. We'll talk soon."

Ending the call, I puff a large breath and run a hand over my face. Even my parents are easy on me. Except for the fights about bull riding and school, they've been amazing. I've lived an almost charmed life. That should make me happy, but I feel like a complete jackass for not being more aware of the people in my life.

Not caring what time it is because I know he's likely awake, I call the one person who will never, ever whitewash his words to me.

"Jamieson, the sun isn't up yet. What the hell are you calling me for?"

Despite the weight on my chest, my lips turn up, and I smile.

"Good morning to you as well, Hunter. Listen, I have a question that can't wait, and I know you'll be honest with me."

"Go on."

"Am I a self-centered asshole?"

He doesn't even pause before he answers. "I wouldn't call you an asshole. You're a nice guy who rarely thinks of how his actions affect others."

"Well, that's...not as bad as I thought it might be. At least I'm not an asshole."

"Why are you calling me to ask this?"

"Because I trust you to be blunt and honest, and I needed to hear it."

Hunter sighs. "Listen, I know I'm not the easiest person to talk to about stuff, but if you need anything, Jamieson, you can ask."

"Thanks, but I just did. There's been a lot of...self-discovery, let's say, over the past ten days. I wanted to confirm that before moving on."

"I'm assuming you didn't think Griff would tell you the truth."

"God no. He's...too loyal for that."

"How's his arm? You both doing okay?"

"Yeah, yeah...there was, um, a change in post rodeo celebration last night and—"

"For fuck's sake, Jamieson, please don't tell me about any of your bed partners. Normally, I'd want to hear it, but it's too early for me to concentrate on that."

I can't help the bark of laughter that peals out, and a man in a suit peers over at me from the check-in desk. There's humour in Hunter's voice, and I smile even as I realize I kind of miss him out here with us.

"I was going to say I miss you, but with a crappy attitude like that, I'm not."

"But didn't you just admit that?"

Hunter chuckles over the phone as I admit internally that it's exactly what I did.

Damn it!

"Oh, I think I'm losing my cell signal." I make some scratchy noises and jumble words over the sound of Hunter's laughter. "Bye!"

I settle back in the chair and tap my phone on my thigh.

Hunter confirmed my suspicions that I've not given the right things my attention and while it stings, I have the chance to make it better. Mend a lot of fences, as the saying goes.

Right now, my focus is on Griff. I can't shake this bone-deep longing to do right by him.

After stopping at the hotel café, I juggle a bag and a tray of drinks back to our room.

It's still dark inside the room, so I catch the door with my foot and ease it closed as quietly as I can, but the wrinkling of the paper takeout bag sounds like gunshots in the silent room.

Griff stirs and I hold my breath, hoping he remains asleep. We both need to wake up and get moving, but if Griff could just sleep for another twenty minutes...

"Jamie? What time is it?"

His voice is thick with sleep, and his uncast arm moves to rub at his eyes. Crossing to the bed in a few steps, I sit on the edge and brush the hair from his forehead.

"It's just after 5 A.M. You should sleep a little longer."

"Can you join me?"

Even though my mind races with all the things I need to do and the long day ahead, those blue eyes draw me like a magnet. I can't look away, and I can't say no.

"Yeah. That sounds like a great idea."

Pushing off the bed, I strip out of my shirt and jeans and slide back next to his warm body. Griff resumes his position on my chest and throws his leg over mine, his cast arm resting on my abdomen.

My fingers dust up and down his spine as he presses against me and for a moment, I consider calling the front desk so we can stay here one more night and forget about the world. That would mean I'd also delay setting things right and I don't want to do that any longer.

"I'm sorry, Griff." The words, so long overdue, fall off my tongue before I can overthink them. "I've not been a very good friend to you, and I'm sorry."

He says nothing, but his fingertips trace random patterns on my stomach and he presses a kiss to my chest.

"It's not your fault, Jamie. I should've trusted you more and leaned on you."

"No, Griff. Don't you dare take any of the responsibility. You've been nothing but generous with your time and comfort to me all these years, and I feel like I let you down. I should've been asking the questions." With a fingertip, I tilt his chin back to meet his eyes. Those eyes are so full of love for me, it's almost impossible for me to accept. "I should've asked how your dad was and pressed for details. I should have asked if you needed me to go with you. That's just the start of things I should've done for you."

Griff's throat bobs, and he pushes until our faces are even on the pillow and his hand comes up to cup my face. His cast scratches my stubble, and he can't lay it flat against my cheek, but he rubs his thumb across my lips.

"Aren't we a pair? You begging for forgiveness, and me begging to be responsible for things you didn't do." He leans in to press a sweet kiss to my lips. "I forgive you, Jamie. Because I love you harder than anything that's ever come into my life. Maybe that makes me pathetic to forgive you so easily, but I can't stand the thought of you feeling like you let me down. Just knowing you were there was all I wanted."

His fingers drag over my tattoo and follow the outline of his initials. "You were there last night for me when I was on the edge of a breakdown. You came through for me. That wasn't just about sex."

"You're right. It wasn't. I wanted it, but I wanted you to know you're invaluable to me. More than anything, I needed you to know that. You've been there for me, Griff. For every single thing, and I've never acknowledged that. All I could think of was that, selfishly, if I had you around, it was all I needed."

Griff shakes his head and presses a finger to my lips.

"Don't. That's what love is, Jamie. I've loved you since that first tutoring session where you needed to learn the periodic table and couldn't accept that there was an element named Germanium."

Even now, all these years later, I snort a laugh at the memory. "I still maintain it's a plant my grandparents had and not an element." We lost a lot of study time that day because I was convinced it was the name of the red flowers my grandfather loved. I was wrong, but we took an unplanned field trip to the local garden centre for Griff to prove to me the plant was a geranium.

Honestly, close enough on a test for me.

Griff's face softens again. "I loved you and I wanted you to be happy. If me not sharing my problems in detail with you kept you happy, I did it willingly. I chose to not come to you just as much as you chose to be happy just keeping me around." Griff smiles sadly. "We both could have used a course in communication or something."

I suppose what he's saying makes sense, but I don't have to like it. I don't want him to do something without support ever again.

"Can I come with you next time?"

His brow scrunches, and I smooth my fingertip over it.

"Where?"

"To meet your dad. To help and support you when you could use someone."

Griff closes his eyes for a few beats. "I'd like that a lot, but—"

"Please, no buts, Griff. We're in this together, and I know things have to change. I want to do that for you *and* for me."

He's silent for a few moments, more pensive than I've ever seen him.

"Yeah. Okay. You can come."

Griff closes his eyes, and I lean in closer to kiss him. He kisses me back, easy and lazy, and it's so perfect my chest warms with a longing to make this my life. To always have this man adore me just as much as I adore him. For lazy morning kisses and random road trips that bring those excited smiles to his face.

To hold his hand through the hard stuff we're about to walk into.

Fuck, I want all that.

"Get some more sleep, babe."

Griff says nothing more and snuggles back into me, and I hold him.

Because holding him has never felt so right.

Seventeen
Griff

"**H**ey, Griff!"

Jackson leans in for a hug, and I accept it. He steps aside and lets me into his home. His two dogs snuffle and jump for attention and don't leave me alone until I give them each a peanut butter pretzel from my pocket.

"Riley just had to run into town for a few things to make dinner." He offers me a glass of lemonade before pouring one for himself and motioning to the living room. "He figured you wanted to talk to just me first. Is that right?"

Jackson settles on the sofa, and his dog Tramp flops at his feet with a loud sigh.

"Yeah, that's right. I mean, I would have been fine with him here, too, but I need to talk to you."

Jackson absently pets the dog with his foot and leans back. He's always been comfortable with his subdued ways, but today in his home, he's so content with his lot in life, and it strikes me how much he has in common with Jamieson, but also how different they both are.

Jackson's parents are amazing, and Jackson is a lot like them. He wants to make everything better and everyone happy. He always has, and it's why I went to him first with my Jamieson issues.

"Um...so I kissed Jamie."

Jackson raises his eyebrows, and I laugh.

"Oh?"

"Yeah." I can't keep the goofy smile off my face. "It was awesome. We, uh...we're together."

"Are you happy?"

"Yeah. I'm elated, you know? Like, I've loved him forever. I didn't even realize how much and once I kissed him, and he kissed me back, it was..." Swallowing, I remember how Jamieson pulled me closer and kissed me like he meant it. "It was everything I ever wanted."

Jackson's smile is one that tells me he knows exactly what I mean.

"I'm happy for you, Griff. You deserve this, but what do you really want to talk about? A kiss and telling me you two are giving it a go is not what brought you here."

He's right about that, too. I sip my lemonade, my throat suddenly far too dry to get the words out. But it's what I'm here for.

"You're right. I guess I'm searching for guidance. You know I've always looked up to you, and I don't have anyone to really talk to about this." Jackson dips his head and bends to pet Tramp. "He asked to meet my dad and to help me, and I'm...I guess I'm afraid of how that might go."

"Your dad? I thought you said he was okay with your sexuality?"

"He is. When he remembers. But he's..." Fuck, just say it. Lots of people have parents worse than mine. "He's an alcoholic. He's not well and I..." My throat constricts, and I take a moment to breathe and swallow while I push away the panic of two people knowing about my dad now. "Nobody important to me has met him."

Jackson seems unfazed by this and simply cuts to the point.

"Are you afraid Jamieson is going to run? Is that it?"

I don't want to say it out loud because then it feels like a betrayal of Jamie. That I don't trust or believe him to be genuine about his promises to be there for me.

"A little. But mostly I'm embarrassed. His parents are successful professionals with a beautiful home, and my mom left us when I was a kid. My dad has been drinking himself to death ever since. I grew up in a trailer park and had clothes from Goodwill. We couldn't be more different."

My hand shakes as I sip the lemonade and will myself to not have an anxiety attack about possibly losing Jamie because I finally dared to show him where I come from.

Jackson moves and comes to sit next to me. He nudges my shoulder.

"Come here." He doesn't wait for me to turn to him. He just wraps his arms around me in a hug. "I know for a fact he won't think anything less of you. We can't change how we grew up or who our parents are. It may have shaped your life in ways he can't understand, but I promise you, he'd never judge you or turn you away."

"You can't know that, though."

"Yes, I can, and I'll tell you why. Because Jamieson may come across as oblivious to things, but he has a heart of gold, and he would never leave a friend over something so trivial. I know that, Griff. He's a good guy, and sometimes it takes things like this for people to really learn about the human condition, you know? He's led a sheltered life in some ways, but not on purpose."

"Why do you always sound so worldly and have an answer to everything?"

Jackson releases the hug and returns to his spot while Tramp runs to the door when it opens.

"I wouldn't say I have an answer to everything, but I know people well and Jamieson is good people."

Keys jingle, and Riley's voice drifts to us as he talks to the dogs. Jackson grins at me with the dopiest smile before he twists to watch Riley settle a grocery bag on the counter before bending over to pet the dogs.

He turns back to me. "It's not always easy, Griff. I won't lie. But it's so fucking worth it. You okay with Riley here now?"

"Yeah. It's okay." Jackson stands, and I follow suit. "Jackson." He turns back towards me. "Thank you. For everything."

"Anytime, Griff. The door is always open."

He greets Riley in the kitchen, and Riley shouts a hello that I return, but I hang behind, and let them have their moment. As I watch them interact, the ache to have a normal domestic life like theirs grows. A shared kitchen. The touches as you move around together, hell, even the arguments over changing the toilet paper and which way is correct. (It's over the top, no debate.)

My phone vibrates in my pocket and it's a text from Jamieson.

Jamie: I know you're over at Jackson's, but I was wondering if I could come over tonight? Totally cool if you're not up for it.

Griff: Do you want to stay over?

Jamie: Yes!

He adds emojis with heart eyes and I can't help the grin on my face.

"Texting someone special?" Riley appears with a tray of veggies and cheese and sets it on the coffee table with a stern finger point at Carrot, the beagle, to go lie down.

"Yeah. Um, thanks for giving me time with Jackson today. I didn't mean to intrude."

"You didn't. Did me a favour, really. He loves nothing more than to make his friends happy. He's a helper, and I love that about him." Riley snatches a carrot from the tray. "Did you know my parents basically gave me up to my aunt because I was a burden to them? They didn't want a gay son...or any child, for that matter."

"Shit. I didn't know that. I'm so sorry."

He waves his hand and keeps munching his carrot. "Don't be. My aunt is way more fun and why should I long for something like two parents and all that crap when my aunt loves me like her own and gave me more than they ever did?" Riley huffs a little and shakes his head. "I'm not saying this well. What I'm trying to say is, you're a worthy human, no matter who raised you or how you grew up. Jackson just mentioned you're worried about Jamieson meeting your dad, and if he's worth his salt, he won't care."

Riley offers a carrot to...Carrot and raises a finger to his lips. "Don't tell Jackson. I give him far too much shit for spoiling these two. He'd never let me live it down."

Riley and I chat while Jackson cooks something that makes my mouth water. I feel a little guilty for not joining Jamieson at his parents' for dinner, but I needed to talk to someone first about

Jamie meeting my dad. I already agreed he could come with me tomorrow, but of course, I had to worry about whether it was the right thing.

I'm a creature of habit in all things. Even my tendency to worry.

Plus, I hadn't seen Jackson for a while, and I've missed him on the tour with us. Riley is a good guy, too, and it's just nice to catch up with them. They're part of a family I made myself, and holding onto that thought will serve me well.

When dinner is over, I offer to help clean up, but they both shush me away. Jackson walks me to the door and hugs me again before I go.

"Have faith, Griff. It'll work out. I know it."

"Thanks. I'm just nervous."

"You're allowed to be, and if shit goes sideways, you have my number." He slaps my shoulder again. "Now get out of here. If I know Jamieson, he's chomping at the bit to see you right now."

I laugh at the accuracy. My phone has been buzzing for the last fifteen minutes with an impatient Jamieson.

"Thanks again, Jackson. I'll talk to you soon."

Before I pull away, I text Jamie to let him know I'm on my way home. He hearts the comment, and I don't know why, but that settles me a little.

When I arrive home and take my usual parking spot at my building, I spy Jamieson's truck on the street.

I live above a small bookshop and coffee bar downtown. It's tiny and all I've ever needed. Parking only needed to accommodate my tiny car, but Jamieson has never seemed to mind parking on the street.

After climbing the short flight of stairs and entering the code to my little sunroom off my apartment, I smell Jamie before I see him. It's a mixture of leather soap and orange, the stuff he uses to condition his chaps. The scent seems to cling to him more than the leather most days.

When my eyes land on him leaning against the wall, I suck in a quick breath.

"Hey, babe." He pushes off my wall and crosses over to me. Hands in his pockets and a shy grin. "I didn't want to sit in my truck. Hope it's okay that I let myself in."

"Of course it is. You could have used the spare key to let yourself all the way inside."

"Maybe I did."

Shaking my head at his cryptic words, I turn the key in the lock and open the door. Jamieson steps in quickly behind me, closing the door and turning the deadbolt while I stare at the giant balloon with a note attached in my hallway.

"What's this?"

"Open the note and find out."

My heart races as I remove the note from the shiny blue balloon.

Griff,

When I met you, you wore a blue shirt like this balloon. I remember thinking how it made your eyes look really blue.

The smile that comes to my face is automatic, and I snort. "Really blue?"

"You know I'm not good at the whole descriptive thing. Keep going, there's more."

The hallway is short, so it's only a few steps before I enter the living room and gasp. "Jamie...did you buy out the balloon store?"

Various colours of balloons fill my living room, all with notes attached.

"They're numbered. See?" Jamieson spins the one closest to us and shows me it's a three. "You need to find number one, then two...it goes in order."

"What is all this?"

He swallows before pulling me to him and placing a soft kiss on my lips.

"A surprise and a way to show you that maybe I've always loved you, too." He pulls a red balloon over with a number one. "Start here."

This envelope has another note in his messy handwriting that really hasn't changed since university.

"The first time we hung out after a rodeo, you ordered a burger with no pickles and told me you aced your sociology exam."

Note two is on a yellow balloon.

"This is the colour of that vile medicine you made me drink when I had strep throat second year."

"You *had* to drink that! I didn't *make* you!"

"If you didn't come over every six hours to make sure I took it, I probably wouldn't have. So yeah, you *made* me."

I work my way through the balloons in order, like he said to, and realize the notes are chronological. Each one is a memory of me or us since we've been friends. Some are funny and some are factual, but once I reach the ones after graduation, the notes take on more feeling.

"The day we fought about Homewrecker, I snapped at you because I was jealous you were helping other bull riders. I was afraid I was losing you."

That one has me huffing a breath, and I look at Jamieson. "Jealous? Really?"

"It was the first time I'd seen you speaking to another bull rider more than me about the bulls. I thought I was just being oversensitive or what not, but I think it was then I realized you meant more to me and I didn't know what to do with that."

I'm almost afraid to read the final three balloons, but I also want to know what else he has to share.

"Why the balloons?"

"Oh. Heh..." Jamieson smiles and the dimple pops on his right cheek, making him look like he's a teenager again. "That doesn't really have any great meaning. I just thought it would be fun because who doesn't like balloons?"

"Nobody has ever given me balloons before."

"Wait until you see the last one, then."

"So mysterious."

Balloon eight.

"You're the only one who calls me Jamie, and the first time you did, it felt like I was special. More than your friend."

Reaching for balloon nine, I pull the note off and immediately feel my eyes water.

"I wish I had stayed with you during spring break. I hate that you were alone."

He passes me balloon ten.

"One night when you were on a date, I got drunk because I missed you."

Balloon eleven gets passed to me as he wipes a tear off my cheek.

"I've laid awake thinking of you every night since you kissed me. Even when I held you, I couldn't stop thinking of you."

"If your intention was to make me cry, mission accomplished." I sniffle as I place all the notes on the table and turn to him.

"Tears of joy, though, right?"

"Yeah, definitely."

"Phew, good. There's one more, and I hope you don't hate me for it."

"I could never hate you," I whisper and hold his gaze. He smiles softly and runs his knuckles down my cheek.

"I'm holding you to that," he whispers hoarsely. "You don't know what I did yet." He wraps an arm around my waist and leads me to my bedroom. The door is closed, which I never do. Jamieson puts himself between me and the door, and I notice the worry flitting across his handsome features.

"I think I can confidently say nothing you do will make me hate you. You filled my apartment with balloons and love notes, Jamie. That's not a bad thing."

"Well, here goes." He opens the door to my bedroom, and a large paper sun is hanging from the ceiling. It's clearly homemade, and that just makes my chest ache in new ways. A small kiddie pool filled with sand is on the floor next to my bed, and seashells cover every surface of my room. They're on my dresser and nightstand, there are stickers on the wall of sea creatures and more shells.

Then I hear it. Over the roaring of blood in my ears, a soundtrack of crashing waves is playing. Jamie's arms circle me from behind, and he rests his chin on my shoulder.

"You really loved the beach, and all I could think of was one day we'd go on a real vacation, and I'd take you to an ocean to find your seashells. Until then, I brought the beach to you. I hope you don't hate it." He pulls over a Mylar balloon in the shape of a heart, and I open note twelve.

"I love you."

Gulping in a breath, I try to calm all the emotions and keep it together.

"When did you do all this?"

"While you were at Jackson's. Riley wasn't just getting groceries in town. He helped."

"You're extra sneaky."

"Do you like it?"

Jamieson's voice carries the nerves of approval, and I turn in his arms.

"No one has ever done anything like this for me. I'm overwhelmed, and I'm wondering how I'll manage to not step into the sandbox, but I love it. I love *you.*"

Pressing my lips to his, I convey my feelings in a kiss. Words are far too hard right now, and thankfully, Jamie understands that because he kisses me back with the same frantic energy.

"I can move the pool to the living room for you," he whispers as his lips brush along my jaw.

"Leave it for now. I've never had sex on the beach."

Jamieson's lips part in surprise. "Shit. I didn't think about the side effects of doing all of this. But I love that idea."

Eighteen
Jamieson

Griff pulls on my shirt and I happily reach down and pull it over my head, before helping him out when his shirt gets stuck on his cast.

We both laugh and continue to make out in the doorway of his bedroom until he grabs my waistband and walks backwards until his legs hit the bed.

We can't keep our mouths off each other while we scramble to unbuckle and unzip our pants. A frustrated growl vibrates from Griff, and I have to laugh.

"You sound like a pissed-off puppy."

"I can't get your button undone with this damn cast covering part of my hand."

Griff's hands are shaking. It's not the cast. Taking his hands in mine, I kiss the back of each one before placing his hands on my shoulders.

"Let me do it."

Griff's fingers press into my shoulders as he ducks his head to watch my hands. With my belt hanging open and my zipper at half-mast, I pause.

"Actually, I have a better idea." Pressing Griff back, he sits on the edge of the bed, and I kneel in front of him to tug his pants off. My fingers slip under the band of his briefs and his breath catches, but he raises his ass so I can take them off.

Leaning back on his elbows, he waits, completely naked, and watches as I stand to remove the rest of my clothes. We've seen each other naked. That part isn't new.

But this spark of emotion and baring not just skin but ourselves is new. I wanted to show Griff how much I loved him when I brought the beach to his apartment, but I also wanted him to know I was all in. Yes, we had words in the hotel, but I know Griff is still nervous that I might nope out at any minute. He's not a passing fling, and the initials etched forever into my skin should have been my first clue that what I felt for Griff was more than just admiration.

But clearly, I'm not always a fast learner.

"I've always thought you were attractive with clothes on, but without them...I might need a glass of water," Griff jokes and motions for me to come closer as he sits up. He runs his hands up over my abs and stares up at me with those blue eyes.

"Griff...I want..." Shit. My throat constricts, and it's hard to swallow.

He smiles the sweetest smile and slides back onto the bed. Patting the spot next to him, I take the hint and lie in the empty spot.

"Nothing you can do with me will ever be bad, Jamie. I want to be with you. I always have."

"Is it stupid to say I'm afraid of fucking all this up and losing you?"

Griff's eyes widen, and he shakes his head.

"No, because I keep feeling that, too. That it's stupid for me to take a chance with you, but I think even if it didn't work out with us, I'd never be able to shed you. I've lived with you under my skin for ten years, Jamie. Like your tattoo...having you in my life is rather permanent now."

"I never knew you were so poetic."

Griff pulls us closer, and my cock brushes his. "Not poetic. Just dying for you to make me see stars." His lips tilt in a playful grin as he rocks his hips into mine. "I love you. I love what you did here tonight, but I'd really like you to make me come."

He pulls me over of him and hooks his legs behind my ass. I get the hint and rut against him. He shifts his hips when I move, and each time he does, our dicks meet differently, every touch better than the last. Griff sighs and pulls my head down, kissing me with a hunger that makes my toes tingle. The man knows how to kiss.

"Fuck, Griff..."

He rolls to his side and reaches for the bedside table. After pawing in his drawer, he has a bottle of lube, and squirts some into his hand. "I want to show you what I like."

"I'm all in."

"Good, because it's always better with a partner," Griff jokes, but I don't laugh because he strokes my hard cock with a well-lubed hand and words are...extremely difficult to form.

After smearing the lube between his thighs, he snuggles back to my chest and lines us up. Instead of holding my cock to his ass, he guides it under between his thighs, and my dick rubs up under his ball sack.

Griff squeezes his thighs together and turns his head over his shoulder for a kiss.

Our harsh breathing and sloppy kisses fill the air, and I hold him so tight to me, it's a wonder we can both still breathe. I bat his hand away from his dick and stroke him in time to my thrusts.

Griff groans, and the warmth of his release coats my hand. "Jamie..." He clamps his thighs together as my balls draw tight and I come so hard the aftershocks of my body shake the headboard.

Jesus. There're men out there who don't like this? Fucking idiots.

"Holy hell, Jamie." Griff laughs softly and kisses the back of my hand while I summon all my mental capacity to form words. I've never felt so wrung out from an orgasm before. Is that what love does?

"I think my brain just went offline," I mumble, and the bed shakes with Griff's laughter.

"Can you at least bring it online enough to tell me if you liked it? There are other positions if you don't like that one."

Turning my head on the pillow, I stare at Griff.

Griff's face glows. Not just post-sex glow. He's truly happy. Or maybe I'm seeing something that's not really there because I'm still so blissed out.

"I think my temporary loss of speech and body convulsions speak to how much I liked it, babe. I've never felt this before, Griff. I'm hot and tingling and feel like the luckiest guy in the world."

"Sounds like you have a fever."

Snorting, I roll onto him and hover over his face. "Just a fever for you."

"Oh my god. Please don't start with all the cheesy sayings and shit. I don't know if I can handle that."

"Okay. How about this...I can't wait to start a new life with you. I love you and you're amazing."

His features soften, and he reaches a hand to cup my cheek. "Better. Shower with me?"

"I'd never turn that down."

Griff's jaw is tight as he drives my truck and even in the light of the early morning hour, I know all I can do is just be here.

I wish I could do more, but after talking to my parents about Griff's dad and learning more about alcoholism, I know it's all I can offer right now. Just to be here and take care of him when he needs it.

The plastic rattles on my licorice package, and he glances over at me.

"How do you eat that in the morning?"

"Licorice? Like this." I rip a piece off with a happy hum and chew it. Griff relaxes a little with a smile, and I hold a piece out to him.

"No thanks. I don't normally eat until after I get to Dad's. I'm too...I just can't."

The tightness returns to his face, and I shift to squeeze his thigh. He immediately grabs my hand and holds it there, his thumb sliding along my knuckles, and I toss the licorice into the bag of snacks at my feet.

"Do you want to talk about anything? I don't even need to respond. I'll just listen."

The radio cuts in and out, so I switch it off with my free hand. Griff's pet peeve is driving where even satellite radio can be interrupted. He'd rather sit in silence than listen to partial bits of song. Or me singing the missing bits. I tried that once and I think if he had a weapon, he would have used it on me.

"He doesn't know we're coming." Griff glances quickly at me. "Even if I told him what day I was coming, he's likely to forget, but I haven't told him about you or that I'll be here."

"Okay. Is he going to be mad?"

"I don't think so. The good thing about Dad is he's not violent. I'm lucky that way. He just gets sad and talks a lot about past stuff. He'll be happy to see me, then sad I'm not around more, then he'll either talk about shit when I was ten or stare at the TV." Griff sighs, and I feel the weight of it. "It's honestly a lot of stress for me. I gave up hoping each time would be different a long time ago. Now I just keep showing up because I never know when the last time will be."

Griff just spews all this out as straight facts, and I want to both cry and punch myself for being so oblivious to his trials.

"I'll warn you, though. Today I'm trying to talk him into going to a doctor. He might agree, and if he does, I need to call the rehab facility immediately. I won't hold my breath because he always fights me on it."

"Is there someone who could come to the house if he won't go? Do doctors make house calls?"

Griff puffs his cheeks and squeezes my hand again.

"I can ask a nurse. There are a few in town that might do it. I've checked, but he needs bloodwork and tests, and...maybe it's best I don't know how sick he is. He needs to detox. But I'll warn you, Jamie...he looks like shit."

I don't know if I'd have the mental strength Griff has if our roles were reversed. To be responsible for the only parent you have is a burden. In every way. Sure, there's love there, but to know he should be in rehab and that Griff has sacrificed his own dreams to help his father...that breaks my heart, and I don't know if I could do it.

"You're an amazing son, you know. You've handled this on your own and a lot of kids might just walk away. This probably sounds rude, but why do you keep coming back when it's so hard on you?"

Maybe that's my selfishness coming out, but I think it's a legitimate question to ask. Especially now that I know he's so stressed he doesn't eat before he visits.

Griff sighs again and squeezes my hand.

"Because I have no one else. He's my dad, and if I didn't keep checking on him, nobody would. He's pushed away all his friends over the years, and he's literally alone. Sometimes I just wish..." Griff's swallow clicks, and I squeeze his hand. "I just wish he'd at least move into a facility. Some place where he could press a button for help, and they'd make him go to a dining room to eat. Where he could be with people and get help to deal with this disease. It's a long shot he'll even agree to the help, I know that, but I just can't ignore him."

He brings my hand to his lips and kisses it before placing it back on his thigh.

"It's hard for me to explain, but I can't walk away like that, Jamie. He's so damn isolated in this shitty town."

Wow. My eyes prick with tears for Griff, and it's not the first time I feel like an asshole. Would I abandon my parents if I were in his place? Probably not, but I've never been in his shoes. Not even a little. His capacity to forgive is something I need to strive towards.

Griff says nothing else, but he still holds my hand, and I'm happy to provide the comfort. My mind wanders in the silence, though. Instead of worrying about how he handles all this, I'm now back to worrying about actually meeting his dad. I've never been in a relationship to meet the parents. Griff knows mine because we live in the same town and they came to the university a few times.

He met my sister and had dinner with us occasionally. They ask about him all the time, and yet I've never met his dad.

Anything close to a relationship I've had never lasted more than a week or so. Definitely not-meet-the-parents material, and they didn't have a connection like me and Griff. They were buckle chasers. You can get laid a surprising amount while doing rodeo. Which I did. God and Griff watched it all go down and never said a word.

"You're thinking pretty hard over there. Want to talk about it?" He grins over at me. "You always chew your lips when something bothers you. Always."

"I've never met someone's parents before. Well, I've met parents, but I've never met them when I'm in love with their child. I guess I'm nervous."

Griff smiles with a sadness so profound I almost wish I never said anything.

"I love that you're nervous, but...don't be disappointed if he doesn't remember your name or ask you much. He might, but prepare yourself for disinterest. He could be in a chatty mood or a silent mood. There's literally no in between. But I'm happy you're here with me all the same."

We don't talk much more after that, both of us caught in our own thoughts. The sign for his town comes into view, and Griff's fingers grip the steering wheel harder.

He makes a series of turns until we're driving down a mixed neighbourhood of houses, fourplexes, and mobile homes. He pulls into a driveway at the oldest mobile home on the street. It has to be a 1960s model with a rusted tin roof and windows that look original. The only thing on the outside that looks new is a small wooden platform deck off the side.

"Well, this is it. Hard to believe it looked better when I grew up here."

"But you had a bed to sleep in at least, right?"

If I don't find something bright about this, I might crack and not provide the support I came here to provide.

Griff nods before opening the truck door. "That's true. Could've been worse." He waits for me in front of the truck, and when I reach him, he takes my hand. "His steps were rotting last year. I looked up a DIY video and made this new deck with a step so he wouldn't trip and fall. I think it turned out pretty good."

"I love a man who's good with his hands."

Griff snorts before puffing another long breath.

"If you want to change your mind, just take the truck and I'll text you."

"I'm not changing my mind, and I'm not leaving you alone."

The open emotion in his eyes leaves no room for words.

"Okay. Let's meet my dad."

Nineteen
Griff

"Dad? It's Griff."

Jamieson lingers behind me as we step into the trailer, and my eyes immediately land on the bin filled with empty beer cans and a 26-oz bottle of rye. He usually sticks to beer, so that's new, and I don't like it any more than I like the number of empty beer cans.

The air is stale in the trailer in this late summer heat, and I smack the window air conditioner unit that's usually running. It probably costs more than it's worth to run, and I should look at replacing it.

"Son?"

My dad's voice sounds from his bedroom, and I whisper to Jamie. "Let me go check on him. I'd say make yourself at home, but..." I gesture to the mess. "I usually clean up a little while I'm here, but I'll be right back."

"I'll be here."

Jamie presses a kiss to my cheek, and I walk down the hall to Dad's bedroom. I almost gag when I step inside. The scent of urine is overpowering, and I wonder how long he's been lying in bed.

"Dad? You okay?"

I crack the old metal slat blinds on the window. The dust floats in the sunbeam as it tries to lighten the room and the atmosphere.

"I lay down for a nap after the Roughriders game, and now you're here. This is a surprise."

The Roughriders game was two fucking days ago. He's been in his own piss for two days?

"Yeah, I wasn't sure if I'd be able to get here this week, so I didn't want to disappoint you, just in case."

Dad pushes himself up. He's a little wobbly, but stronger than I expected if he hasn't moved in two days.

"Why don't I help you with the shower, Dad? It will wake you up a little, and we can have lunch. It's warm in here, too. You should get some water into you."

"Oh, I don't need help in the shower. I'm a grown man."

His voice still carries that tone I hate. It's a mix of denial that nothing is wrong with him and pride that he'd need help. It makes me want to scream. To yell at him that grown men don't spend the day drinking and pass out in a bed full of piss, but that anger would get me nowhere. Instead, I push away his words and root around for clean clothes for him.

"Okay. I'll get your sheets changed while you're in there, but if you change your mind, call out."

My dad shuffles down the short hall, and I set the clean clothes on the bathroom counter for him. He mutters his thanks and once the water turns on, I walk down the hall to look for Jamieson. I find him in the kitchen, emptying the garbage and taking the pile of empty cans outside.

"You don't have to do that."

"No, I don't, but I want to. Is he okay?"

"He says he is, but I think he's been passed out for close to two days. His mattress is soaked in piss and he's shaking pretty bad."

Jamieson reaches for my hand. "If you need me to do more, just ask. Anything, Griff. I'm here for you, and you don't need to do this by yourself."

My throat closes, and I throw myself against him, burying my nose against his neck. "Thank you," I croak. "For...you. For this. This is the worst I've found him, and I'm scared."

He rubs his hands up my back, and his arms provide strength I don't feel right now. I never realized how much I needed someone to lean on until now. Jamieson hasn't turned up his nose or run away screaming. He's here for me in every capacity and I wish I had asked for his help sooner. Even if I never kissed him, he'd be here for me, and I should never have doubted that.

"I'm gonna change his bedding while he's in the shower. If you want to grab the bags of groceries and bring them in, that would be great."

"You got it."

Jamie kisses my cheek and turns to head out to the truck.

"I love you." My voice, clogged with emotion, barely squeaks out.

"I love you, too."

The door clicks behind him, and I stride down the hall towards dad's room, my mind whirring about the conversation we need to have. With his soiled sheets in the hamper, I spray the mattress with Lysol before placing a clean sheet and checking his comforter. It needs washing too, but that requires a laundromat. Maybe I'll just buy him a new one and take this one back home with me to deal with.

"Griff?"

My dad's voice sounds from the bathroom, and I hurry over to the door.

"Yeah, Dad?"

"Could you come in?"

I step into the small bathroom and dad sits hunched on the toilet bowl, looking far older than his sixty-one years. "What do you need?"

"Do you think you could help me shave? I tried, but I dropped the razor and…" My dad's bloodshot eyes well up and I notice how much more his hands are shaking since he's been awake.

"Dad," I whisper as I kneel in front of him and take his hands in mine. "You're not well, and it's okay to ask for help. But I want you to listen while I help. Can you do that?"

He remains silent but I stand and fish the shave cream from the shower and find a new razor in his cabinet. Dad never liked electric ones and hasn't even progressed to a five-blade razor. He buys bags of disposable ones from the dollar store that have no forgiveness in the blade, and I'm scared to shave him with one.

After lathering on the foam and filling the sink with warm water, I kneel back in front of him. He's in an early stage of withdrawal. That much I'm aware of with my research. He's also probably still in denial. A thin sweat breaks on his skin while I shave, and I launch into the speech I prepared for him today.

"Mom isn't coming back. I know you're sad. I am too. We're two amazing men she turned her back on. It's her loss, Dad. Remember that, okay? That's the only thing that makes it hurt less sometimes for me. That I'm amazing without her." I scrape the razor along his face, and he closes his eyes. "I don't fault you for turning to booze,

Dad. But I want my dad to meet the special people in my life, and I want to help you."

"I've been a shitty father." His voice cracks with a deep sorrow. "Sometimes I wonder why you keep coming back."

My hand jerks at his words. He's never spoken like this, and I take a moment to wipe the shave cream off the side of his face while I gather my thoughts. My pre-planned speech is no longer needed.

"Because I love you. You're my dad, and if you let me help you, we can have more years together." Taking his hands in mine again and I squeeze and force him to look at me. "I know you don't want to admit it, but you're sick. I came here today to force you to listen to me."

Dad attempts a smile, and his body shivers. I'm scared out of my mind that he might actually die before I can get him to the rehab facility that I paid for in advance. I wasted too many years leaving him like this, and I regret not being more firm over it, but it's time.

"I have a spot at a facility in Kissing Ridge reserved for you. It's a rehab place. You'd have your own room and access to doctors and therapists. All I need to do is make one phone call, and they'll be on their way to pick you up."

Dad's shakes and shivers worsen, but there's strength in his grip on my hand that gives me hope.

"It's closer to you? I'd see you more?"

"I wouldn't be able to see you for the first few weeks, but after that, yeah. Do you want to stay in Kissing Ridge?"

Dad stops trying to hold the tears back and breaks into an ugly cry. "I don't want to die alone, Griffy. I'm so sorry I've done this to you. I want to see you at the rodeo and be there for you. I'm sorry. I'm sorry."

"Hey...stop that." Reaching over to the toilet paper roll, I tear off a bunch and wipe at his wet cheeks. "Right now, I need to know if you'll go to rehab. One call, Dad. I have it all ready. I just need you to say yes, and we'll get started."

"I want to."

I know he's probably only agreeing because he's scared and feeling like shit as he sobers. But I'm holding on to the promise of his words. If he's truly sorry, he should do this. I just hope like hell we aren't too late.

"I'm going to make the call, and then I'll finish your shave. While we wait for your pickup, I have someone I want you to meet."

Standing, I grab a towel from the cabinet and drape it over his shoulders. His shaking is escalating, and it's painful to watch him suffer through this. After taking my phone from my pocket, I dial the contact and speak to Justin.

"Hey Justin. It's Griff."

"Hi Griff. Are we a go?"

"He said yes, and he's already in withdrawal. He passed out for over 24 hours, maybe longer, and hasn't had a drink since the football game on Tuesday."

"Okay. We can deal with that. I have a unit on the way already for his pickup. I was confident you'd get him to say yes, and they left thirty minutes ago."

"So, about an hour until they're here?"

Justin and I confirm a few details, and after ending the call, I kneel in front of Dad again.

"You're going to get through this, Dad. Want me to shave the other side, or do you want to start a new trend?"

Dad smiles a little, and it makes me hopeful that better days are ahead.

"I'm n-no trend setter, Griffy. Go ahead and sh-shave it."

Now that I've had the hard conversation, I can concentrate on shaving the rest of his face. I help him get dressed, and when we step out of the bathroom, the aroma of chicken noodle soup greets us.

My dad's body is so frail it breaks my heart, but together we make it to the tiny kitchen table and find Jamieson's six-foot-two frame taking up most of his kitchen while he stirs soup on the stove.

My dad immediately sits at the table, and Jamie turns to greet him.

"Mr. Shepard, it's a pleasure to meet you." He offers my dad a hand and I notice my dad assessing Jamieson. Judging if he's good enough for his son and while I wish they met under different circumstances, I'm just happy they finally have.

Dad takes the offered hand with a single shake. "Got a name?"

Jamieson blushes and stumbles over his words. "Oh, yeah, so sorry. I'm Jamieson."

"If he cooks, he's already a keeper, Griff."

The first smile I've had in my dad's home in years graces my face. Despite the situation and worrying about my dad, I can't hide the smile if I tried.

"He's really not bad," I say as I kiss him on the cheek and reach for the soup bowls. "Think you can try a bit of soup, dad?"

"I can t-try."

My dad continues to glance between me and Jamieson and suddenly blurts out, "Do you love my son?"

Jamie places a bowl in front of dad and lowers himself to the chair next to him. "I've never loved anyone more. Did you know he saved my life once?"

"I'm not surprised. Griff is the bravest person I know. Is that when he got the stitches in college?"

"You remember that?" I ask as I sit across from him.

"I do. You didn't call much, but you called that day, and I knew there was something more to it. I figured you'd tell me, eventually. So it was because of this guy?"

My dad's hand shakes far too much to get the soup to his mouth, and the liquid falls off the spoon. Jamie, without missing a beat, takes my dad's spoon and brings a spoonful of soup to his mouth. For a moment, I think my dad will tell him to piss off and he doesn't need spoon feeding, but he doesn't.

"Yeah, it was me. If it wasn't for him, I wouldn't be here today. Seems like you and I already have a lot in common, Mr. Shepard." My dad opens his mouth for another measure of soup and Jamieson just keeps feeding him like it's not weird to meet your boyfriend's father and start spoon feeding him.

"Call me Charlie."

Jamie smiles. "Okay. Charlie, it is."

Dad coughs on his next swallow and shakes his head that he's had enough.

"Sorry. Two young bucks like yourselves shouldn't be here acting like n-nursemaids to an old man." He slides a shaky and age-spotted hand across the table to me and offers the other to Jamieson. "But thank you. I hope we can do this again and I'll be able to feed myself instead."

"I'd love that," Jamieson says, and I know he means it.

"Hey, babe. You okay?"

After the rehab workers picked Dad up and we had a tearful goodbye, Jamieson and I spent several hours cleaning dad's place. We even ran his old mattress to the landfill, and I'll get him a new one when he needs it.

If he needs it.

We came home to my place late last night and now after breakfast I'm staring at the wall with my hands in a sink of cold dish water.

"I think I will be. I'm just running through so many scenarios and hoping for something good. He liked you. I want him to know you like I do."

Jamie circles his arms around my waist and rests his chin on my shoulder.

"Keep thinking good thoughts. You've done what you can."

"You're right."

He laughs and turns me around. "Of course, I am. I'm doing some weight training with Hunter and Jackson today. Want to join us?" He kisses me softly and I sigh. Fuck, I cannot get enough of him kissing me.

"Not today. Could we meet up later? Maybe at the Thirsty Cow? It's been ages."

"That's a great idea. I'll text you with the plan later?"

Jamie gathers up the stuff he left lying around the living room and before he leaves, he runs back to me in the kitchen and kisses me breathless.

"What was that for?"

"To let you know I'm yours and I want to get naked with you for the rest of my life."

Laughing, I push him off me.

"Noted. Now get out of here or you'll be late."

Jamieson leaves like the whirlwind he sometimes is and when he's gone, I miss the space he takes up.

Twenty
Jamieson

"**J**amieson, goddammit you're going to hurt yourself."

Hunter lifts the barbell from my shaking arms and replaces it in the cradle.

"I really thought I could do a few more. Guess not."

Hunter lifts his eyebrow in that way that calls my bullshit, and I roll off the weight bench, feeling like a bowl of Jell-O.

"How did the day go yesterday? Griff was pretty vague when he texted me." Jackson tosses me a towel, and I roll into a sitting position. Hunter leans against the wall after replacing our weights and chugs Gatorade like it's his job while scrolling on his phone.

"It went very well. His dad is here now at White Oaks."

Griff had shared with Jackson about his dad a few days ago and finally our little group understands everything Griff has been going through. It stung a little less when I learned he kept it from everyone and not just me.

"That's great. He must be relieved." Jackson leans next to Hunter on the wall and bumps his shoulder. "Why do you keep checking your phone so much? Are you going to share what's going on with you soon?"

Hunter huffs in exasperation and shoots Jackson a withering look.

"We aren't all like you, living in a delightful land of love and rainbows."

Jackson frowns, and I don't like the tone Hunter is using with his closest friend and the nicest man I know.

"Hey. That's uncalled for, and you know it. We're not against you here and Jackson would literally give you the shirt off his back anytime and anywhere, so maybe don't be such an asshole."

Hunter mutters an apology, but Jackson just...explodes.

"You know what? Just once in your life, look at the people around you. We're your friends, Hunter. I speak for all of us because I've never felt more sure of anything, but we're here for you. We will stand beside you, behind you, or fucking hold you up. Whatever help you need, we can give it if you'd just let us in!"

I've never heard Jackson angry. Well, once, when he dropped a dish of hummus because of me bumping into him, but that was more sadness at not having hummus. This is new, though, and it feels like they've been arguing before about something I'm not aware of.

"Do you have a hundred thousand dollars you can loan me to keep my home? Because that's what I need, Jack." Hunter's face flames red with anger, and Jackson's mouth drops open.

"What? How? Is there —"

"Oh, I'll tell you." Hunter swallows hard before sagging against the wall and sliding to the floor. Jackson immediately sits beside him and presses his shoulder against him.

"I still meant what I said. Let's work this out somehow." Jackson's voice is soothing, but I'm not sure how we can help financially. I know Griff is using most of his savings to pay for the rehab he took his dad to. I have some saved, but not nearly enough to even put a dent in what Hunter needs.

"When my grandfather died, he left everything in trusts. He controlled it all, even after he died." Hunter's lips twist in a sneer. "Even dead, he's still messing with my life, and I can't access the money to pay the property taxes. The bank said no to refinancing since the property is in a trust, and I've maxed all my credit trying to keep the remaining horses and bulls fed and cared for."

"Riley's friend, Gabe, is a lawyer. Maybe there's a loophole or something? He could look at the documents if you'd like."

Hunter thuds his head against the wall with a sigh. "I don't want to lose the ranch. As horrible as it was growing up there, it's all I know. It's who I am."

The three of us sit silently until Hunter pushes up off the floor.

"You said something about The Thirsty Cow? Why don't we get cleaned up and head over there? I could really go for a massive piece of cheesecake right now."

I'm definitely not against eating your feelings. But as he stalks out of the gym, Jackson and I share a concerned look.

No cheesecake in the world will solve this issue.

The Thirsty Cow is a local coffee and dessert place. Music always plays softly, and they have shelves of board games.

Various paintings of cows and photos of desserts cover the walls, and the furniture is mostly overstuffed armchairs and love seats rather than tables with chairs. It's only been operating for a few years, but it's a massive hit for Kissing Ridge. Baristas wear tight cutoff jean shorts and revealing shirts, which also helps to keep the place busy. It's not just the cows that are thirsty, if you know what I mean.

Griff took me here for my birthday, just after it opened, and bought me an entire blueberry pie. That was almost two years ago, and I remember it like it was yesterday.

He's waiting for us, along with Riley and Riley's friend Gabe, in a small sitting area near the back. Two couches face each other with a coffee table between them, and it's a lot like being in someone's living room.

Except your friend doesn't keep selling you seven-dollar coffees and giant slabs of cake.

Taking the seat next to Griff, I lean in and kiss him. "Hey, babe. Did you already order for me?"

"Aww, I'm so happy to see you guys together." Riley sighs and Griff grumbles something I can't quite hear.

"Thanks. I know it's weird but...it's right."

Griff's lips tilt in a tiny smile, and he shakes his head. "I ordered for you. We haven't been here long."

Gabe wags his finger between us. "Is this new? You weren't together last year at the rodeo when I was here, were you?"

"Nope. But we should have been." I drape an arm over Griff, and he smiles back at me. The lines around his eyes crinkle, and his gaze is all for me. *He's* all for me and I wish I'd have seen this sooner.

Sometimes love sort of bites you in the ass, though. Or kisses you in the middle of a bar and blows your mind.

Either way.

"Where are Hunter and Jackson?" Riley checks his phone before looking back at me. "He said he was right behind you."

I'm about to reply, but the barista arrives with my coffee and two blueberry custard tarts.

"Griff, you spoil me. Two?"

"It was the last two they had, and I knew you'd want a second one if we were here longer for an hour."

Griff does this little shoulder shrug, like he doesn't know me better than myself sometimes, and I press a kiss to his lips and linger there.

"I love that you spoil me with blueberries."

Griff laughs and playfully grabs my shirt and pulls me closer. "If I knew all it would take was blueberries to win you over, I'd have done it sooner." He pecks another kiss on my lips before letting go, and I straighten to find Riley clutching his hands to his chest in absolute glee.

"You two are so fucking perfect. This makes me so happy."

Riley is still grinning as I take a bite of my tart.

"Do you think Jackson could grow blueberries for me in that gardening setup he has?" I ask Riley.

"I don't actually know if he could. But I could ask."

We chatter on a bit more, but the whole time, Gabe is tuned out, and it feels almost rude. He's not even listening to the conversation, so I turn my head to find out what he's looking at.

And all I see is Hunter and Jackson at the counter and I know he's not eyeballing Jackson. Interesting.

"So, Gabe. Are you in town for long this time?"

He snaps his gaze to mine, and I smirk. Yeah, I caught you looking, big guy.

He raises an eyebrow, cool as a cucumber, and his gaze shifts back to the two men while he speaks. "I might be here longer than expected."

Riley, who had been talking to Griff, chimes in. "He might be staying, actually. Permanently."

"No shit? I thought you were a city guy and hated all the big trucks and animals in these parts."

Riley laughs with far too much enthusiasm, and Gabe finally gives us his attention.

"I don't hate the animals. That's not true."

Jackson and Hunter arrive, and I lean back and watch with amusement as Riley gives his seat to Jackson and snuggles on his lap, while Gabe shifts to create extra space for Hunter and raises that damn eyebrow again.

Hunter would rather sit on the floor, I think.

"To answer your question, Jamieson, while I may be '*city*,' as you put it, I like the small-town vibe, and I like the animals so far. Especially the wild ones."

Hunter stiffens and stares into his mug like it's the most fascinating thing in the world.

"Tell them the good news, Gabe. Quit stalling." Riley pokes Gabe's shoulder behind Hunter, and we all turn our attention to Gabe, who leans forward and places his now empty mug on the table.

"As you all know, I miss Riley. He's my best friend and I hate being in the city without him. Visiting him here has made me reevaluate my life goals." Gabe puffs a huge breath. "I've left my law office, and I purchased a small law practice here. I'm moving here permanently."

Riley is absolutely thrilled and kisses Jackson as he laughs. His two best men will now be in the same town, and he could only be more excited if he were a kid on Christmas morning.

Griff and I stand to offer Gabe a handshake and congrats, which he accepts with a genuine smile.

Hunter grunts.

"Have you found a place to stay? Riley, is your place available?"

He shakes his head. "No, I rented it last month to my assistant, which works for both of us since we've been finishing part of the floor for an office now that we have condo approval for it."

Hunter finally feels the weight of my stare and shakes his head. After all Griff has shown me the past few weeks, and what I've learned from this group of men I call friends, I can't believe he'd remain quiet.

He's gonna kill me, but I'm saying it, anyway.

"Don't you have an extra room or two? You could rent to Gabe while he finds a place of his own? There aren't a lot of quality properties for sale right now, and I'm sure Gabe would prefer to take his time before he buys."

Jackson tilts his head in thought. "He's right, Hunter. And he's an extra set of hands to look after the place if we go to a rodeo."

Hunter glares the sharpest of knives my way, but I don't care. If he won't speak up to take something that could help him, I will. It might not help him keep the ranch in the end, but it's still money to pay some bills.

"He wouldn't know what end of the horse to feed," Hunter grumbles, and Gabe just smiles.

"Sounds like you could teach me since you're so good at knowing everything then."

"I'm very particular about how I keep house. You can't just leave stuff everywhere."

"Okay. I'll keep everything in my room."

"No overnight guests."

"Not a problem."

"You pay for your own groceries."

"I don't expect you to feed me."

Hunter's jaw clenches and unclenches as we watch their exchange like a tennis match.

"I'm difficult to live with." All of us laugh, and Hunter throws his hands in the air. "I'm being honest!"

"If you're being honest, then tell me why you don't want to rent to me so badly."

If I had a bag of popcorn right now, it would be perfect because there's something going on here, and I'm done with secrets. Griff's were enough to break me. I don't want Hunter to be like Griff and carry all his burdens alone.

"I like my space." He raises a hand when I open my mouth. "I'll try it to keep these three quiet, but it's short-term, and we agree on a price after you see the place."

Gabe beams the brightest smile and holds out a hand.

"You've got a deal."

Hunter shakes Gabe's hand once before stalking off to the counter, complaining about his cheesecake taking too long.

"What the fuck was that about?" Griff asks.

Gabe relaxes back into his spot, a pleased smile on his face.

"Nothing. He just wants cheesecake, and can you blame him? This place makes the best."

We all chatter about anything and everything. Griff even fills everyone in about his dad, and Gabe offers him help if he needs to step in to act as a power of attorney. We talk about the next rodeo and the Kissing Ridge Rodeo in two weeks' time.

Jackson says he's excited to get out there with Hunter again, and it's nice to hear the excitement in his voice as he talks about the hydroponics and the crazy stuff the dogs have been up to.

Eventually, I ease back into the couch with my second tart, and Griff cuddles a little closer.

And I fucking love my life.

Twenty-One
Griff

Watching Jamieson sleep in my bed and knowing he's naked under the covers, *my covers*, is almost surreal. Since our road trip, he's spent every night at my place, and I'm certainly not complaining.

A crack in my curtains shines a sliver of sunlight into the room, just enough to make you open your eyes if you're dozing. Well, as long as you're not a deep sleeper like Jamie.

Today, he surprises me and cracks one sleepy eye open.

"Stop staring at me when I sleep. It's stalker vibes, Griff."

Laughing, I lean forward and press a kiss to his lips. "Sorry, I couldn't help it." I trace a fingertip along his chest. "I like waking up to you."

Jamie wraps a hand around my wrist and pulls on my arm. "Get your sexy ass over here."

With some rustling of blankets and laughter, we wrestle until I pull him on top of me. "Well, this is good, too," he whispers as his hips move and press our morning wood together.

"Part of my master plan," I whisper as he kisses my neck and ruts against me. When I told Jamie penetrative sex was off the table, I wasn't sure if we could be compatible. I'd spent years watching him with both men and women, but I never asked for intimate details about how it went down behind closed doors. I assumed he was like his bull rider personality and liked the thrill of a fast ride.

Many times, my imagination sent my jealous brain into a tailspin with thoughts of him bending people over—literally—at his whim.

Turns out Jamie kept his own secrets and prefers to take things slow, and he likes to touch...a lot. For Jamieson, the greatest buildup is teasing exposed skin and simply being against another body. Every single caress has a purpose, and there's just something about his attention to the little things that ignites the flame I've always kept for him.

His lithe body undulates against me, lighting up every nerve in my body, and I arch up into him with a sigh. His lips smile against my skin as his fingers brush over my hardened nipples, and a sudden puff of air escapes my lips.

"I love how you gasp like that when I touch you."

He does it again, and I shamelessly grip his ass and push him harder against me. "I l-love it when you do."

"Wrap your legs around me." When I do as he asks, Jamie shudders. "Fuck, yes." He plasters himself against my chest, and I hold on to him tightly as we both move in an erotic slide, chasing our orgasms.

He rests his forehead against mine, and our pants mix in the space between us. Jamieson kisses me, his tongue parting my lips with a gentleness I crave, and I moan against his mouth.

"Griff..." Jamie tenses, and the hot splash of his release hits my skin.

"Oh, fuck!" My balls draw tight, and I unload between us with an orgasm that catches me by surprise. Jamie always seems to do that to me. He gets me to the edge without me noticing how close I really am. It's intense, and I wouldn't change a thing.

"You get his pinkish tint all over after we have sex, and it's the most adorable thing I've ever seen."

Jamie pushes up and hovers over me to survey my body as much as he can, clearly pleased with himself.

"Adorable? Really?"

He settles back down over me and kisses my nose. "Really."

"I guess I could be called worse things."

"Absolutely. Besides, I like adorable." He rolls off me and finds my hand on the bed, clasping our fingers together. The mood changes and, like the flow of electricity through wires, Jamie's nerves channel through his hand to mine. "I need to talk to you about something."

Turning my head, I take in his profile. Handsome, with a light scruff along his jaw, and when he turns his head to meet my gaze, his expression makes me want to hand him my heart on a gilded platter.

"What do you want to talk about?"

"I want us to move in together."

No preamble, just...here it is. That's Jamieson.

"You're already here every night. If you want to change your address to mine, I'd not be opposed."

Jamie's lips quirk into a half smile, and he bites his lip.

"I probably should have waited until we weren't covered in drying cum to have this conversation, because that's not what I mean." He brings my hand to his lips for a kiss. "Just give me a minute. I'll be right back."

He leaves me and I hear the water running in the bathroom before he comes back with a warm cloth to wipe me off. There's something about Jamieson that's just different now. Not in a bad way. Or maybe I'm seeing this side of him because I didn't allow myself to before.

He's extra gentle. Almost...soft in that giant teddy bear way.

When he's finished wiping me off, he kisses my belly button and then raspberries my belly, so I laugh before he flops beside me again.

"What's on your mind, Jamie?"

He lies on his back and grabs my hand again.

"I want us to get our own place. A new start."

"Okay. We can look at places with more parking. I'm totally up for that." He turns his face on the pillow again, and his brow dips a little. I run a finger over it, then pry the bottom lip from his teeth. "What's bothering you?"

"The couple who rents my grandmother's house have given their notice."

"You want us to move there?" It's a cute house in town with a little yard and garden, if I remember. I helped him mow the lawn once when his dad's property manager didn't send someone.

"I want to buy it."

"Oh." Buying a house needs money, and I don't think I'm in that position anymore. "I spent my savings on Dad's program. I can't help with that."

He rolls over and pulls me to him. "You don't need to. But...I have an idea and if you're on board, I'd really like to do it."

"I'm not sure if I want to have you carry the burden of a mortgage, Jamie. We can always find a bigger apartment. I can afford that."

"Listen to me first." He kisses me before drawing back. "I have enough for a down payment and my dad will sell the house at fair market value privately. No extra real estate fees. The mortgage I can cover on my own. I was pre-approved, and it's a number I can manage. You can contribute to other bills, so you don't feel like it's charity, because I know that's where your mind is going."

"It was," I admit. "But what else aren't you telling me? This isn't just you asking us to live together, which I one hundred percent want to do. There's nothing better than waking up to you every morning."

Jamieson bites at his lip again, and I run my thumb over it and rescue it. "Stop doing that. You'll make it bleed."

"The basement of the house has an in-law suite. There's a separate entrance and we just need to do some renovating to freshen it up."

"I don't understand? You want us to live together but on separate floors?"

Jamie remains silent for a moment, cupping my cheek with his palm.

"I want your dad to live there."

"What? No." I try to push out of his arms, but he holds me closer.

"Griff, listen to me. I've thought about this, and I want to do this. You said it yourself; your dad will need you more than ever. He's isolated in his trailer and that town. He can live downstairs, and we'd be able to help him. He can even pay rent; I don't care how much, but whatever it takes to make you both feel like this isn't a handout."

"Jamie...that's a huge...we can't."

It's not possible that this man can offer so much to me and a man he doesn't even know.

"But you *can*, Griff. You've already been driving to his place and taking care of him. Having him here will be safer for both of you. If he needs medical care, it's here and you can take him."

"He's not your burden, Jamie. I can't let you do that."

"Babe, it's not a burden. It's a gift. I want to be with you and fight over the blankets every night. I want to sneak into the shower with you when you think I'm not awake yet, and I want so badly to see you smile more." Jamieson brushes his knuckles across my cheek. "You deserve good things, Griff."

"Why?" My voice cracks, and I squeeze my eyes closed. I don't know how to handle this. "Why would you do all this?"

Jamieson shifts until he blankets his body over mine. His thumb wipes at the tear that escaped to roll down my cheek.

"Because I love you and I'd do just about anything to make your life easier. I will stand by you in the hard times, Griff, and right now...it's a hard time. You've always been the one taking care of me, and now I can help you. Too many years have passed with me stuck in the clouds, not even knowing the real you. Please let me take care of you."

My chest heaves as I inhale and release a shaky breath. Jamieson never wavers, and his gentle touch on my cheek finally makes me open my eyes.

"The bravest thing I've ever done wasn't stepping into rodeo rings with ornery bulls. It was kissing you. But you've been the best chance I've ever taken, Jamie."

"Is that a yes?"

Sometimes I think just having Jamie like I've always wanted is enough of a gift in life. The ray of sunshine in my darkness has already helped me do so much. I'd be a fool not to let him do more if he wants to. Who am I to turn away love? Not just for me, but for my dad.

"Yes." The smile that fills Jamieson's face is more beautiful than the sunset on our boat cruise.

He throws his head back with a howl before kissing me while laughing.

"I love you, babe. You've just made me so freaking happy. Is it okay if I call my dad to let him know? Oh, and will you come over for supper next week? Mom said it's been too long since she's fed you."

"Yeah, to all of it."

Jamieson peppers my face with kisses before bouncing off the bed and grabbing his phone.

I just lie there a little longer and feel the weight of my past finally break up and drift away.

"Griff!"

Jamie stalks my way, chaps flapping as he walks, arms swinging at his side.

"Yeah?"

"I need you to vibe with this bull. I can't believe I drew Lemonball." He points a finger at me. "Yeah, that's the face I made, too. Please tell me this bull isn't about to live up to his name today."

Lemonball is one of those bulls who just make the cut to be on the circuit. When he performs, he's amazing, but when he has an off day, he can break a bull rider's heart. There's no bull with a more appropriate name.

"Of course. Lead the way."

Following Jamie down the path to the pens, I admire his ass in his jeans and this time I don't worry about hiding it. If anyone notices, they say nothing, and that just makes me smile.

A real one because I'm at the rodeo with Jamie and it's no longer a secret that I love him.

"He's right over..." Jamieson tilts his head. "Why do you look like that? What's wrong?"

"Look like what?"

He swirls a finger around my face. "This. You look crazed or something."

Jamieson's brow dips as he tries to decode whatever he sees, and I throw my head back with a laugh. "I was staring at your ass if you must know and happy that I didn't have to hide it anymore."

Jamie huffs and drops his head with a smile. "Seriously, Griff?" He shakes his head, but the smile never fades. "I didn't peg you for a one-track mind while working. Get back to work." He points at Lemonball, and brushes his hand over mine when I step closer.

The bull in question is almost docile in its pen, barely doing much, and Jamieson sighs. "He's a dud today, isn't he?"

"I feel like he won't bring his A game tonight."

Jamieson's shoulders sag. "Dammit. I guess I just need to wow them with my technique then."

"And hang on for eight seconds," I add with a laugh. Jamieson does too and we look at each other sideways, right there next to the bull pens, and it finally just slots into place. This man is mine and while I'm still here protecting the riders in the ring, there's something extra about it. Maybe it's no longer carrying the secret, but whatever it is, it clears this weight that's always been with me at rodeos.

"I don't know what just happened, but I feel it too, Griff. Things just shifted, but not in a bad way. Is that where your mind went?"

"Yeah. There's a lightness to this I've never felt since..." Pausing, I scan his face, and he waits just as patiently as he ever has. "Since before I fell in love with you. It's sort of cheesy, but knowing you know how I feel and what I carried every rodeo, it's kinda freeing to have you to talk to about it now."

Jamieson remains quiet for a moment, and his hand brushes mine again.

"Can I take you out tonight? Not to the bar with the others or someplace loud. Like a date? Something away from the rodeo."

My heart flutters against my ribcage and I'm certain I'm blushing, but I don't fucking care.

"I would love that."

With a tip of his hat, he grins. "It's a date."

Someone calls my name, and I step away from Jamie to get to work. As I'm walking away, I call back over my shoulder, "My favourite flowers are roses."

His voice is far away, but I still hear him.

"I know! I'm a wonderful boyfriend that way."

I snort a laugh as I turn the corner towards the entrance into the ring. He's an amazing boyfriend in every way.

Twenty-Two
Jamieson

Three Weeks later

Today is a really fucking great day.

Before I pull away from the house I've bought for us, I text Griff to let him know I'm on my way. Today he gets his cast off and I can't wait.

Not that I haven't enjoyed helping him wrap his cast for showers or minded the odd bonk when he'd toss in his sleep. Now I get to feel both his hands on me, and that excites me more than anything.

This weekend, Griff and I are having dinner with my family, and Griff finally gets to visit his dad in rehab on Sunday. He's only been able to speak to him on Sundays since he was admitted, and Griff desperately wants to hug his dad.

But first, I need to get him to the hospital for his cast removal. One step at a time, Jamieson.

Griff is already outside his place waiting, and after parking on the curb, I lock the door and press the button to lower the window.

"Hey sweet thing, do you need a ride?"

Griff always has this sweet flush on his neck and cheeks whenever I get playful. It's the cutest fucking thing ever and I'll never tire of it.

He tries the handle and raises an eyebrow. "Really, Jamie?"

"Well, I don't want to give you a ride for free, sugar."

"I swear to god if you pretend to solicit me any longer you won't see my dick for a week."

Pressing the unlock button, I pretend to pout as he slides in. "What if I just ask for it? Is that better?"

"Lord, is that what my future holds? You making deals for sex?"

Griff sounds pissy, but he's smiling, and before he can buckle himself in, I reach over and fist his shirt in my hand, tugging him over the console so I can kiss him.

"No sex deals unless it's what room to do it in first in our new place."

"Did you get everything signed?" Griff's lips dust over mine, and I steal one more kiss before leaning back in my place and putting the truck in gear. "Yep. The tenants are moving out next week, too. Once they give the keys back, we get in there early since it's still my dad's property. We can start the renovation almost a month early!"

"That's great news, Jamie!"

Griff's smile is truly one of his best features. When he smiles, it sort of makes his blue eyes more blue if that's possible, and he exudes this lovable personality that I'm completely in love with. He's beautiful, and he's mine.

He reaches for my free hand as I drive to the hospital, and I fill him in on my morning with lawyers and arranging for materials at the home improvement store. After I park at the hospital, he takes my hand as we stroll inside and check into the orthopedic suite.

"Mom wants to know if you want her to make anything special for dinner."

Griff stops flicking through the gossip magazine he grabbed off the table and faces me. "Did you ask for the macaroni salad you love?"

"Of course I did. Then she asked if you still liked apple strudel or if you'd prefer something else."

Griff swallows hard, the click audible even in the busy hospital. "She remembers that?"

"Babe, you ate half the pan and told her she should sell the stuff. She remembers."

"God, that was...what? Six years ago?"

"At least. She likes you and wants you to feel like you're part of the family."

Dinner with my family has happened a handful of times over our friendship, and every time it did, Griff was polite and charming. My mom loves him, and so does my sister. My dad was harder to read, but once I told him I wanted to buy the house and that Griff and I were in a relationship, a small smile appeared.

My dad approved, and that meant the world to me. We bumped heads a lot when I insisted bull riding was my goal, and sometimes I wonder if he stopped fighting me on it simply because he grew tired of me arguing. Or maybe I'm just a late bloomer, and I've finally figured out my dad's arguments just came from love.

Either way, we've had some great conversations since he texted me that morning to say he was proud of me, and we've mended a lot of our differences.

"Anything your mom makes is great, but you can tell her I still love strudel."

"Griff Shepard?" A nurse calls out, and Griff stands.

"Need me to come hold your hand?"

Griff rolls his eyes. "I can handle it. See you soon."

After he leaves me in the waiting room, I open the Pinterest app on my phone and scroll for decorating ideas. My sister told me to make boards and pin things, and she'd help me figure out what we'd need to turn my grandmother's old one-hundred-year-old home into something modern that suits me and Griff.

Owning my own home and building a life with a partner wasn't something I thought about. I rented a tiny studio apartment I wasn't attached to, and its purpose was to hold my stuff in the summer and give me a place to sleep in the winter.

I only had sex when someone attractive literally asked me to. It never turned into more because it was usually while I was travelling with rodeo, and it was just sex.

There wasn't a lot of stability in any part of my life.

It's funny how I drifted through almost thirty years and not once thought I was missing something. I was mostly content with my life until Griff kissed me and flipped my life around.

Suddenly, I'm excited to choose paint colours and pick out light fixtures and wake up in our bed every day. This longing for something sits nestled in my chest, and it only goes away when I'm with Griff.

"Hey. I'm done." Griff appears in front of me and holds out a very pale arm. "The nurses had a great laugh at your doodles, by the way. Thanks for that."

I snort laugh and peek around to see the nurses snickering, and I wave at them.

"I never claimed to be a Van Gogh. It takes skill to draw anatomically correct stick figures. Cock and balls are hard." I snicker at my joke, and Griff shakes his head.

He scratches at his arm as he leaves the waiting room, and I trail behind him.

"Skill which you didn't have, but they appreciated all your hearts."

Last night, I drew at least a dozen different hearts with our initials in them on his cast. He just let me and said nothing; well, he didn't like my incredibly hung stick man with a caption claiming bull riders swing to the left, but he watched and passed me coloured markers when I asked.

"I couldn't let you get your cast off without signing it. Isn't that what you're supposed to do? Sign it and make the person wearing it feel special? I couldn't let you go in there with a dirty, unmarked cast."

Griff stops in the hallway of the busy hospital, his blue eyes welling with an emotion he's only recently shown me.

"You make me feel special every minute of every day, Jamie."

A woman bustles by and brushes against me with an apology, and I reach for his hand.

"Let's get out of here." Once outside in the summer sun, I stop Griff and kiss him softly. "You *are* special, Griff. Never stop believing that."

"My boys!"

My mom rushes to us before we're even in the house and hugs Griff, then me. The scent of cinnamon lingers when I lean down for the hug and squeeze her back a little longer, knowing she probably made Griff's favourite strudel.

"Hey, Mom."

"Hi, Mrs. Carr."

My mom takes Griff's hands in hers. She's so damn tiny next to us. It's like she's a kid and her small hands are lost in Griff's giant ones. "You can call me Viv, or if you're comfortable, call me Mom."

Griff sucks in a breath and I watch as my mom and the man I love share a truly special moment. "For now, I'm good with Viv, but...one day I'd like to call you Mom."

My mom squeezes his arm and smiles, beaming her sweetness at Griff. "I'm okay with that, but don't get angry with me if I call you son. That's just going to slip out, and I won't apologize."

"I won't."

Mom tilts her head to the living room. "Everyone else is in there. Go have a seat, and I'll join you both in a few."

Mom bustles off, and Griff wipes at his eyes. "Should have warned me your mom would make me almost cry."

"I didn't know." Tugging on his hand to bring him in for a hug, I whisper, "There's no shame in crying when you find something that's missing, babe."

After slipping off our shoes, I lead Griff to the living room where my dad and sister sit watching last year's National Final Rodeo on TV.

"Hey, guys. Getting in the mood for Kissing Ridge rodeo next week?"

Dad stands and shakes our hands. He's always been more reserved than my mom, who hugs complete strangers, but he smiles when he takes Griff's hand and holds on a little longer, squeezing his other shoulder before releasing it.

My sister pats the seat on the couch next to her for Griff and sticks out her tongue at me. Griff takes the seat with a smile, and I settle into the armchair next to Dad.

"I guess you could say that. We're looking forward to it, that's for sure. Are you two ready?" My dad glances between us, and I reply first.

"I am. It's been a fantastic year. One of my highest point years ever, and after next week's rodeo, as long as I stay on and have a qualified ride, I should get to nationals."

My dad hums and nods with a smile.

"What about you, Griff? Will you be working the Kissing Ridge Rodeo, or will you be watching?"

Griff turns away from my sister with a smile. "Oh, I'll be working. If all goes well, it will be the first rodeo my dad will be at watching. No way I'm turning down the job."

"Jamieson told me he was in the rehab facility. Is it going well?"

Griff shifts with a sigh, and his gaze darts to mine. "The counsellors have said yes, and I spoke to him last week. He sounded positive, but I'll see for myself tomorrow."

"We're here for you if you need anything. If you take on my son, you get us too."

I whip my head towards my dad, who has never said anything like that. Ever. Even my sister, Kara's eyes widen.

"I didn't agree to that." She elbows Griff. "One brother is enough to handle."

Griff nods and thankfully finds words to accept my dad's sentiment before my sister asks Griff to come with her. She babbles about needing to bring in something from the garage for my mom, and Griff goes off with her.

With the sounds of last year's rodeo in the background, I clear my throat.

"Thank you for that, Dad. It means a lot to hear you say that. I know I've disappointed you —"

"You've never disappointed me, Jamieson."

"But you never approved of the university and rodeo. The bull riding for a career. Even where I lived. We've always fought about it, and I guess I felt like I didn't live up to your expectations."

Dad frowns and sighs. "That wasn't disappointment. That was me failing at telling you how proud I am of you for reaching for the dream. I wanted to force you into something safe and practical. Bull riding is dangerous and often short-lived. I just...I wanted you to fulfill your potential, and you have, son. In spades, you have."

"Really?"

"Really. I'm sorry I wanted you to be more like me. You're your own person and you live life in a way I envy."

My dad is so straightforward, and I take a moment to let his words sink in. I've made so many wrong assumptions all these years.

"For what it's worth, Dad, other than me thinking I let you down, you're a great dad."

The TV blares loudly as the announcer's excitement calls the tie-down roping event. We pause to watch, and my dad says, "It's your year, Jamieson. Griff and the house are only the beginning. You have great things coming."

My dad never held love back or anything like that. I had an amazing childhood, but my dad always stood on the sidelines while my mom reassured me I was good and she was proud. She put the Band-Aids on and shipped me packages at university. Dad always remained at a polite distance.

I thought it was because he disapproved, but that wasn't it at all. Mom is just better at showing love than my dad. That's something I understand now more than ever since I've been with Griff.

"Thanks, Dad."

Normally I can talk your ear off, and I want to ask my dad all the things, but I settle in, and we talk about rodeo in between suggestions for the house. It's bonding on a level we've never had before.

And another piece of my life clicks into place.

Twenty-Three
Griff

S tanding over the kitchen sink, I shove another forkful of Jamieson's mom's apple strudel into my mouth.

It's so fucking good. When Kara showed me there was another pan in the garage fridge for me to take home last night, I might have done a happy dance.

The soft light over the kitchen sink is enough for me to move quietly and pour a glass of milk while Jamie sleeps. Normally, it wouldn't be a bother that I'm restless. I'd just wake up and read or watch a mindless show.

But I can't stop my mind from running over scenarios today with Dad.

Is he going to be angry that I finally got him to this place? Or is he going to jump right in and try to fix our relationship like I desperately hope?

Dinner with Jamieson's family last night was both amazing and heartbreaking. His mom telling me to call her that if I wanted, almost made me cry. His sister told me in the garage that his parents were thrilled Jamieson finally got his head out of his ass and noticed he was in love with me all along.

That bit blew my mind. To know his sister noticed long before he did was just more proof that we were both living in the clouds.

But sitting at the dinner table, eating a home-cooked meal with people who care about you, people you call family, was something I've always longed for. Listening to school kids talk about family Easter or Christmas dinner and visiting families...that wasn't my life, but it sounded great, and I wanted it.

Now I have it, and this euphoria that contradicts my entire mindset for all these years has me feeling like I'm two people living in the same body.

"Hey, babe. Everything okay?"

Jamieson stands at the doorway of the kitchen, naked as the day he was born, with his hair sticking in every direction. He's like an angel lost on his way to a Sleep Country mattress photo shoot. He's more attractive than anyone should be after rolling out of bed in the early morning hours.

"Okay. That's an odd word, isn't it?"

After rinsing my cup, I set it in the sink and when it tumbles over, only then do I notice the shake in my hands.

Jamieson's calloused palms gently grip my shoulders and turn me around, pulling me into his chest.

"It's fine if you're not, Griff. I'm here for you and all you need to do is tell me what you need from me. I'll try to figure it out, but sometimes I can't. Apparently, I miss a lot of obvious stuff."

That draws a small laugh from me, and I clutch at Jamie like he's the tether keeping me standing.

"I'm nervous and scared. What if he hates me for getting him to rehab? What if the dad I knew before was never there, and it's just me making stuff up?"

"I think those are all normal things to feel, babe. The only way you'll get answers is when you visit this afternoon. Whatever you remember of your dad in good times isn't made up. It might feel like it, but I know it's not true."

He presses a kiss to my temple and holds me until my shakes finally disappear.

"Sometimes I wonder if you being here is real or just a dream. This, us, standing here in my kitchen like this is…" Swallowing, I shake my head against his chest. "I was prepared to accept I'd never get to have this with anyone."

"I'm not perfect, Griff. But I love you, and it hurts that you never met someone to treat you like the amazing man you are." He kisses my temple again. "I'm also really fucking happy you never did, because I wouldn't be the one holding you right now."

A hoarse laugh escapes my lips, and I push back to look at Jamie's handsome, sleepy face.

"I ate half the strudel."

"Is that a confession?"

"No. I plan to eat the rest for breakfast without sharing. *That's* a confession."

Jamie laughs before cupping my face and kissing me softly. "Come back to bed. It's lonely without you."

"I didn't want to wake you, sorry."

He tugs my hand and pulls me back to the bedroom. "You wake me when you're not there. Somewhere in the last few months, having you next to me in bed is what settles me to sleep. I like knowing you're close by."

Jamie pulls the blankets back and slides in, turning to open his arm for me to spoon up next to him.

"Thank you," I whisper before clutching his arm tight against me.

"Don't thank me for loving you. It's my privilege."

"Griff, hello! I'm Miles. We spoke on the phone about your dad."

"Hi, Miles." I take his hand, and he motions for me to sit in a chair opposite his desk. "Thank you for keeping me updated. Is he...is he looking forward to seeing me today?"

"He is. Very much, but before you two have a visit, I wanted to prepare you for what to expect."

It's odd to be so nervous to visit Dad. I used to visit with a pit of dread and sadness, wondering what I might walk into at his house, but today that ball in my gut is a writhing pit of anxiety. Why am I not happier about it?

"Your dad is progressing well, and he gave me permission to speak with you." Miles smiles softly. "He loves you a great deal."

"I love him too. It's been hard, but I just..."

"It's hard to watch a parent decline, and he feels a lot of guilt for what he put on you, Griff. I want you to know that. He's working hard on that, and it looks like you might have guilt of your own to sort through?"

"I feel like I should have pushed him harder or gotten him here earlier. I always felt like..." The familiar frustration bubbles up, and I wish Jamieson were here to help me get a grip on it.

"You're always welcome to have therapy with someone here as well, if you need. Your emotions are just as valid, and sometimes it's hard to work through it all. Your dad may have a substance addiction, but it's your problem, too."

I've never thought about it that way. It's always been what Dad needs, or Jamie, or anyone else but me. It's never been a problem, but more of an obligation and maybe that might make a difference to change the way I think about it.

"I'll think about it."

"Are you ready to see him now?"

Nodding, Miles motions for me to follow him out of the office and after walking down several hallways, a bank of windows appears, looking out into a gorgeous, landscaped area complete with vegetable gardens.

I spot my dad before Miles even opens the door.

"Can I just go out there?"

"Absolutely. He has about an hour before he's due for a checkup. I'll find you when it's time."

Stepping out into the sunny, late summer day, I head towards the very skinny man swinging on the wide swing, facing a series of bird feeders. He turns his head my way when my steps crunch on the short gravel path nearby and immediately bursts into tears.

"Hey, Dad."

He stands and I hold out my arms. "Son." He hugs me while he cries, and he doesn't need to tell me what the tears are for. I understand and shed some of my own.

"I didn't mean to just cry all over you like that." He wipes at his tears as he steps out of my arms, and I reach for the tissues I stuffed in my pocket.

"Don't be. I think we both have a lot to talk about and it's okay to cry."

Dad takes the tissue I hand him, and dabs at his eyes. He's lost so much weight, a light wind could blow him away, and after he resumes his spot on the garden swing, I join him.

"You always liked the birds. I remember you had that big feeder with the spinner thing to keep the squirrels out when I was a kid."

"Yeah. I like to watch them. They're so...I don't know. Cool with the feathers and the tiny feet." Dad huffs. "Tiny feet. What the hell am I even saying?"

"That you like bird feet. Hey, I won't judge, Dad." My tone is teasing, and he looks over at me with fresh tears in his eyes.

"Hey...don't cry."

"I've missed your entire life, Griff. You're my son, and I missed it all. How do I even make this right?"

Taking his hand in mine, I squeeze it and don't let go. "This is a good start. You do what the counselors and doctors say and work at being sober. That's what you do right now."

"You never gave up on me."

"I couldn't. You're all I have, Dad." My voice cracks, and I clear my throat.

"Don't hide how much pain I caused you, Griffy. I made you grow up too fast, and you did things no kid ever should."

While that may be true, things could have been a lot worse. At least I knew he still loved me.

"You were never abusive or mean. You drank to escape the pain and sadness of Mom leaving." Dad inhales sharply, and I squeeze his hand again. "I don't blame you. It had to hurt an awful lot, and while I may have been a kid, I was aware enough to know your actions weren't because you didn't love me."

"When did you get so smart?"

He has a small smile, and it lifts my heart to see his eyes finally not clouded by alcohol and to know he really means that. He's proud of me.

"Well, I've always liked having my nose in a book, and I went to university."

"I missed your graduation."

"Technically, yes, but I also didn't tell you."

Dad's lips quiver again, and I hold his gaze. Miles and all the stuff I read online advised me to be truthful, and this is one of those times where the truth hurts. A whole fucking lot. "I only told you I was graduating. I never told you the day or invited you because I knew you wouldn't come, and I didn't have it in me to deal with that. So I just left it out."

He sighs and nods, taking a moment to find the words.

"I'm sorry I wasn't there for you, but I want to be now."

My smile is genuine, and Dad returns it. "I'd love for you to come to the Kissing Ridge rodeo next week. You can watch me be a bullfighter and Jamieson ride a bull. It would mean a lot to me."

"I'll be there, but I need a ride, I think."

"I'll arrange it for you."

Dad nods, and we watch the birds fly around from the feeder to the trees and into some sunflowers. We still hold hands, and for a moment, I imagine this as a little boy, holding my dad's hand in the park or crossing the street. He did that once, and even though I'm close to thirty and we've barely hugged over the years, this is something I've missed.

"So, this Jamieson. He seems like a nice fellow. How did you two meet?"

My smile comes easily when I hear Jamieson's name. "At university. I was bored and went to the rodeo team practice during my first year. Someone asked if I wanted to be a bullfighter, and it paid a bit of money, so I tried it. Turns out I'm pretty good at it, and Jamieson was a bull rider."

"But you never said you were dating. Did I miss that, too?"

"No, that's new. He's been my best friend since that day. I've loved him for years, but only just told him this summer."

Dad shifts to look at me, still holding my hand.

"That's a long time to carry a torch for someone."

I shrug a little and sigh. "I know, but I was scared. I didn't want to lose him as a friend if I told him I liked him, and he rejected me."

"But he didn't, and now you're together?"

"We are. Moving in together soon. He bought a house and I'm going to see it tonight."

Dad's face is the happiest I've seen it in the last twenty years, and I hope to see more of that. "That's wonderful! Congratulations! I can't wait to visit you there."

The crunch of gravel alerts us to someone, and we both turn to find Miles approaching. He taps his watch and turns back to the residence.

Dad and I stand and stroll the path back, still holding hands.

"I'm really happy you came today, Griff. I know we have a long road ahead of us, but I can't thank you enough for giving me this gift and staying with me all these years. Jamieson better treat you right because you're something special, son."

My throat tightens, and I nod. "Thanks, Dad." I open the door for him, and Miles stands waiting.

"Did you two have a good visit?"

"We did, and he can still come to the rodeo next week, right?"

Miles nods and pats Dad on the shoulder. "Definitely with some stipulations, but we will work out the details and get him there."

After hugging my dad, he leaves me with Miles to attend his therapy session. I stare after him for a few beats, still in a bit of disbelief that we got this far.

"I can't thank you enough for what you've done. He's not a hundred percent, but it's the closest I've been to the dad I know I have for a very long time."

"He's putting in the effort, Griff. You should be proud."

Miles and I discuss the rodeo part and getting dad to the venue before I leave, and when I exit the building, Jamieson waits for me. He's leaning against his truck, scrolling on his phone, but puts it away once he sees me.

"Hey. How did it go?"

I fold into Jamieson's arms and take a moment to enjoy being there. The fabric softener outdoorsy scent still clings to his shirt, and I breathe it in along with everything else Jamie.

"He looks better than I thought he would. It went well."

"That's wonderful, babe. If you're up to it, I thought we could swing by The Thirsty Cow. I hear they have blueberry cobbler today, and I think it's the best way to celebrate."

Chuckling, I press a kiss to his lips and step back.

"I think that sounds perfect."

Twenty-Four
Jamieson

"**I** wish I knew what it is about blueberries that makes me crave them so much."

Honestly. What is it about this little round berry that makes it so tasty? Is the blue part? Is there research on this?

"You just like blueberries. It's totally okay to like something so much it's all you can think about."

My fork pauses at my lips, and I raise a playful eyebrow. "Oh? And what do you like so much that it's all you can think about?"

Griff shakes his head with a smile and sips his coffee. "Don't fish for compliments, Jamie."

We share a secret glance, one that carries more weight than it ever used to. Griff and I have always been able to communicate without words. But now there's a whole other level to his expressions, and it blows my mind that I understand him without a single word exchanged.

Those soft blue eyes and shy lowering of his chin, a lick of his lips. I read you loud and clear, Griff, and I'm going to make up for so much lost time with you. I promise.

"I can see you two mooning at each other from across the room." The barista, Diamond, sets another plate of blueberry goodness in front of me. "Compliments of me because I have tea to spill and needed a reason to come and sit for a minute."

He wedges himself on the seat next to Griff and beams a smile at us both. Diamond owns The Thirsty Cow and is the most colourful and over-the-top person I've ever met. I wouldn't call him a close friend, but we've gotten to know him well the past year because when we're home, we come here far too often.

He makes some of the best damn blueberry creations around and always finds time to ask us about our lives. Which would normally feel like small talk, but Diamond carries himself with a genuine warmth. He cares about his patrons, and I love that about him.

"You don't need to bring me free food to gossip. It's appreciated, but unnecessary."

Diamond snort laughs and crosses his long, toned legs. Both Griff and I ogle them before glancing at each other with a shared look. The man has amazing legs, and those little jean shorts show them off well.

"Eyes up here, boys." Diamond gestures to his face. "Listen, you need to know this."

"Okay." Griff shifts sideways to face him. "What's going on?"

"Your super hot friend, the one with the ranch. Hunter, right?"

"Yeah, he's the one who owns the ranch. I don't know if he's hot, though?" I say between bites of free dessert. "If you're into the silent, broody type, I suppose he is. What about him?"

Diamond tsks and shakes his head. "Silent and broody is hot all day long in my books and extra when there are two of them!"

"Two Hunters?" Griff's eyebrows scrunch and Diamond huffs in exasperation.

"No. Hunter was here for almost two hours last night with another man who fans the flames, if you know what I mean."

Diamond raises one perfectly manicured eyebrow with a smirk.

"He fans your flames or Hunter's?" I'm sort of confused about what he's trying to tell us.

"Hunter was here with another tall, dark, and handsome. They sat here for two hours and had multiple coffees. Hunter had a slice of lemon cheesecake, and mystery man had deep-dish apple pie." He points to the cozy corner with two giant overstuffed chairs. "Although I shouldn't say he's a mystery man. I've seen him here with Riley before, and one of my employees mentioned a new lawyer in town. I'm betting it's him. They sat there and there was a lot of talk. *Heated* talk. It seemed big, so I wanted to mention it. I've never seen Hunter with another man who's not any of you before."

Griff shrugs. "He hasn't said anything about being involved with anyone. Especially Gabe, if that's who it is. Maybe he doesn't want us to know yet."

Diamond snort laughs and pats Griff's shoulder. "That's cute. If he wants a secret, he shouldn't have come here then. The man should know that I keep track of everyone's business." Diamond wags a finger between us. "Like you two. I wasn't sure if Jamieson was just too thick or you were too shy. But there was always something."

"A little of both, but I was definitely too thick." Or, more accurately, self-absorbed. If I had paid more attention, I would've noticed there was more to the extra touches from Griff.

"Doesn't matter now. We're, ah...we're moving in together." Griff beams when Diamond slaps his hand to his chest with a happy gasp. "It's fast, but we have history. Jamie is my person, so why wait, you know?"

"Absolutely right. Hey, if you have a housewarming party, I'd love to bring you some baked goods. Maybe blueberry?"

Laughing, I stand and stretch. "I'll never decline that. And of course we'll let you know. We never talked about a party, but perhaps we should."

"We're on our way right now to see the place." Griff stands to join me, and I press a quick kiss to his cheek.

Diamond pushes off his seat. "That's my cue to get back to work, then. Enjoy the night and make sure you give me notice to bake something!"

He struts back to the main counter, and we both watch after him. Griff reaches for my hand and slides our fingers together.

"I like him, don't you?" Griff says as we walk past the coffee-making bar with a wave and exit the building.

"I do. He's fun and apparently a spy on Hunter."

"And those legs..." Griff bites his knuckle in jest, and I open the truck door for him. "Never pegged you for a leg guy."

He kisses my cheek before sliding into his seat. "I'm more a Jamieson kind of guy."

"Well...that works out well for me, doesn't it?"

The drive to our new place is only ten minutes.

My late grandmother's older home, our home now, sits at the end of a cul-de-sac in an older residential area of Kissing Ridge. I've always loved it and have fond memories here as a kid. From the backyard water balloon fights during summer vacation to the Easter egg hunts around the house that my grandmother loved to organize; nothing but happiness lives here for me. My memories sometimes make my heart hurt for Griff, since he never had the same happy childhood I did.

That's been nagging at me a lot the last few weeks. It's not something I can change, but it compels me to provide him with more. To give him the experiences I've taken for granted. Even a damn Easter egg hunt, because the simple joy of finding hidden plastic eggs would mean everything to Griff.

"This is our new place."

Griff leaps out of the truck before I even kill the engine. He smiles at the tidy little row of flowers lining the walkway to the front door and the paved but bumpy asphalt driveway. He stands on the lawn gazing at the house. The shutters need replacing or repainting, but the light beige siding is newer, along with the rain gutters. Something I didn't think was important a few years ago when Dad had it done, but now I do.

It's a modest home. Nothing fancy or overly large. Average in every way.

"It's perfect, Jamie."

Griff's smile is blinding as he rushes to the back of the house. The yard is smaller, but there's a single raised vegetable bed and a tiny shed for storage. It definitely needs a spruce up. The back door opens onto a small deck barely big enough for the BBQ. But Griff doesn't see the deficiencies I do.

"We can go in, right? The tenants left?"

"Yeah, babe. That's what I brought you here for. Come on."

After fishing the keys from my pocket, we return to the front door, and I lead us into the empty house. Griff kicks off his shoes in an excited rush. "Give me the tour, Jamie. Show me everything."

He's breathless with excitement that spreads to me, and I'm smiling back, but my emotions are rocking like a ship in stormy waters.

"Okay, it's not a huge house, so it won't take that long. This is our living room." It takes up the entire front of the house, and if we wanted, half could be the dining room. Griff runs his fingers along the edge of the mantle of the gas fireplace.

"We can hang stockings from the mantle at Christmas." His voice wavers, but that smile never fades.

"Yeah, we can."

We walk into the kitchen, which is big enough for a table for us, but I'd like to make a kitchen island instead. The door to the back deck is in the corner and another door leads to the pantry. Griff opens and closes cupboards and runs his fingers along the countertop.

"I want to upgrade the cupboards and put in an island for us to eat at and use for extra counter space. Instead of a kitchen table."

We've discussed some of the renovation ideas I have, but not all of them. Griff doesn't want to have much input because his name isn't on the mortgage. I respect his feelings about that, but I also want him to make this his home. It's *our* home no matter whose name is on the piece of paper.

"I like that idea." He bounces on the balls of his feet. "Show me the rest."

Leading him down the very short hall, I show him the linen closet and the bathroom. "This definitely needs an upgrade. I want a bigger shower and to have the laundry machines here. We don't need two sinks."

Griff pokes his head into the shower before laughing. "There's no way the two of us will fit in here. Good call."

At the end of the hall are two bedrooms. One will be ours, and the other is for us to discuss, but I think he'll agree with my plan.

"Oh, I love the window in this one. Is this our room?"

Our room.

Those words from his lips are the ultimate confirmation that this is real. Griff and I are in this together. I never have to worry when he's away or miss him at night when we sleep in separate places. He'll share this space all the time and be next to me in bed.

Holy shit.

We're actually a couple.

"Jamie? Are you okay?"

"Yeah, I'm...it just sort of hit me that this is happening."

I'm not spiralling into doom. I'm sitting somewhere on the edge of spontaneous laughter or breaking out into dance. It could go either way.

"Are you...is this still what you want?"

Griff's smile fades, and I reach for him before his happiness disappears completely.

"More than I thought I ever did. It just sort of hit me that everything is changing and you're not just my best friend, you're my partner in this life. It caught me off guard that this is our forever."

Griff breathes out and presses his forehead to mine. "You've always been my hope, Jamie, and I couldn't walk away from you. I got as far as applying for my master's program, and then dad..." He sighs again. "I'm still here because I don't think I can ever walk away."

"The only time I want to see the back of you is when you're going to the kitchen to get me a snack." He huffs a laugh, and I take his face in my hands. "Preferably of the blueberry kind. But the Griff kind is my favourite."

Pressing my lips to his, I sink into this moment. We're creating a future that wasn't even on my radar three months ago. Now I'm consumed with a Pinterest board I started, and showing Griff all my ideas to make it *our* home. To give him and his dad a new start, because they're a package deal. To build a little family of our own.

Griff's fingers curl into my shirt. "Are we going to have sex in every room of the house when we move in?"

"Is that a thing?"

"Maybe. If it isn't, we should totally make it a thing."

Griff chases my lips while he fumbles with my belt buckle and suddenly the heat just turned on. He walks me backwards until my back hits the wall and I growl in frustration when I can't get his pants open.

He steps back and quickly gets his pants shoved to his thighs and does the same to me. Griff is confident, and it's hot as hell when he gets that look in his eye. I've seen it before in the ring. His take-no-shit game face, and when his rough palm grips my cock, my head thuds against the wall.

"Jamie...lips on me." His hand grips the back of my neck and I comply with his request now that my brain is back online.

His hips pump into mine, nudging his hardness against me. Never have I felt so consumed by someone like I do now. Griff pressing against me, his lips and hands everywhere. It's like I've melted into him, and every cell of my being is caressed by some part of him.

"Fuck, Jamie..." His lips falter on my skin when my hand closes around his dick.

"Fucking hell, Griff," I croak when he bites into my shoulder. How can something so frenzied and carnal feel so fucking perfect?

We're both racing to bring each other to the finish while trying to climb inside each other, and I've never felt so connected to anyone. So in tune without words.

Griff groans into my mouth as the warmth of his release coats my hand. "Jamie..." His breathless plea breaks me, and I push up on my toes, forcing him to squeeze me tighter. And then I'm over the edge. I come with a shout that echoes in the empty room, and my free hand clutches the back of Griff's head, holding him to me as we both try to catch our breath.

"Thank god I have a wall holding me up because that was fucking intense."

Griff laughs into my neck before pressing a kiss there. "That was...unexpected. I don't know what happened. I just...god, I just wanted to..." He swallows, and his silence drags on. "I needed to make sure all this is real."

"Nothing is more real than the cum cooling in my hand."

Griff barks a laugh and separates us carefully. He shuffles into the bathroom, and we clean up the best we can with warm water and squares of toilet paper.

A splash of pink still sits on his cheeks, a leftover mark of his desire for me, as he pats his hands dry on his jeans.

"I didn't plan on us having sex here right now. I would have planned better if I knew you'd go all feral on me."

That pink tinge turns a little brighter and I pump an internal fist. I fucking love Griff like this. Like him anyway, really, but demure and blushing is one of my favourites.

"I've never told you this, but you're the first guy I've been with who calls what we do sex. I don't think you understand what that means to me."

"Why wouldn't it be sex? We both came. We helped each other to get there. That's sex to me. Every time is sex."

Griff puffs a long breath and leans on the counter. "Jamie, when we were in university, I went there thinking I'd get to discover what it was like to be a gay man. I had plans. Filthy ones." His lips tilt in a small smile. "The first guy I ever hooked up with, the very first one, laughed at me when I asked him to stop because I didn't like what he was doing. He stopped, but not before he made me feel like I was a freak. I wasn't worthy because sex meant only one thing to him. If I didn't want a dick in my ass or to bury myself in someone else balls deep, how could I call myself gay, right?"

Griff hangs his head, and the absolute heartbreak comes off him in waves. "I never told you that happened. Or that it happened a few more times before I gave up trying to meet people."

He lifts his head, a sad smile on his still flushed face.

"I wish you had said something. I'd have been there for you." Something clicks in my brain, and I step closer to him. "That night we were both fooling around with that cute blonde guy...you left. Was it because of this?"

Griff quickly nods once.

"Mostly. I didn't want to be in a situation like that and have you find out. It wasn't something I wanted to share. Plus, I already knew I loved you. Seeing you intimate with someone else up close...I couldn't handle it. I thought I could, but I lied."

"I'm sorry. If I had known..." Fuck, if I'd have known, I don't know how different things would have been, but I would never have suggested a three way.

Griff wraps his arms around my waist and kisses me.

"Now you know. It's the past, and we've both grown. I just wanted to tell you how you make me feel so seen. It's such a tiny thing, but it means the world to me."

He kisses me again, and minutes pass with us lazily kissing each other and sharing whispers of promises. The storm of my emotions from earlier calms, and it's the most settled I've felt in years.

When my stomach growls, the tender moment ends. Griff laughs and pats my stomach.

"Let's get you fed."

We don't even finish the house tour. Griff leads me outside and suggests we grab a pizza to bring to his place so we can watch TV and eat in our underpants.

And honestly, that sounds perfect.

Twenty-Five
Griff

Kissing Ridge rodeo is always my favourite rodeo of the season.

The energy is somewhere between immense pride and chaotic celebration, and I love it. Everyone welcomes you like an old friend, and there's nothing like it. Especially if you're a hometown hero.

I feel like Kissing Ridge is my hometown, even though I wasn't born and raised here. Just a transplant since Jamieson lived here, and I followed him home after we met. Living with my dad once school finished wasn't an option.

But all that has changed. Kissing Ridge has become my home more than Fox Grove ever was. I'm part of this community and not just the rodeo. Until Jackson's parents offered to help my dad around today, I didn't know how much I was truly part of this town.

"Hey Griff, you ready to go?"

Jamieson pulls his shirt over his head as he enters the living room. "I'm gonna eat something first." He thumbs over his shoulder to the kitchen, and I chuckle.

"I figured you would. I grabbed an extra pizza from the store yesterday. It's pre-cooked so just heat it up."

"Ah, you're the best boyfriend ever." Jamieson removes the pizza slices from the carton and rips a bite from a cold slice.

"Too hungry to warm it up?"

"Cold pizza is the bomb. It doesn't need warming." Jamieson tucks into the second slice as I gather our bags of gear. "Are you nervous?" His voice is softer, and I turn my head towards him. His remaining pizza sits untouched on the counter while he focuses on my response.

"Some," I admit, but Jamie shakes his head and steps closer.

"Tell me, babe."

Jamieson's soft touch to my arm has me sinking into his embrace. "Just overwhelmed with everyone's help. With you, the house, and Dad. It's a lot of stuff that's out in the open now, and as happy as I am to have it, I feel like I'm a gutted fish on the dock." His hands move up and down my back as I pour out this overwhelming tide of emotion I can't put a name to. "I've been so used to just being on the fringe, you know? My entire life has changed, and while they're all good things, it's catching up, and I feel overwhelmed."

Jamie kisses the top of my head and hugs me tighter. "Thanks for telling me. What can I do to help with that?"

People shouldn't need to ask for help when they're happy. It makes no sense, but it also makes perfect sense to me. My heart is full, but my brain needs extra time to process it all. It's a weird place to be.

"I...I'm not sure, Jamie. But this definitely helps. Holding me and just making me feel like I'm deserving of this life."

Jamieson sucks in a breath and steps back so he can press his forehead against mine. "You deserve to have a reason to smile, and I will hold you anytime you need it, okay?"

"Okay."

We stay like this for a few beats before I pull away first and playfully push him back to the kitchen. "Go finish eating. We have lots to do today. Are *you* nervous?"

I throw the question back at him because it's a big day. Hometown heroes are always under extra pressure to perform, and Jamieson needs high scores for an invitation to the national finals. He's had a strong season, but so have a few other riders in our tour, and it's a deep field.

He leans on the counter with his pizza and chews slowly, uncharacteristically quiet for him. Jamieson usually talks a mile a minute and eats just as fast. There *is* something on his mind, but he usually saves the nerves until he's at the event and can pace it off behind the chutes.

This is new for him to be almost...reserved.

His soft gaze meets mine, and the tenderness he aims at me makes my breath hitch in my throat. "I'm not nervous in a bad way. Maybe I'm so excited I don't know what to call it." He huffs a small laugh as he cleans up his pizza mess. "My parents and sister are so eager to help your dad. They want to make sure he has fun and experiences his son doing his job that he's really fucking good at." He grabs a glass from the cupboard and pours a glass of milk. "I think I'm a cross between over-the-moon excited our families are mixing and nervous about not having a great ride." He chugs his milk and laughs. "I want to impress your dad, Griff. Is that lame?"

Of all the things I thought Jamie might say, that wasn't it.

"I think you already have, and it's not lame at all."

Jamieson rinses his glass and leaves it in the sink. "Have I?" He strides over to the door and grabs his boots, the last thing he needs before we head to the rodeo grounds.

"Yep. '*My son's dating a fancy bull rider. Does that mean I get good seats at the rodeo?*' That's what he said, and no, it wasn't a joke. He was so puffed up about it, he went online to watch some of your rides."

Jamieson smiles, and his dimple pops. His eternally boyish grin will never stop making my heart flutter. "Really?"

"Really."

"Well...cool." Jamieson is genuinely lighter with that knowledge, and it's beyond sweet that he wants to impress my dad. "We should get going, though. I've got that meet and greet thing with Jackson and Hunter."

And just like that, we're in the normal pre-rodeo groove with Jamieson chatting away while he tosses our bags into his truck and I yank the keys from his hand to drive. Just because I let him drive more when my arm was in a cast doesn't mean it's the new norm.

I'm still not a fan of his driving, and that's never going to change.

The shuttle van from Dad's rehab pulls up to the curb in front of the rodeo grounds, and I jog over to meet it.

"Are you Griff?"

"That's me." The woman smiles and glances in the back. "I've got a very excited man here who claims he's your dad."

She hands me a clipboard, and I sign the consent that Miles reviewed with me. Dad is free to leave the rehab anytime he wants, but he opted for more accountability and asked for them to make him stick to tighter rules because he doesn't want to mess things up. That means I have to sign a form that Dad already did, agreeing on a curfew and pickup times.

I'm actually proud of him for taking his recovery so seriously.

"Yep. I'm waiting for him."

Dad opens the door of the minivan and steps out. My grin damn near splits my face when dad stands in front of me with a red-checked bandana around his neck and a straw cowboy hat. I don't know where he got the overalls that sag on his skinny frame, but it's clear he's tried his best to fit in with his version of rodeo.

He holds his arms to the side. "Well. What do you think? Am I country?"

"You're something." I step up to hug him and we both linger in the hug. After releasing him, I gesture towards the entrance to the rodeo grounds as the shuttle van pulls away. "How are you feeling today?"

Dad places the straw hat on his head as we walk up the pathway. Screams of people riding the midway drift towards us and my dad's mouth drops open as he turns to me. "There's a fair here, too? Not just a rodeo?"

"Yeah. I thought you knew that. Is there—"

"Can we get cotton candy? I took you to a street fair thing once when you were maybe four, I think? Just a wee thing and you begged for cotton candy. You were fascinated watching the lady spin it on a paper cone right in front of you."

Dad's eyes glass over as he gets this faraway look, and it's the first time I've ever heard him talk about something from my childhood.

"You took one bite and then you sort of got it everywhere and were one big sticky mess. But I remember..." His throat clicks as I steer him towards the fairground entrance away from the rodeo. "I remember you offered me a slobbery blob of it, and it was really good."

I smile and laugh, choosing to paint the happy picture in my head and not dwell on the lost memories. "Yeah, we can get cotton candy, Dad. I promise I won't even lick it before you get some."

He laughs, a sound I've not heard in a long, long time. I think he startles himself since he cuts off the sound just as abruptly as it came. "That would be wonderful," Dad says and I lead us to the cotton candy booth.

"Do you want it on a stick or in the bag?"

"Are you eating some, too?" We step closer to the order counter.

"Of course. I love the stuff. I haven't had any for years."

"Then make it a stick."

After passing the money to the woman, my dad stands to the side watching the woman wind the spun sugar on a paper cone through the plexiglass. He's lost in more memories and I only hope this isn't another moment my mother steals from us in her absence.

After she passes me the cotton candy, Dad and I walk around the midway, eating the fluffy sugar on a stick and just enjoying this new thing we have. The counselors warned me he may have some memory loss because of his prolonged addiction, but it seems like the cotton candy memory is one that stuck, and I have no reason to doubt it.

After strolling through the flower and produce exhibits—dad had never seen pumpkins that big!—we head to the seating area at the rodeo that Jackson's parents sponsor.

"So, Dad, you're going to meet some people tonight. Don't worry about remembering who they all are, okay?" I turn to him for his acknowledgement before continuing. "Jackson Sutherland is a steer wrestler. Every year, his parents sponsor the seating you'll be in. He's a good friend and his mom and dad are nice."

He nods along, but I notice the slip in his smile, and I reach for his hand.

"Dad, please don't compare yourself to them or go on a guilt trip. These are people I've met as an adult, and they mean a lot to me. So do you."

"I can't just turn it off, Griff. It's not like that. I've let you down and I'm a drunk. Hardly anything to parade around to your friends."

Okay. They also warned me about this, and while it goes against everything I really want to say, I stick with the truth.

"That was true before, yes. I was embarrassed, and you let me down. But that's the past, Dad. We have the chance to start over. That stuff doesn't matter now. You're my dad, who is brave enough to work at being better, and I'm proud of that. *That's* the dad I'm parading around."

"It's just...I'm not good at making friends. I've had none for years, you know?" His eyes water, and I pull him in for a hug and just say it.

"Dad, it means a lot to have you here to watch me. If you don't want to talk to them, then don't. Just sit and watch me. I want my dad to see what I do." I release him and step back. "Please, Dad."

He swipes at his eyes. "I'll do anything I can for you, Griffy. It's just a little harder. Sorry."

"Don't be sorry. Would you feel better if I told you someone is nervous you're here?"

Dad cocks his head. "Who?"

"Jamieson. He wants to impress you. I'm not sure where he ever got the idea, but he seems to think him having a great ride in front of you will earn him dad points or something."

My dad laughs again, and this time he doesn't cut it off. This time, he squeezes my hand and smiles. "Let's meet these friends of yours."

"Thanks, Dad."

We finish the walk to the stands, where Jackson's mom and Riley talk at the bottom of the stairs. When they see us, it's Riley who comes forward to introduce himself.

"Mr. Shepard, welcome. It's nice to meet you. I'm Riley, a friend of Griff's."

"Call me Charlie," Dad says in a tone that hides his nerves.

"I can do that, Charlie."

Riley smiles at me as Mrs. Sutherland introduces herself and chats up Dad like he's a long-lost friend. Of course, everyone in the stands tonight knows my dad is a recovering alcoholic, and without me even asking, they agreed to not have liquor in their seats tonight, even though they're in the only seating that can.

"Jamieson asked if you could meet him in the signing area before it's over." Riley says, while I watch my dad with Jackson's mom.

"Oh? That's odd. Thanks." My gaze follows dad into the stands where Mrs. Sutherland introduces him to Jamie's parents and I can't hear what they're saying but my dad laughs again. With his straw cowboy hat and too-big overalls, he waves at me and gives me a thumbs up.

"We'll take care of him, Griff," Riley whispers as he squeezes my arm and I blink the wetness away.

"Thanks, Riley. I'll go find Jamie then. Time to get ready for the show. Are you excited to see Jackson back in the ring?"

He sighs with a smile. "Oh yeah. I love watching him on a horse. He doesn't even have to fall off it and wrestle a steer. Just him on a horse...I could watch that for hours."

His gaze darts to the ring, searching for Jackson, and I laugh softly.

"Sounds like you need some riding lessons."

"I've got some! I think he's looking for a horse as a surprise to me. Don't tell him that, though. It's just a hunch."

"I won't." With a last glance up at the stands, Dad has a water bottle in his hands and for a guy who was worried about making friends, he seems pretty chatty as he nods along to whatever Jamieson's dad is telling him. "Dad!" I shout, and he looks down at where I'm standing and smiles.

"That's my son!" He points and the biggest smile splits my face.

"I'll see you at the end. Stay out of trouble."

My dad nods and returns to his conversation.

"Good luck tonight, Griff." Riley bounces up the stairs to join the crowd and I leave to find Jamie.

Finally accepting that the good in my life is mine to keep, I jog to the signing tent to get to my love faster.

Twenty-Six
Jamieson

They never tell you how much you'll love meeting your fans and how much you'll hate it at the same time.

It's been a long two hours and while I love smiling for photos and making people happy because they met a real bull rider, I hate how shitty my handwriting is every time I sign something. I really need to practice that more. Seems a shame to muck up a nice photo with my chicken scratch.

"Are you ready for tonight?"

Jackson has been signing with me in this *Meet the Rodeo Stars* thing they always put on. It's nice to have company, but I wish I was with Griff.

"Yeah. It's always nice to be home. My parents are here, and even my sister came out. Are you looking forward to being back?"

Jackson semi-retired last year after he met Riley and restarted his hydroponic gardening business. He only attends a few rodeos a year now instead of making it a full-time career, and I couldn't be happier for the life he's building. I sure miss him on the road sometimes, but I can't deny him his happiness.

"I am. You know my parents come up for it every year, and it's sort of tradition for them to watch me. I'll probably enter this rodeo until I physically can't anymore." He elbows my side. "Plus, Riley loves watching me, and there's no downside to that."

"No, I don't suppose there is."

A few stragglers enter the signing tent and momentarily distract us from the conversation. Both of us engage with the kids a little longer since there's no line up and I like to think that adds an extra thrill to their rodeo experience.

"So..." Jackson begins. His voice carries both a smile and a question, and I know what he's asking.

"Yep." I nod and hope it implies I'm happy, and answers the silent question on Jackson's face.

"Griff is a great guy. He loves you more than you might realize."

Three months ago, I would have agreed, but not anymore.

"Oh, I realize. I'm sorry it took so long, is all. I guess I'm more of a pretty face than a scholar."

Jackson scoffs. "Don't be so hard on yourself. Sometimes it's harder to pick out the obvious because it's too good to be true."

Damn, if that doesn't sum it all up for me the best way possible. "Sometimes I wonder how I got so lucky to have my best friend in love with me."

Jackson wants to say more, but his gaze shifts to the tent entrance, and when I follow his line of sight, my heart dances.

"Oh, thank god you're still here."

Griff rushes over, still dressed in jeans and a T-shirt and not at all ready for a rodeo. Which makes sense, since he was with his dad and getting him settled.

"Hey, babe." I press a quick kiss to his lips and grab his hand. "Is your dad settled in okay?"

Griff turns to Jackson with a laugh. "Oh, yeah. Riley was on it, along with Jackson's mom." Griff's voice softens. "He's good. We had a nice walk and...I'm optimistic."

Jackson squeezes Griff's shoulder before he leaves us. "Good luck tonight, you two. If you need us to help with anything you make sure you ask. That goes for both of you. Riley and I will be happy to lend a hand." With another pat to my shoulder, Jackson excuses himself to saddle his horse for tonight.

The tent clears out and staff bustle around cleaning up for the autograph session that comes after the events. I usually do both signing sessions, but this year I passed on the evening session because of the man in front of me and his father.

"Riley said you wanted me to meet you here. Is everything okay? We usually do our pre-event routine after we're dressed."

Griff's brows furrow as his kind blue eyes roam my face, and I realize my mistake.

"Ahh, shit. I'm sorry to have worried you. It's nothing...I...I just wanted to see you before we go back to all the pre-rodeo bustle." I rest my hands on his hips and press my forehead to his. "I also wanted to ask you how it went with your dad and have a bit of privacy to do it."

Griff sighs, and his hands slide around my waist, hooking his fingers into my belt loops.

"It was something I didn't know I missed. Just walking and eating cotton candy. We shared a bonding moment, I think, and then he was angry for a bit. Nothing we couldn't work out, but the emotions were everywhere."

My thumb sneaks under his shirt and rubs small circles across his hip bone.

"And you're doing okay? I know that's not a great word, but...do you need to talk about anything?"

Music blasts from the speakers as the pre-rodeo entertainment, which is a clown telling off-colour jokes, starts. I know we don't have a lot of time left before we need to get to work. This feels like a moment I needed too, not just for Griff, but for me. I need him to know he's my priority.

Griff ducks his head, pulling us just a step closer. Our chests touch, and he pauses a few breaths before leveling me with the warm gaze I misread for almost ten years. I'm not sure how I didn't see beyond the affection Griff holds there. Maybe I just never wanted someone to look at me like that until now. Now I don't want it from anyone else.

"We have some difficult times ahead with my dad. If you're still in this with me, there will be tears. *Lots* of tears." Griff's lips tilt in a lopsided grin as his fingers grip my belt loops tighter. "So if you want to change your mind, you'll have to tell me before we go any further."

His tone suggests a joke. Maybe an unserious attempt to give me an out because of all his insecurities, but there's no way I'll ever let him down.

"I'm not changing my mind." Closing my eyes, I inhale a soft breath and rest my forehead against his. "I can wipe your tears and hold you when it gets too much. I don't want you to do this alone, and I want to be the one you turn to when it's hard."

"I might have to stay away from some rodeo jobs," he whispers, and I know that was hard for him to say. He might have fallen into this career by accident, but he's grown to enjoy it, mostly. Now that I know his heart was with me more than the job, it's easier for me to hear those words and accept I might not always have him at events with me. "You'll have to go without me sometimes."

"I'm an adult. His recovery is a priority. I get that, Griff. I only want one thing from you."

Those blue eyes meet mine and I could get lost in them if I let myself. "What do you want, Jamie?"

"I just want to love you."

Griff swallows hard and puffs a shaky breath. His lips part and then close, not saying a word. But he doesn't have to. Instead, I press a soft kiss to his lips and feel his fingers pull my belt loops tighter before releasing them with a sigh.

Griff takes my hand, lacing his fingers in mine.

"Let's do this. It's your night, Jamie. I can feel it."

Bumping his shoulder as we leave the tent, I kiss his cheek as we turn towards the back of the rodeo area. No matter what happens on the back of a bull, he's right. It is my night.

I broke my usual routine tonight preparing to ride. Breaking a superstition should have me all kinds of messed up, but the truth is...I'm fine.

Griff and I chatted while he taped up his ankles and changed into his bullfighter gear of loose shorts and rodeo-branded shirt.

It was easy to just talk about nothing, and it felt like it was what I should have been doing all these years.

It wasn't his assurance before every ride I needed, or his bull intuition. The longer we prepared alongside each other, the more it became glaringly obvious to me that it was simply his presence that settled me.

"So, what bull do you have tonight?"

"Um...Morphine Dream, I think."

Griff pauses his stretches and raises an eyebrow. "You think?"

"No, I know. That's the one." Griff glances around before taking a few steps over to stand in front of me. "Jamie."

Griff wastes no time calling me on my shit, and I kind of like it when he does that. He's a very smart man. I knew that in university, and I know it now. Griff waits for me to let him in on why it's a new routine tonight and why suddenly I'm not dragging him to look at a bull and tell me how it will ride. When I meet his gaze, he studies my face for what feels like hours when it's barely been seconds.

"Okay." He returns to his place and gives me a pass on not putting it into words. I'm sort of happy about that because I don't really know how to explain it. Bursting into a sea shanty doesn't seem like the right option, but I need to say *something* so he doesn't worry.

"When I was signing autographs tonight, I had this thought." Griff continues his stretches, and I smirk when he bends over to grab his ankles and sticks his ass out. "I thought, what if I didn't put so much pressure on you to soothe me...to boost me up before events and I just..." I rush on before he can assure me that's not what all this was. "I loved knowing you'd be there for me, and I think I might have used it as a crutch. I know how to read a bull,

Griff." I suck in a breath. Then another. "Maybe it would be nice if I took that off your shoulders."

Griff's face remains unreadable, but his eyes...they really are a window to the soul. Pushing off the bench, my chaps swish with the few steps I take to reach him. "These shoulders." I rub my hands over them and continue when I have his full attention. "They've carried more than enough, and I unintentionally added to that. I just want you to know that if you want to quit or walk away to take care of your dad or any other scenario I haven't thought of yet, it's okay. That's why I changed my routine tonight."

When Griff remains silent, I step back. "Please say something."

He graces me with a smile, and the relief is like a glass of water on a hot day.

"I think I love you even more, and I didn't know until now that was something I needed to hear from you, Jamie. I didn't want to disappoint you—"

"You never could."

"I thought I was staying because I was weak and couldn't walk away from this. What we have here. That still may be partly true, but...hearing you tell me it's okay to not be here is, fuck, it's like a weight lifted."

"Hey! You two need to get going. Bull riders start in fifteen!" A volunteer motions down towards the ring before jogging that way himself.

"Start a new tradition with me?"

Griff cocks his head. "Of course, but make it quick."

Taking his face in my palms, I kiss him, taste him and hold him in place until his hands are on my chest, trying to find purchase on my flak vest. When I pull away, Griff blinks, then laughs, a joyous sound from the bottom of his feet, before grabbing my hand and pulling me along the path to the ring.

He pauses at the gate to the ring and beams a bright smile.

"Hold on tight and do what you do best, Jamie."

Then he disappears into the ring.

And that's what he's been telling me all along.

Twenty-Seven
Griff

The last rider of the first flight exits the ring safely, and I finally allow myself to search the stands for my dad.

While the rodeo clown sets up for a skit, I grab water from a volunteer and wave at the crowd where my dad sits. He's still wearing that ridiculous straw hat, and he and Riley wave back.

Even from a distance, it's clear he's enjoying himself, and when he waves back, the little boy in me surfaces with mixed emotions. All the science fairs or public speaking that he missed, I can't forget how much I wished he were in the audience for. But tonight feels like a new beginning. Like the ten-year-old who wanted his dad to be at the library for his speech on hermit crabs, I use this moment to insert him there and wave back.

And that's the moment I know I can't walk away from this part of my life completely. Bullfighting was never my end goal, but in some sort of way, having Dad here to see me fills a hole I've long ignored. Jamieson's confession that he didn't need me to prop him up surprised me, but in the best possible way.

With all the changes and emotional fragilities of my life the past few months, I'm standing in a rodeo ring experiencing the greatest epiphany of my life.

I can still have everything I've ever wanted.

The man. My dad. Rodeo... and the dream I tucked away when I left university because I was being pulled in too many directions and couldn't possibly stretch any further.

The revelation settles over me, and for the first time since I was a kid struggling to grow up far too soon, I finally see a light on for me.

The short intermission ends, and I get back to work, vigilant of all the bull riders, but with a new restlessness for Jamieson's ride. He has a lot on the line with tonight's ride, and choosing to go with a new pre-ride routine hopefully doesn't backfire.

"Give it up for hometown rider, Jamieson Carr." The announcer's voice blares over the speakers, drawing out the 'r' in his name so it sounds like a growl. The crowd roars so loudly it drowns out the announcer. Jamie's black helmet and long torso are visible as he works to position himself on the bull, Morphine Dream. The bull has a good chance of bucking him off tonight because he has a winning record and has only seen the end of eight seconds with a rider still on board three times all season.

Nothing about Jamieson's posture shows he's nervous. He's all confident moves and sharp instructions to the people at the top of the chute helping him. Then he's nodding his head, and the men pull open the gates.

The massive black bull with mismatched horns launches out of the gate, hell bent to throw Jamieson off. It bucks high and hard, sideways and back again. My heart is in my throat because this is the best ride of his life. His form is perfect, and every muscle in his body must be on fire while he fights to survive the ride.

The buzzer sounds, and from the corner of my eye, I see the stands with our friends and family jump to their feet clapping, and

I'm pretty sure my dad's straw hat goes flying. Jamieson works to free himself and holds on just long enough to grab onto a pickup man while Morphine Dream simply trots to the end of the ring and down the corridor like a respectable loser.

"Jamieson Carrrrr...." The announcer draws out the end of his name again as the man himself stumbles towards me while ripping off his helmet. "Get on your feet because the hometown hero just rode Morphine Dream for the biggest score of the night!"

Then Jamie is right in front of me with his smile and those damn dimples that make my knees weak.

"Ninety-five points for the bull rider, folks!"

"Holy shit!" Jamie's eyes widen as he reaches me, and we both laugh.

"Holy shit is right! You did it. You're going to the finals, Jamie."

"I'm going to the finals, baby!" He tilts his head back and howls like a wolf at the moon, and I'm so happy for him that my chest aches with a joy I don't know how to express.

But Jamieson does.

His hands grip my shirt as he pulls me into his chest.

"That ride was for you, Griff. You're it for me." He crashes his lips to mine, and we let ourselves fall into a passionate kiss in the middle of the ring with the roar of the crowd surrounding us.

My hands shake as they clutch at his waist, and when we finally break for air, we find a line of cowboys waiting, applauding with smiles on their faces.

I duck my head against Jamie with a groan. "Oh god. This is embarrassing."

Jamie just grins with that mischievous glint in his eye and tugs me towards the exit. "As embarrassing as that time I made you sing karaoke with me and the prompter broke, so we made up the words?"

Despite my embarrassment, I bark a laugh and take his hand in mine as we exit the ring. "Not quite. Although if you kissed me then like you did just now, I'd probably think it was the best karaoke performance of my life."

Jamieson takes a few minutes to receive congratulations from some of the bull riders, and I stay with him because he doesn't let go of my hand, and I'm not one bit mad about that.

We end up changing, with me removing the tape off my ankles while having several conversations at once with other rodeo cowboys. Some even express their happiness to know we're a couple, but most just want to fanboy over Jamieson and offer their sincere wishes for a great national final.

And I couldn't be happier about that.

He's still chatting with one of the bull riders when my frequent bullfighting partner, Mitchell, plops into the seat beside me.

"So...it finally happened, did it?" Mitchell grins and my answering smile is probably all he needs for confirmation.

"Yeah. It hasn't been a secret. It was after I broke my arm, but I didn't think he'd kiss me in the ring like that."

"I knew something was changing when he was waiting for you at the hospital. Call it a hunch."

"I didn't know you were at the hospital."

"I brought Jamieson food, because I knew he'd be hungry. He was...more upset than seemed normal for a broken arm, and when I asked him if he was okay, he said he would be when he could hold you again. Not usually something a friend might say."

I don't know what to say to Mitchell as he slaps me on the shoulder. "I'm thrilled for you, Griff. I like Jamieson, and I hope this answers questions you never found the answers to."

Mitchell is far more observant than I've ever given him credit for.

"Thanks. I'll still be around. You won't be losing me as a partner forever, maybe just sometimes."

He grins back. "I like the sound of that." With another slap on my shoulder, he says goodbye and heads out.

"Hey, we should go find your dad, right? Isn't the shuttle coming for him soon?"

Glancing at my phone, I'm shocked at the time and throw my things in my bag quickly. "Yeah, thirty minutes. Riley said he'd wait with him."

Jamieson and I speed walk around to the stands and find everyone still waiting for us. Jamieson's family is the first to congratulate him, and his sister gives me a punch to the shoulder with a firm nod. That's Kara language for *'good job protecting my brother.'*

"Dad, did you have fun? Jamieson did great, didn't he?"

"It was a lot of fun, Griff. You did great, too."

"I don't really do much most of the time."

My dad looks at me with an expression I'm not familiar with. "You keep them safe, Griff. That's a lot. Maybe it's only one bull a night that gives you trouble, but without you, those riders might not be so confident if they didn't know a guy like you was out there to save their butts."

"I've never thought of it like that."

"You should. You do more than just stand around in the sand, son. I'm proud of you. Thank you for giving me a chance to see you like this."

Dad's eyes shine with unshed tears, and I feel like in the brief time he's been active in my life again, he's seen more than anyone ever has. Which is doing all kinds of things to how I'm feeling.

"You're welcome. I hope it's not the last time you'll watch me."

Jamieson interrupts and slings his arm over my shoulder while offering his hand to my dad. "It's nice to see you again, Mr. Shepard."

"You had one hell of a ride, Jamieson. And I told you, call me Charlie." Dad shakes Jamie's hand, and Jamie's arm around me relaxes.

"Thank you, sir. I couldn't have done it without Griff."

I don't know what to do with that. Jamieson is a talented rider by his own merit. I didn't force him to practice or do his strength training. That's all on him. Thankfully, nobody waits for me to reply to that, and Dad says his goodbyes to his new group of friends while we walk him to the entrance to wait for his shuttle.

"Uh, so, Dad there's something I have to talk to you about." I glance at Jamie, and he nods. "Have you thought about what you'd like to do after the rehab program finishes?"

Dad stuffs his hands in the pockets of his too-big overalls and stares at his feet. "I've thought about it, yes. But I don't know what to do about it. Miles said I should attend meetings and keep up with my therapy at the centre, but I'd have to move here, and I don't know if I can find a place I can afford with my pension."

"I've thought about that a lot, too, Dad."

He raises his gaze to mine, and while I wish he'd made better choices, I'm also grateful I never gave up on him.

"Would you let me help you again?"

His lips press into a tight line, and I brace myself for an outburst of anger.

"It's not easy for me to admit that I need my child to help me out of the spot I'm in." His voice cracks, and Jamie reaches out to him before I do.

"Your child has helped many people, Charlie." He takes my dad into a hug like he's an old friend, and I swallow the growing lump in my throat. "We want to help you."

Dad releases Jamieson and finds a tissue to dab at his eyes.

"I'm listening."

"I'm moving in with Jamieson soon."

"Really? That's wonderful!" Even in the middle of all his problems, he still finds a genuine smile for my news, and that's the bit of Dad I used to know. That's the dad I want more of. To have him watch the birds and flowers and kids throwing baseballs at the park down the street. To find some of the joy he had when I was small.

"Thanks, Dad. Um...we have a house and there's a suite in the basement."

"You'll have a private entrance," Jamieson adds.

"We're renovating it, and we'd like you to move in there."

My dad stays silent for so long I'm concerned he had a stroke standing up and perhaps forgot to speak. "Dad?"

"You want me to live with you?"

"I'd like you to sell the trailer and have you live here, yes. We'll make it work with your pension, so it's not you taking advantage if that's a worry. I want to help you through this part, Dad. I miss you, and I don't want you to be alone." God, the tears are hot on my face as my dad pulls me to him, probably rougher than he meant to. We both stumble, and Jamie's hand on my waist stops me from tumbling over.

"I don't know what I did to deserve a kid as good as you, but right now, I'm thankful you're mine. I love you, Griffy. Thank you."

Dad sobs into my shirt as the shuttle pulls up, and then he turns to Jamieson while he wipes at his eyes.

"Thank you. I don't know what else to say right now because I need to unscramble my head and thoughts."

"We have lots of time to talk, Charlie. You just take care of yourself first."

Jamieson steps back and lets me have a private moment with Dad before he leaves.

"Dad...I'll come by next Sunday and we'll talk more, but tonight is one of the best nights of my life. Just know that I'm beyond happy to do this and so is Jamieson, okay?"

"Don't worry about me, Griff. Go enjoy this night. You both deserve it."

Dad steps away and into the van without prolonging the goodbye, and I'm left watching the taillights disappear for a moment before Jamie's arms wrap around me from behind.

"Are you up for celebrating, or would you rather just have some quiet time at home?"

"You want to sing, don't you?" I chuckle.

"More than I think you know."

"Then let's go sing."

Twenty-Eight
Jamieson

My favourite part after any rodeo is the after-party.

The energy is high, and if any of our crew had great performances, we ride that post-performance like the biggest wave in the ocean. Tonight, I might as well be an Olympic-level surfer.

I had the best ride of my life, and I'm finally making it to the National Finals. But that's not the best part. The best part stands in the corner chatting with a barrel rider from town. As if he feels my gaze on him, Griff swivels away from the pretty brunette and meets my stare. He smiles at the woman again before politely excusing himself and walking my way.

Griff, I've only recently come to realize, is my lighthouse. At the rodeo, in the bars, and even just in life. When things are tough or uncertain, it's always Griff I've reached for. My heart should burst right now, but it's heavy as I watch him work his way through the crowd towards me. All the nights I put him through watching me hook up with people, keeping me safe, when all this time it should have been him.

"Jamieson! Are you singing tonight?"

A nameless roper slaps my back a little too hard, but I smile at the mention of singing, anyway.

"You bet! Just need to figure out which one."

The man leans in closer and slides a hand across mine. A gesture I never would have picked up on before unless Griff pointed it out to me. Stepping away from the touch, I search for Griff again, and I meet his blue gaze only a few steps away.

When he reaches me, he slides his hand into my back pocket and presses a kiss to my lips. "You're on your third drink, Jamie. Shouldn't you be singing by now?"

"That's what I said!" The nameless man grips my shoulder and leaves his hand there for an extra beat and I want to think it's just him being friendly, but there's more to it. When I glance at Griff, his eyebrows furrow, and there's a spark in his blue eyes as he takes in the man's prolonged contact.

"He's not available, Pauly. In case the kiss didn't give it away." Griff almost growls, and that's sort of hot.

Pauly laughs and removes his hand while stepping back. "Sorry, sorry. I heard you two might be a thing, but a guy can hope."

When Pauly leaves, I turn to Griff. "You can use that voice anytime, babe. It's hot." Dipping my mouth next to his ear, I whisper, "I like it when you get all possessive, and I like that flush on your neck right now. Why did we come here when we should've gone home and gotten naked?"

Griff's lips, so close to my ear, send a shiver down my spine. "Because you want to sing and celebrate like always, Jamie. I'll still take you home after."

He presses a kiss to my neck, and the only thing I want to sing right now is his name as he comes all over me.

"Follow me?"

"Always."

Turning on my heel, I head to the hallway towards the bathrooms. It's cliché and not romantic, like Griff deserves, but I just want to have him to myself for a few minutes. The hall is quieter than the bar, and Giff laughs.

"You want to get off in the bathroom? Really?"

"If that accessible bathroom is open, yes. But just for a few minutes. We don't even have to come. We just have to..."

My words trail off as we reach the bathroom in question because Hunter charges out of it like a swarm of bees is on his ass...with Gabe right after him. They both notice us and say nothing, but Gabe runs to catch up with Hunter.

"Wow. So Diamond was right about something going on with those two," Griff says as he grabs my hand and pulls me away from the door of the bathroom. "That's not who I am, Jamie, even with you. Let's sing your song, then I'll dump the rest of your drink and take you home."

"You always take care of me, Griff," I croak.

His smile is soft as he cups my cheek. "That will never change, Jamie."

"I'm sorry. I never noticed how much this hurt you."

Griff smiles and presses a kiss to my lips that lingers. "Don't be sorry. I put myself in that position and yes, it hurt, but I kept you safe and that was far more important than my feelings."

Resting my forehead against his, I sigh a shaky breath. "I don't want you to do that anymore. I want to know how you feel, and I don't want you to hurt because of me again."

"Okay."

"Promise me, Griff."

Griff nods against me and runs his hands up my chest. "I promise."

My tongue feels thick, and the warmth of his hands on me is all I can think about. When he moves to drop his hands and step away, I grab his wrists and pull him back to me.

"I...I'm...fuck, I don't know what I am, but I..." My heart feels broken and mended all at once, and my skin feels too tight. All I want right now is to be lost in Griff in a way I never have before. "Can you take us home?"

"Yes, of course. That's what you want? No singing?"

"I want to be alone with you. You make me sing."

Griff's gaze never leaves mine, and he might as well wear a neon sign with his feelings. His throat bobs, and he gives a single nod.

"All right. I'll take you home. Let's go."

We don't pause for goodbyes, but we wave if anyone shouts or waves as we weave through the crowded bar. Once we're outside and the late August air hits my skin, I shiver, but not with a chill.

Griff, always confident and protective, holds my hand as he fishes the key fob from his pocket and points it toward the parking lot. Lights flash as my truck comes to life, and when we reach it, he holds the door for me. He's done it a million times before. Held the door and buckled me in and just fucking cared for me, but I don't know why this feels so different.

Is it because I know what his dick feels like in my mouth and we've made each other come every morning for the past few months? What changed tonight for me to feel so out of sorts and so fucking emotional?

Griff drives us out of the parking lot, and I watch the streetlights dance over his face as we drive the short distance across town to his apartment. The one he's moving out of soon to be with me.

"You're moving in with me. To my house. Our house," I blurt, and Griff huffs a laugh.

"I am. I'll start packing this week if you want."

"I want."

Griff laughs low as he parks my truck on the street close to his apartment.

"You're being weird, Jamie. What's wrong?"

"Nothing is wrong. Not even close."

He rounds the front of the truck and meets me, taking my hand as we walk to the back stairs up to his apartment.

"Okay. If nothing's wrong, can you tell me why you gave up your bar singing? You love that. Tonight was a big night for you. You should celebrate."

Griff holds the door open for me, and I step inside, kicking off my boots and grabbing him as soon as he locks the door behind us.

"I'm celebrating with you instead."

I want Griff naked, and I don't know how I want him after that. I just know I need to feel him against me and hear his moans. My name on his lips and his on mine as we lose ourselves to this electricity between us.

Our teeth clash and we stumble down the short hall to his bedroom, pieces of clothing left in our wake until Griff pushes me on his bed and tears my jeans and underwear off in one smooth motion.

"Fuck, you're beautiful Jamie." He presses a kiss on my knee. "So fucking beautiful."

His lips trail paths over my legs while his hands lazily roam, and I finally find the words to tell him what I want.

"I want you to make love to me, Griff." My cheeks burn with the words. They sound so juvenile, but I don't know what else to say. I don't want a quickie or a hard fuck. I want Griff to crawl inside me and stay there.

"I can do that." He presses a harder kiss on my thigh. "In fact, I'd love to do that."

Maybe it's the drinks I had tonight or the buzz from the rodeo ride. Or maybe it's both, but I've never felt so much at one time as I do now. Every touch of his skin against mine and every breath shared between kisses feels like nothing we've shared before.

Griff kisses me with a passion that burns my lips and stokes a fire so deep I might combust. This is love. I get it now. Everything he's kept inside for years pours out. This isn't our quick frots or blow jobs, this is so much more than that.

"Lie on your side, Jamie."

The snick of the lube cap is impossibly loud as I shift my back towards him. His firm hand taps my thigh, and I lift my leg, gasping as he slides his cock through, brushing against my balls.

Griff's arm holds me as he moves slowly, stroking my dick. It's agony, it's bliss, and I feel like I'm the luckiest man in the world to have this.

"Squeeze your thighs a little tighter, Jamie," Griff breathes next to my ear, and when I do as he asks, the answering moan is better than any shanty I could sing in a bar.

"I'm so close, babe. Fuck, that feels amazing. Don't stop."

There has to be a way to do this next time, so I can face him, because even though it's an intimate act, I feel like we have an opening between us when I want none.

Griff stops moving and rests his head on my back.

"I said don't stop," I whine, and Griff chuckles.

"On your back. I want to kiss you when you come."

"It's like you read my mind."

He spreads my legs wide and lowers himself closer. This time I'm the one trapped in the mercy of his thighs and I think I squeak in surprise as he tilts my throbbing cock back and squeezes it between his thighs.

"Wrap your legs around me." Griff shudders when I do and I pull him as tight as I can.

Griff lowers himself over me, and I surge up to kiss him. "Holy fuck, it feels like my dick is in a vise."

"Need me to loosen a little?"

His cock drags along my belly with every movement, and I shake my head because all language has now vanished. I'm flying.

"I got you, Jamie. I got you."

Griff's words are in a tunnel as I come so hard I feel like my body left Earth and crashed down harder than gravity allows. It's only the warmth on my stomach and Griff's words that have me tethered to earth.

"You're shaking. Are you okay?"

Clearing my throat, I test my voice. "More than okay. I've never had such an incredible orgasm." We both laugh softly, and I finally let my legs flop to the side. "For real, Griff. I'm almost sad I didn't know sex could be so good."

We lay there a little longer, just kissing and not caring about the mess that's growing uncomfortable. Neither of us wants to break this perfect moment.

Until my stomach growls.

Griff drops his head to my shoulder, body quaking with laughter.

"Your pillow talk needs work."

"You know I can't control my stomach. If it's hungry, it's hungry."

"Let's get cleaned up, and I'll make you mac and cheese."

Smacking a giant kiss on his lips, I flip him onto his back. "You always know the way to my heart."

Griff's fingertips brush my cheek and then my lips. "I've never been brave enough to travel the whole way there. But now that I have, I don't plan on ever leaving."

"I like that plan."

"How can you possibly think it's okay for Donald Duck not to wear pants, but Mickey has to? It's so bizarre."

Griff made a giant pot of Kraft Dinner, and rather than dealing with the mess in the bedding, we took the pot of pasta, extra blankets and made ourselves comfortable on the couch for several hours watching old cartoons.

The pasta is long gone, and the cartoons are looping back to replay. Our eyes are heavy, but neither of us wants to sleep.

"The sun will rise in another hour. Want to stay up for it?" Griff's voice slurs with exhaustion, and as much as I want to do that, I'm not sure I have the strength to stay awake longer.

"I'd love nothing more, but there's a problem."

"What's that?"

"I can't hold up my eyelids," I whisper with a laugh.

A beat of silence passes before Griff speaks again in the same tired voice.

"Mickey has to wear pants because mice have dicks. Ducks don't."

"What?"

"The pants thing. It's not bizarre. It's dicks."

"This conversation makes no sense. Of course, ducks have dicks."

When he doesn't reply, I roll my head his way and find him fast asleep with his mouth parted and his cheeks still flushed. Rather than wake him and force him to carry on with the conversation about mice and duck dicks, I decide it's better to just let it go.

If anyone knows that kind of information, it's Jackson. If I'm still awake in an hour, I'll call him and ask.

After dragging the blanket over, I snuggle in next to Griff as best as I can on the couch and let the cartoons continue playing. One episode blends into the next until my eyes no longer stay open. I forget about the pants-less duck, and finally fall asleep with Griff in my arms.

In my arms, my heart, and my life.

As it should be.

Twenty-Nine
Epilogue

Two years later

Griff

"Did you check in at home? Everything okay?"

Jamieson sets a fresh piña colada in the cup holder of my beach chair before settling next to me in his. Jamieson in his swim shorts, stretched out in the Dominican sunshine, is a sight I'll never tire of.

"Yeah. I spoke to Dad, and he's doing well. Said he's walking dogs with Riley today, and tomorrow your sister will drive him to therapy."

He hums under his breath and sips his cocktail. A pineapple mojito, I think he called it. Something about needing to test the theory of copious amounts of pineapple.

"She's good that way. She might end up taking him shopping, though. Maybe you should give your dad a heads up."

Smiling at the thought of my dad shopping with Jamie's sister, I lower my sunglasses and lean back. After Jamieson went to the National Finals and won, our lives moved almost too fast.

First, we hired help to finish the house renovations with his prize money. Then we moved my dad into his basement suite and sold his trailer in Fox Grove. It took a while to sell, but in the end, it gave me and Dad a chance to really mend a lot of our relationship. Sometimes just the two of us would make the trip to the trailer and pack up a few things while checking on the place. Other times, Jamieson would join us.

Dad used that time to work through a lot of the other relationships he broke with co-workers and friends. It wasn't perfect, and some were happy he was doing well. Some didn't care, and that was okay, too.

When Jamieson came with us, Dad would tell stories about me as a kid. Jamieson loved every single one.

We had our first Christmas together as a family in a home I could call my own. It didn't matter if the mortgage was in Jamieson's name. It was *our* home, and I knew that. Jamieson, with help from his sister, had personalized stockings made that we hung on the mantle.

It was a small thing, really, to have our names on brightly coloured stockings, but to me, it was yet another gesture from my best friend. If I asked for something, he delivered, and it wasn't just tasty drinks on the beach in the Dominican. He was in this thing with me, and he proved it every single day.

This trip is a late gift for my graduation. I finally finished my master's degree in social work. I landed a position at the rehab centre my dad still attends for therapy. It's been a change from dodging bulls and keeping riders safe, but it's filled the last crack in my life. I still work at the Kissing Ridge rodeo, though, and I probably will until Jamieson quits riding bulls. Which might be sooner than we both thought.

"Do you think we could look for seashells somewhere? The beach doesn't look like it has much."

Jamie smiles like he knew that question was coming.

"Oh, I asked the bartender, actually. He said every night they physically comb the sand here and clean up anything like that, but we could walk around the corner where the trees are thicker, or he said to just wade out and look in the water."

Jamieson's hand covers mine, and I turn my head towards him. "We'll get you some shells, Griff. Even if I have to buy them at the market on the resort, I'll get you seashells."

There's something extra about sitting here together on a sandy beach I never thought I'd get to visit. It's not quite what I imagined when I was a young boy hoping to play along an ocean's edge and searching for treasures only oceans could give up. It's infinitely better.

"I might want to make a sandcastle."

Jamie huffs a laugh and pulls my hand to his lips. He feathers a kiss on my wrist that makes me forget about the sandcastles.

"I'll make sand angels if it makes you happy."

Sliding my glasses back on my head, I shift in my chair towards him.

"What else would make *you* happy? So far, we've done all the things I want. What do you want, Jamie?"

He sips from his drink, and I watch the bob of his throat as he swallows.

"I want a lot of things, Griff." He turns his head, and his lazy smile melts my insides. "I want to fuck on the balcony at night if you can stay quiet." He laughs softly and dusts his fingers down my neck. "You can't blame that blush on the sun, babe."

"No, I can't." I laugh. "That's all for you."

His warm gaze travels down my naked chest as his fingers stop at the waistband of my shorts, and I know I'm blushing even more. Jamieson will always get that reaction from me. I can't help it.

"This trip is for you. There's nothing else I want from it than to give you something you never had and always wanted; the beach, seashells, and a break from life. I'm completely happy just being here to share it with you."

When he says shit like that, it's so hard to not want to climb into his lap and drown myself in him. But it's a public beach, and while no one's been rude to us, I know it's best to keep things on the down low here. Instead, I take his hand and lace our fingers together between us.

We sit like that for a while, just listening to the waves and the sounds of people on the beach. Couples splash in the water and tour boats float by while we sip fruity drinks and occasionally brush our feet together, just happy to be here.

But Jamieson has something on his mind. He's been chewing his lip for days, and while I think I know what he wants to talk about, I don't want to come out and ask. It has to come from him.

"I heard from the school board. If I refresh my teaching certificate by August, the job is mine." Jamieson swallows hard. "I think it's time I look at leaving the rodeo behind. My shoulder isn't what it used to be."

Jamieson ended his season last year with an injury, and before we went on this vacation, he had some serious talks with doctors and friends. He didn't want to live in pain when he was still a young man. While it devastated him to admit he was at the end of a career he loved, he knew he'd get to mentor other riders and be involved with the sport.

"I thought something was on your mind. How do you feel about that?"

Taking his hand in mine, I squeeze it, and he looks over at me.

"It's hard. But it would be harder to get on a bull and risk worse right now. I want to be there for you."

His voice wavers, and I rub his hand with my thumb. "You will be. This has to be a choice that you want, Jamie. Make the choice for you and nobody else."

He sips his drink, and we return to staring at the ocean for a short time. A group of young men runs past, joking about the loser buying drinks, and it's an old joke on an all-inclusive resort, but I guess it's humour that never fades.

Jamieson loves bull riding. He was made for it, but what he's also made for is teaching. He's more afraid to face a room of 16-year-olds than a raging bull. To be fair, I would be, too. It was easier for me to step away from bullfighting. I didn't live and breathe rodeo like Jamieson did, but I'll get him through the hard times just like he did for me.

But first, he needs to get back in the moment and remember why we're here.

"Let's go look for shells."

Jamie follows me to the water's edge, and we walk to the trees the bartender told him about. A flash of white in the sand draws a gasp from my lips, and I burst forward, bending to pick it up before it's washed back with the waves.

"Ohmygod, Jamie! It's a shell! I found a shell!"

Jamie smiles in that way that wraps around me like a blanket, and before I can respond with a kiss, more shiny pieces show up, and I drop to my knees, digging through the sand for more shells. "There's more! This one is whole!"

I'm a 31-year-old man on my knees in the ocean sand digging out pieces of seashells with the enthusiasm of a five-year-old...and I couldn't give a single fuck what anyone who might see me thinks.

Then Jamie is next to me doing the same thing, and we laugh when we both reach for the same shell and knock our hands together. Our pockets are full when we walk back towards the beach, and the shells shift in pockets that are only big enough to hold room keys.

I'm so happy I could burst, and Jamie leans down to kiss me. "I love you, you know. Thank you." He lingers like he wants to say something else, but kisses me again and takes my hand as we walk the path back to our room. "Think we can test out the pineapple theory before supper, or should we wait a little longer?"

His dimple pops as he grins at me, and I bark a laugh.

"We're here for another four days. I think we have ample time to test several theories."

He stops at the door to our room and swipes the key while I hold my breath. I hope they had enough time to set up what I asked. Jamieson steps inside, and I follow close behind until he stops, and I run into his back.

"Griff...what is this?"

Our room has multiple vases filled with birds of paradise, and the housekeeping staff made hearts out of towels on our bed with our initials inside. I wasn't sure how far they would go with my request since we were two men, but I guess money talks.

Or rather, kiwi does.

Jamieson walks over to the tray of fresh fruit and stares at it without a word. Too many beats pass, so I launch into my speech.

"Um, you know I love you more than anything, Jamie. You're the one constant in my life, and some days, I don't know how I can breathe without you around. I want to spend the rest of our lives together, not just sharing a house. I want for us to share our names."

Jamieson finally turns to look at me, biting his lip, and I reach out to pull it away with my thumb. "Please say something."

He points to the plate of fruit. "I think they ran out of kiwi slices or couldn't read your writing."

When I glance at the plate, it doesn't say *Marry Me* like I hoped. It just says 'Merry?' and I burst out laughing.

"I guess that's my fault for asking kiwi to do the talking."

"I honestly couldn't figure out why fruit for someone named Merry was here." He cups my cheeks in his palms. "But you need to clarify the question, Griff. Say it."

"Will you marry me, Jamie?"

He closes his eyes with a small laugh. "Will you spell it in blueberries next time?"

I laugh softly. "I'll write it across the sky if you want me to."

"Yeah, I'll marry you. There's no one but you, babe. It's always been you."

I run my fingertips over the tattoo on his chest. The one over his heart with my initials inside a bull's hoof.

I don't wear a tattoo for him on the outside, but he's tattooed on my soul and at some point, I think the universe knew that or it never would have put me in his path all those years ago.

Fate is a funny thing. We like to celebrate it when it brings us good things, and curse it for the bad. Every trial I endured brought me closer to Jamie in ways neither of us processed in real time.

The past few years have still thrown us bad things, but it's easier now. Soulmates are a thing, and he's mine in every way.

"It's always been you, Jamie."

With his lips on mine and my heart in his hands, I know we can take on whatever fate throws at us next.

Jamie's stomach growls, and we break apart, laughing.

"Dinner first and naked hot tub later?"

"Sounds perfect, Jamie."

And it really is.

Thank you so much for reading! Are you hoping Hunter finally gets a happy ending?

He's up next and guess what!? He's part of a fake marriage with city slicker Gabe in Ropers Can't Tie Knots!

Acknowledgements

Hello again dear reader,

Thank you so much for reading and I hope you enjoyed Griff and Jamieson's journey. Fictional characters are a funny thing. This was supposed to be another light and funny book, but Griff told me something else every time I tried to write his voice. After the third time, I went with it and this is the story that was born.

It's a little different from my usual lighter stories, but I hope it was just as fulfilling. They really were meant for each other. It might have taken them longer than most, but it came at the right time.

Thank you to my friends who heard me moan over this one far too often, and talked me out of scrapping the entire thing more than once, lol. Thank you for believing in me, Jenn. One day I'll buy you pompoms because you're the best cheerleader an author could ask for.

Hunter's story is next, and I can't wait to get it to you all. I've not been this excited for a character since Heath.

As always, if you enjoyed Bull Riders Don't Swoon, please consider leaving a review or rating on the platform of your choice.

Thank you for being the best readers.

Much love, RM

About the author

R M is an introverted Canadian author who likes to write about love while freezing in the winter. Her mission is to always make you swoon and snort laugh, sometimes even in public.

She talks to her cat, Moon, and sometimes people. She married her prince charming, who often inspires her characters, but still can't place dirty clothes in the hamper.

When she's not writing swoony men to fall in love with, she's in her garden providing mosquitoes with an alternative food source. She can also be found inventing new swear words on the golf course.

Also By

Want to read more by me? Scan the code
to find my back list.

Visit my website for signed paperbacks and merch!
rmneillauthor.com